Book 4: Hero Rising

Also by Shane Hegarty

Darkmouth, Book 1: The Legends Begin

Darkmouth, Book 2: Worlds Explode

Darkmouth, Book 3: Chaos Descends

Book 4: Hero Rising

SHANE HEGARTY

Illustrated by James de la Rue

HARPER

An Imprint of HarperCollins*Publishers*

Darkmouth #4: Hero Rising

For information address HarperCollins Children's Books, a division of HarperCollins Publishers, 195 Broadway, New York, NY 10007.
www.harpercollinschildrens.com

Library of Congress Control Number: 2017939012
ISBN 978-0-06-231138-2

18 19 20 21 22 PC/LSCH 10 9 8 7 6 5 4 3 2 1

Originally published in the UK by HarperCollins Children's Books in 2017
First US Edition, 2018

For Aisling & Laoise

DARK
ICE CREAM
DENTIST'S OFFICE
ROCKY BEACH
PET SHOP
MR. GLAD'S SHOP
SCHOOL
CHIP SHOP
Welcome to Darkmouth

MOUTH
DOOM'S PERCH
LOOKOUT POST
CAVE
FINN'S HOUSE
EMMIE'S HOUSE

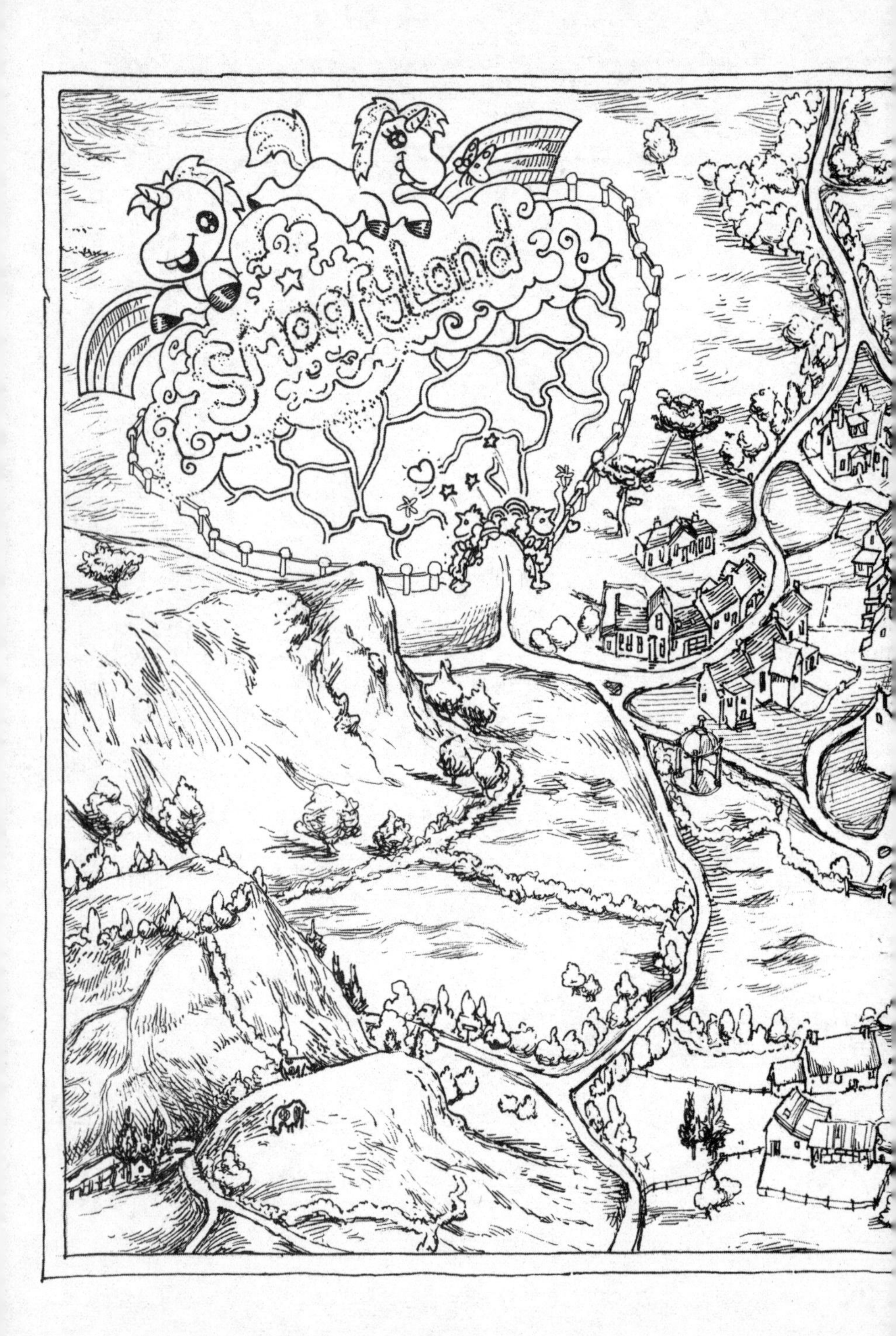
Snoofyland

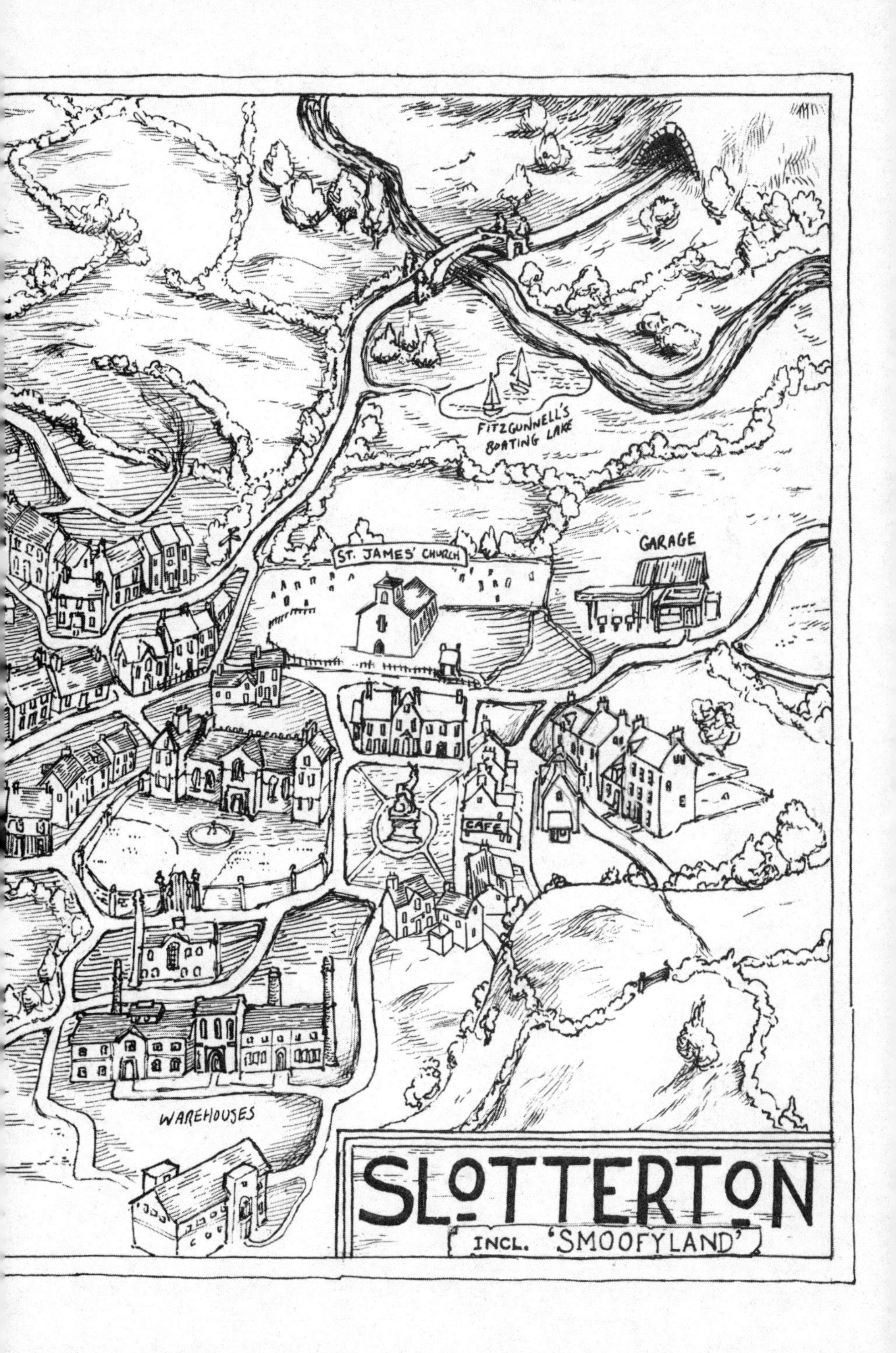
FITZGUNNELL'S
BOATING LAKE
GARAGE
ST. JAMES' CHURCH
CAFE
WAREHOUSES
SLOTTERTON
INCL. 'SMOOFYLAND'

Tornclaw

Previously in Darkmouth

(How it was won. And lost.)

They had won the battle but lost Darkmouth.

There had been an invasion, a fight, death, victory . . . and when it was all over Finn was accused of being a traitor.

When this shocking reversal began to sink in, Finn's mother, Clara, suggested that the awful situation should force them to do something they'd never done before.

"Let's go on a vacation," she said.

Worse than that, she thought she knew exactly where they should go.

"Let's go to Smoofyland."

Smoofyland was a theme park based on a popular TV unicorn she kept telling Finn he loved. It was fifty miles up the road from Darkmouth and yet, because Legends kept getting in the way of their plans, they'd never been.

"You would love Smoofyland," Clara told Finn.

"I would not," Finn insisted.

"You love Smoofy," Clara told him.

"I do not," he said, deeply unamused by the very suggestion.

"Well, you used to," she said.

"When I was a baby," he conceded.

"You had a Smoofy cake for your ninth birthday," Clara reminded him.

"You promised not to mention that again," said Finn.

"You used to love the *Smoofy the Magic Unicorn* TV show theme," his mother said, before bursting into it.

"*Who's the sparkly unicorn with magic in his mane? Smoofy! That's who.*"

"If you sing one more line—" Finn warned.

Clara sang two more lines.

"*Who's the flying unicorn who's friends with a rainbow train? Smoofy! That's who.*"

Finn did not want to hear the *Smoofy* theme song. He did not want to go to Smoofyland. He did not want a vacation at all.

He wanted Darkmouth back. For his family. For his dad. For himself.

They had saved the town from an invasion by Fomorians led by the particularly brutish Gantrua, who had brought with him a house-crushing Hydra. They had rescued a group of Half-Hunters, including Emmie's father, Steve, who had been trapped between worlds by the spectral traitor Mr. Glad. This had occurred on Finn's birthday, when he was supposed to be made a proper Legend Hunter. But that did not happen because a man named Lucien had turned up and stolen Darkmouth from them.

An assistant to the Legend Hunters' leaders, Lucien had seemingly spent too long in a small office off a narrow hallway in a tall building in Liechtenstein, and wanted some proper action for once. He had struck lucky when all those leaders—the Council of Twelve—were desiccated at the same time.

It cleared the way for him to give orders and take control of the shell-shocked and confused Half-Hunters who had survived the Darkmouth invasion, and who didn't know who to believe. Lucien pointed out that a boy who had spent time palling around with Legends should be the last one to trust.

Estravon Oakbound, the rule-obsessed assistant who had once journeyed with them to the Infested Side, agreed.

That sealed Finn's fate.

Lucien captured Broonie the Hogboon and took him away for Desiccation. He stripped Finn and his father, Hugo, of their right to defend Darkmouth and forced them to move into a small house with Emmie and Steve.

In the weeks that followed, that house saw disappointment, anger, bewilderment, and several arguments about who ate the last of the biscuits.

What happened next? Steve was sent to Liechtenstein to report back on his strange experiences. The Half-Hunters had gone home too, as the threat was over for now—besides, most of them had to go back to their jobs as accountants or washing-machine repair technicians or balloon-animal makers and the like.

Lucien stayed in Darkmouth though, bringing loyal assistants with him. He claimed to be looking for the truth of what happened. But nothing about Lucien rang true.

It was clear to Finn and Emmie that Steve had been sent to Liechtenstein not just for information but to get him out of the way. It was even clearer that there had been a conspiracy to take Darkmouth for the assistants. Knowing how to *reveal* this truth was another matter.

Finn would not let it go, though. He would fight to get Darkmouth back.

There would be no vacation yet.

"You really would love Smoofyland," his mother kept insisting. "You know it's in Slotterton? It was an old

Blighted Village, once filled with Legends, so you never know what might happen."

"I'll be bored and embarrassed, that's what'll happen," said Finn.

"Smoofyland has a roller coaster." She smiled. "The sparkliest roller coaster ever built."

"Exactly," said Finn.

DO NOT PUBLISH

Report by Tiger-One-Twelve

Location: North Africa

By the time we arrived, the sun was as high as it would get, the heat ready to strip the skin off anyone crazy enough to go for a stroll in it.

It roasted steep ridges of sand dunes in a desert that stretched for five hundred miles in every direction. Except, that is, to the south, where it stretched for a *thousand* miles with only a brief break for boiling mud. This was not a place for life, apart from the very hardiest of creatures.

The man they called Warmaksan the Unflinching was about the hardiest of all.

Our jeep had bounced over dunes to reach him, shuddering and shaking while three of us clung on inside. Our destination was Warmaksan's village, apparently long abandoned, its collapsed stone huts as bleached as the landscape swallowing them up. I could not pronounce the village's name, but it translated into something like "Death and Maiming Is This Village's Specialty."

The driver asked my translator something.

"Lady," said my translator, "are you sure this is the right place?"

I nodded and the vehicle threw up a spray of sand and flies as it ground to a halt at the edge of the crumbled settlement. The translator and I stepped out wearily, preparing ourselves for the flaying heat. He waited a moment while I adjusted the brim of my hat before striding toward the one remaining hut with a fully intact roof.

Stepping into its relative cool, I let my vision adjust. It soon revealed a pair of eyes, glinting in the dim light leaking through a high window. The man behind those eyes stayed sunken in a creaking chair. This was Warmaksan the Unflinching.

He had been here for many decades, the one remaining Legend Hunter from the village. The others were long gone, but his duty was to remain at his post should the day ever come when he would be required.

That day had come.

His eyes told me he was deeply afraid.

"Ask him what happened here," I asked my translator.

The two began a conversation in a language I couldn't hope to comprehend.

"He says the lights came," said the translator. "From the sky. And that when they left, the ground began to cry."

Warmaksan kept talking, louder, faster, until it became a babble.

"What is it?" I asked the translator, impatient.

The translator held a hand up to me to ask for more time, then got into some kind of animated discussion with Warmaksan. When that had concluded, he considered carefully what he should tell me.

"Lady, he says the dead walked."

This did not faze me. In fact, it might have looked as if I was expecting that answer. "Ask him how many of the dead walked."

The translator lifted his eyebrows, skeptical, but repeated the question nonetheless.

Warmaksan responded, calmer now that he sensed I might take him seriously.

"All of them," said the translator.

Warmaksan gestured toward a door at the rear of the house.

Following his direction, I stepped into the cooker of this desert day and the three of us walked through the crumbled remains of what was once a Blighted Village, a place that had long ago said good-bye to its only business—killing Legends. Once that had stopped, its inhabitants had either left or died off. Only Warmaksan remained. As a sentinel. A watcher. Just he and the buried dead.

Those dead were no longer buried.

At the eastern end of the village was a circular site where slabs of stone marked the graves of those who had been placed here many decades before. But where there should have been undisturbed ground, a carpet of bones glinted under the bright sun.

Skulls.

Ribs.

Leg bones.

Hips.

Ancient and bare, each rough pile of bones seemed to belong to an individual. There were maybe forty such scattered heaps in all. It looked as if each had been pushed up from directly beneath the surface.

The translator took a step back from this gruesome sight. I couldn't blame him. I have seen a few things in my time—a worrying number of those things recently—but this was on a level of strangeness even I had not expected. Or wanted.

Warmaksan the Unflinching shuffled up to my shoulder and said something. I looked to the translator.

"He says that this is not yet the strangest part," the translator said.

Warmaksan directed us to a small rock pile where sand had rested in drifts. Something was sticking out from it, a shocking artificial red among the desert's bleached monotony. I pulled it free, shook the sand away, and held it up.

"A bag?" asked the translator.

"A schoolbag," I confirmed.

"What's that writing on it?"

I turned it over and read a scrawl that was made up of three distinct parts.

EMMIE SMELLS, read the top line.

NO I DON'T, read the next in different handwriting.

Finally, in neat block letters at the base of the bag: **IF FOUND, PLEASE RETURN TO FINN**.

Smacking a fly on my neck knocked me from my trance. I realized I needed to get back into the shade before I combusted under the sun. Retreating back into the hut, I motioned to the driver to hand me our satellite phone. Yanking the antenna to its full length, I dialed a number. After three rings so distant they might as well have been calling another planet, a voice answered.

"Bubble Blast Car Wash," said a very chirpy voice. "How can I help you?"

"Reptile-Three-Seven," I said. "This is Tiger-One-Twelve. What is the status of Ugly Duckling?"

The phone glitched, hissed, and squibbed to life again.

"Roger, Tiger-One-Twelve. Ugly Duckling is within half a klick of his home and eating a Whammy Bar." There was a pause. "Correction, Tiger-One-Twelve, make that a Squishy Bar. Repeat: Ugly Duckling is eating a Squishy Bar."

I hung up, thanked Warmaksan and, with the schoolbag in my hand, returned toward the Jeep. I needed water. Not just for the heat, but for the headache that this discovery had brought on.

As I walked, I gazed at a horizon rimmed with vast, shifting dunes and thought of people far off in that direction, wandering through a small town in a distant land.

I knew that thousands of miles away, in a Blighted Village on the east coast of the island of Ireland, the boy Finn was walking while eating a Squishy Bar.

More than that, I knew something big was coming his way.

"Hello," Finn said as he passed a man sponging down a car.

"Hello," said the man from Bubble Blast Car Wash.

If Finn had stopped to think about it for a moment, he might have noticed that the Bubble Blast Car Wash man was washing the same part of the car over and over. And that he wasn't really washing it too well anyway, just sort of waving a hand over a windshield that looked shiny enough as it was.

But Finn was distracted. First because he had managed to get a glob of Squishy Bar stuck between his teeth, which required trying to dislodge it with his finger. Second because he was following two people through the many back lanes of Darkmouth while trying not to be seen. Or heard.

Hanging back, with a baseball cap pulled low, he dialed

a number on his phone. It was quickly answered.

"They're talking about cakes, I think," he whispered into the line.

"Cakes?" asked Emmie's voice loudly.

"Cakes," replied Finn.

Ahead of him, two assistants were walking purposefully toward some unknown destination. They wore the grayest of gray, as if someone had designed it specifically to be the least interesting color ever invented. There were too many of these suits, and the assistants wearing them, around Darkmouth these days. Finn had begun to recognize these two, though. She was Scarlett. He was Greyson. Finn had made it his business to find out what they were up to.

Scarlett and Greyson stopped.

Finn ducked behind a Dumpster, pressed in tight against the wall, and listened.

"Why hasn't it worked?" Greyson asked. "It should have worked."

"We can't talk about this in public," said Scarlett.

"We've added the sherbet," replied Greyson, tapping his head as if hoping an answer would fall out. "We've added chocolate. We've even experimented with custard."

"Please, we can't–"

"And no one likes wasting custard."

"Stop," Scarlett ordered him, looking around to see if anyone was listening.

Finn was so close to them, crouched behind the Dumpster, hardly breathing for fear of being caught. He pressed a hand against his mouth to stop himself from making any noise.

"We have to be careful," said Scarlett. "The walls have ears."

Greyson examined the wall, ran his hand along it.

"I don't mean they *actually* have ears," said Scarlett. "Come on, let's go."

"If it doesn't work at the cliff today, we should try rainbow sprinkles."

"What did I just say?" Scarlett asked, exasperated.

They resumed their walk again. From behind the Dumpster, squeezed into the darkness of the narrowest of gaps between buildings, Finn breathed again, mightily relieved they hadn't heard Emmie on the far end of the phone asking repeatedly, "What's happening?"

"I don't know," answered Finn, because he didn't. All he knew was that something was going on. *Something* had been going on for a while now. Something strange. He'd spotted assistants moving suspiciously in and out and around the town. These two especially.

"They're heading for the cliffs. Meet me there," he said and hung up.

Using his local advantage over the assistants, Finn ducked into the alleys that crisscrossed Darkmouth. He knew that if he ducked in at Scraper's Lane there would be a shortcut to Red Alley. And if he slipped into the gap between two houses off Red Alley it would bring him to Stump Street, which in turn would allow him a quick route to Limper's Rock.

He emerged at the beach road ahead of the assistants. At the same time, Emmie arrived from another of the narrow lanes.

"Hey," she said. "What do you think those assistants are doing? And why are you wearing a baseball cap that says *Cool Dude?*"

Finn took her elbow and pulled her around to face a shop window.

Scarlett and Greyson approached along the path. Hunched, with his baseball cap pulled down, Finn hoped they hadn't noticed him and Emmie or that the two of them were looking in a shop window long empty except for dead flies and dirt.

"They're up to something," Finn said after the assistants walked past. "They've been up to something for a while.

We need to find out what."

Emmie kept looking at his hat.

"And the best disguise I could do on short notice was this dumb baseball cap, okay?"

"You should have grown a mustache or something." She smiled.

"This is serious," Finn said. "Whatever they're doing, we need to find out what it is so we can have our old lives back. Do you like sharing one bathroom with loads of people every morning?"

"Good point," she said. "Come on."

The assistants climbed a path toward what remained of Darkmouth's cliffs, a slumped mass of rock and earth on which grass grew and trees clung at precarious angles. They had collapsed when Finn's grandfather Niall Blacktongue had returned from the Infested Side and exploded in a cave below the cliffs to destroy an army of invading Legends. During that adventure, Finn had also turned into a walking bomb, and while he'd had a few explosive moments since, in the months since Gantrua's invasion he was beginning to feel like the strange energy had finally dissipated, that he had gradually returned to something like normal. The cliff, though, would never be the same again.

Finn and Emmie took another shortcut, dashing along the stone shore, carefully making their way across the narrow strip of beach squeezed between the soil and the sea. They clambered up the long, steep slope of weeds and grass just as the assistants arrived from the other direction. The breeze carried their curses as briars caught at their suit pants, as they stumbled over ground that had come crashing down in one terrific, almost catastrophic implosion.

The *cave.*

That's why they're here, thought Finn. That was what they were looking for. The Cave at the Beginning of the World, as it was once known. A place where crystals had grown, where gateways to the Infested Side had popped open and shut.

But it had been destroyed, pulverized by the exploding Niall Blacktongue. Hadn't it?

The assistants paused to look around them, and Finn and Emmie dropped behind the tendrils of a half-uprooted tree, still heavy with leaves, but its branches almost touching the ground on one side, as if it might topple fully at any moment.

They carefully maneuvered themselves so that they were behind the web of roots that had been thrust into unwanted daylight and peered through them. The assistants were gone.

"Where are they?" asked Finn, pushing himself up for a better view.

"They just kind of dropped out of sight," said Emmie.

They crept into the open again, carefully at first, presuming they'd see the assistants' heads over the crest of the land. But there was no sign. They moved past a couple more lopsided trees, toward where they had last seen them, and Finn noticed a patch of ground that looked out of place, like a wig on a bald head.

He carefully pulled at it and the grass and dirt fell away like a kind of mat. It revealed a hole that, if he was to guess, was large enough to fit an adult with relative comfort.

"Is that a rope ladder just inside?" Emmie asked.

Finn knew every inch of Darkmouth—above ground and, more recently, the tunnels and caves below. "This was never here before," he said.

From the collapsing trees angling behind them, birds sang, noisy. Something sticky landed on Finn's neck, and he swatted at it while trying to concentrate on the voices he could hear rising from the hole in the ground.

"That didn't work," they heard Greyson say, and Emmie moved back instinctively, her feet pushing away a sliver of rocks and soil so they formed a tiny avalanche as they tumbled down the slope.

"We'll try again," they heard Scarlett reply from deep down below, in the ground.

Feeling a little braver, Finn stood higher, craned over the hole to listen better.

"Do we hold it this way, or that way?" Greyson asked.

"Well, we held it that way last time," Scarlett replied, "so we should probably hold it *this* way this time and see what happens."

Finn and Emmie looked at each other, frowning.

All went quiet. There was only the sound of the breeze and birds, and the pebbles sliding away from their feet. Finn began to wonder if the assistants had left the cave and headed out some other way.

Then a spark rose up from the darkness, a burst of light, lasting just a millisecond.

"What was that?" asked Finn.

It happened again.

And again.

"Again?" he heard Greyson ask.

"Again," confirmed Scarlett.

There was another momentary burst of light.

Finn placed his hand on the bark of the tree to keep his balance as he leaned over the hole in the cliff, but the sap's stickiness was enough to pull at his skin. The birds were making a lot of noise too, above them and across the trees scattered over the crumbled cliffs.

He stood to gather his thoughts, trying to pick the drying sap off his hands while figuring out exactly what to do now. "What do you think, Emmie?"

"I think there's something very weird going on with that little bird over your head," she said.

He looked up. A tiny finch was hanging upside down from a leaf, desperately pecking at the branch and beating its wings, unable to pull itself free.

Finn reached up to the branch and felt the sap covering the bird, and he realized it was seeping from every part of the tree. As gently as he could, he helped free the small bird. It did not fight him, its exhaustion overpowering its fear. He felt its heart beat at a panicked pulse, held it out delicately to show Emmie.

She took a bottle from her bag and gently squeezed water over the bird's back and wings while he massaged it as carefully as he could, until the sap gradually eased out and, with a shake, the bird found freedom again in its wings.

Finn held the bird out on the palm of his hand, where it stayed for a little while longer, regaining its energy.

Eventually, it spread its wings and flew, dropping low along the grass before picking up and rising higher as it disappeared across the hill toward the town. They followed its flight, Finn feeling pleased that they had freed it, saved it from certain death.

Until he realized that in every tree in sight there were birds fighting, struggling, failing to free themselves from the sap that oozed from the leaves and bark. He nudged Emmie and showed her.

"That's weird," said Emmie.

"Are you spying on us?" asked Scarlett, her head popping up through the hole in the ground.

"I think they *were* spying on you," said Estravon, appearing behind them, flanked by two assistants, stocky men who filled their suits, thick necks spilling out over their collars. "And I've had to ruin a good pair of shoes spying on *them*. Come with me, you two. Lucien will not be happy."

Lucien was annoyed with his kids. Lucien was *always* annoyed with his kids.

"Put down that head, Elektra," Lucien ordered his daughter, an eight-year-old girl with seemingly inexhaustible batteries. She had an eye for trouble. And another eye for mayhem. Right now she was wandering around the wide, circular library of Finn's house with a 250-year-old stuffed Minotaur head on her thin shoulders, wobbling and giggling, while her six-year-old brother, Tiberius, hit her with a large spear.

Finn and Emmie watched from where they stood in the long hallway, right beside the bare spot on the wall where Finn's portrait was supposed to be hanging. Beside it was the square in which his father's portrait was meant to be, and alongside it the dark rectangle from where his grandfather Niall Blacktongue had once gazed. He was gone too, considered the first bad apple in what Lucien had decided was a rotten crop.

"Put down that spear, Tiberius," Lucien ordered his son.

Tiberius brought it swinging down on his sister's head, and she staggered backward into a shelf of ancient desiccated Legends.

From the hallway to the library, Lucien strode angrily to the door, gripped it with knuckle-whitening frustration, considered saying something, but reconsidered before slamming it shut just as Elektra hit the floor and Tiberius leaped on her tummy.

"They'll get tired eventually," he said.

From the other side of the door they heard the sound of a spear hitting a stuffed Minotaur head, followed by a muffled sound of pain.

Lucien drew a long, steadying breath and turned his attention to the other problematic young people in his life.

"You know the writer for *The Most Great Lives* is due to visit?" he said to Finn. *The Most Great Lives of the Legend Hunters, from Ancient Times to the Modern Day* was the most prestigious, popular, and long encyclopedia. Its publishers had waited years for Finn to become a proper Legend Hunter so they could print, and sell, a new version.

Unfortunately, *The Most Great Lives* had a section on traitors.

"They want to write an entry even though you are not yet

a proper Legend Hunter," continued Lucien, unblinking. "There is such demand for your story. Everyone wants to hear it. But the rumor is they have not yet decided if you should be among the heroes at the front, or the traitors hidden under black pages at the back of the book."

Lucien rubbed a palm over his few wisps of hair. "So I wonder, young man, why you look so satisfied for somebody on the verge of destroying his family's legacy?"

Letting that thought sit, Lucien set off down the hallway so that Finn and Emmie were forced to walk alongside him.

"How many times do you have to be told to stay out of things in Darkmouth?"

"Dunno," Finn answered, as insolent as he could manage. "How many times has it been so far, Emmie?"

"Quite a lot," she said.

Lucien stopped, and even though he was neither tall nor imposing, he radiated a menace that made Finn bristle all the same. He felt the hair prickle on his neck, hoped it hadn't been noticed.

"You are a cocky young man these days," Lucien said, his breath as sour as his mood. "You weren't always like that. I know this from previous reports. From everything Estravon told me."

"That was before you kicked us out of our home." It

hurt Finn to know he was only *visiting* his own house. He missed every part of it, and it all seemed so much sharper to his senses now that he was hardly ever in it. The distinctive must of the corridor, of metal and wood and peeling portraits. The vinegary odor of Desiccator fluid that had leaked into the walls over the years.

Lucien's kids had filled much of this place with their toys and clothes and stench. It made Finn nauseous to even contemplate it. But he needed to keep his mind focused on one job right now. Which was being really obnoxious to Lucien.

"I have been very lenient on you and your family given what you have done," Lucien told him with a wave of his hand while walking on again.

"We've lost everything because of you," said Finn.

"I have allowed you to stay at home here in Darkmouth."

"The other house is *not* my home," said Finn, unable to stay patient, and stepping in front of Lucien.

There was a thud and a wail from way behind them at the library door, as Elektra or Tiberius succumbed to some inevitable stuffed-Minotaur-related accident.

Lucien did not flinch. "I have allowed you to stay in Darkmouth while we examine exactly what happened, how and—most importantly—*who* was involved. You forget that I could have sent you and your parents to Liechtenstein HQ to be imprisoned. Or far worse."

"Like how you sent Steve away," said Finn.

Emmie's face tightened at that.

"As someone who was trapped between worlds, he is helping us understand the threat we all face, that is all," said Lucien.

"Or you're getting one more problem out of Darkmouth," said Finn.

"There are many worse things we could have done to your family. Many, many things that are allowed by the Legend Hunter punishment book." Lucien paused, then called out. "Estravon?"

Estravon stuck his head out of a small training room off the hallway. "In 1867, Jan the Intolerable was made to eat forty rotten boiled eggs in under three minutes as punishment for his cowardice at the Battle of Little Death." Estravon retreated back into the room to finish whatever he was up to in there.

"Something's going on," Finn said. "You've sent the Half-Hunters home. You've sent Steve to Liechtenstein. It's almost like you want them all out of the way."

"That's clever. Exactly the kind of quick thinking I would want if I was, say, a traitor working for the Legends," said

Lucien, pausing at the top of the hallway at the first, and oldest, portrait of one of Finn's ancestors. The painting itself was so ancient it was merely a square of varying brown blobs. A worn plaque beside it declared it to be of long-dead Legend Hunter Aodh the Handsome.

"You're doing something in the cave," said Emmie.

"It's a place where incredibly important and dangerous crystals grow," explained Lucien. "The only place on Earth, in fact. Those crystals have the power to spontaneously open gateways to the Infested Side. Of course we're doing something. We're looking into that strange phenomenon."

Finn felt cornered, trapped by Lucien's logic.

"You're looking a little annoyed now," Lucien said to him. "Be careful. I know you haven't exploded in a while but I've only just had this door painted and I wouldn't want you ruining it."

"You can't keep doing this," Finn told him.

"This is your final warning," said Lucien. "The next time you look like you're spying on behalf of the Legends, your family will have to go. You. Your mother. Your father. All gone. No more Darkmouth. No more home."

"You're framing us," said Finn.

"Emmie will be gone too. And it will be your fault." Lucien looked at her. "I don't even have to ask how upset you would be about that."

Finn retreated into silence.

Lucien eyed him, pushed his glasses up his nose. "It doesn't need to be this way. Think about that. Think about your future."

He casually closed the front door after Finn and Emmie.

They walked down the street a bit, quietly furious, until they were at the corner of the house they now shared.

"We'll go and check out the cave later," Finn said. "We know how to get into it now. They're up to something else, for sure."

"You heard him, right?" Emmie said, sympathetic but reluctant. "We're in danger of getting into worse trouble than we're already in."

"I remember when *you* were the one pushing *me* into things," Finn said to her.

"And I remember when you were the sensible one," she said, but he was already jogging on down the street.

"Where are you going?" she called after him.

"To see Dad at work," Finn called back over his shoulder. "He'll know what to do."

So it was that, five minutes later, Finn was in the back of a shop called Woofy Wash, looking at a very grumpy Hugo giving a labradoodle a bath.

3

The labradoodle was shiny, its tongue hanging loose, its eyes covered by wringing-wet black curls, while Hugo—still officially the last and greatest Legend Hunter on Earth—cursed as he pulled a large comb through its sopping coat.

"This morning was a real mess," Finn explained to his dad.

"Stupid, hairy, knotted mutt," hissed Hugo, the comb tangled in doggy curls. "Why people don't just shave their dogs bald, I don't know."

"Something's up," Finn continued, wincing at the sight of his father's struggles. "And just because I tried to find out what it is, Lucien threatened to kick us out of Darkmouth altogether."

"You have no idea how long it took to clean this animal's paws," Hugo griped without pause. "I think it walked through wet tar to get here, or something. I had to use a toothbrush to get in the gaps."

He pulled again at the dog's coat. The labradoodle yelped.

"Brush it first, before washing it," said Finn.

Hugo stopped–the comb snagged in the dog's newly shampooed hair–and looked hard at his son in a way that suggested he didn't want advice but might have to take some anyway.

"You should brush dogs before washing them," repeated Finn. "It makes it easier to comb them afterward."

At another time in his life, Finn had wanted to be a vet instead of a Legend Hunter. It wasn't that he'd given up on that dream; it was just that for a while now he'd had no choice.

Silently, Hugo seemed to accept the advice and began to calmly untangle the comb from the dog's coat, as if he'd had his rant and let off the required steam.

Hugo's boss, Mr. Green, passed behind and, without stopping, without even looking at Hugo, said, "You should have had that labradoodle polished up and out by now, Hugo. You have two cats to primp and a guinea-pig haircut to do, all before midmorning break."

This kicked Hugo back into grumpiness and he pulled a little hard on the comb, causing the poor dog to yelp again.

"And next time you should brush the dog *before* you wash it," said Mr. Green, disappearing into the front of the shop.

"I was in school with that self-important fool," Hugo murmured so that only Finn could hear. "He never liked me. He's loving every minute of this. The second I'm done with this job, I'm going to give *him* a soaking so strong it'll shrink him to a size no bigger than this dog's—"

He stopped, glancing at Finn.

"We could have used you out there this morning," Finn said. "We could use you out there every time this happens."

"I *know* that," his father hissed. "I want to be out there, not here, up to my elbows in dog fleas. But without access to our own house, this is the only way we can get enough of the chemicals to make our own Desiccator fluid. Without this, when an invasion happens again—and it will happen—we'll be fighting off Legends with nothing but guinea-pig hair clips. I just wish the right combination of chemicals could be found in, I don't know, the ice cream shop or somewhere. Not here, with these poodledors—"

"Labradoodles," Finn corrected him.

"Whatever they're called," said Hugo, pulling at the dog's coat. "Either way, these things have . . . too . . . many . . . curls."

The dog whimpered, but was finally free of the combing.

Hugo let it down off the table to scamper to a basket and chew on a rubber bone.

Mr. Green appeared once more in the washing area, again passing by without stopping. "A rabbit's done its business on the shop counter," he said. "Wipe it up before you move on to Killer."

"Killer?" asked Hugo.

"The guinea pig."

Hugo looked like he might swing a fist, or maybe an entire labradoodle, at his boss.

"But we had better get Darkmouth back soon," Hugo said. "If I have to wash another mutt's you-know-what, I'll go insane. More insane than I am now anyway."

Finn knew his father had sacrificed many things over the years in order to fulfill his duty as a Legend Hunter. He'd never vacationed. He'd never been able to relax during a rainstorm. He'd never stopped training, thinking, planning, day and night and the next day again. But this seemed to be the greatest sacrifice of all. Swapping his dignity for a couple of bottles of doggy shampoo.

Hugo looked around to make sure Mr. Green had gone, then pulled six small plastic bottles from under the table and pressed them into Finn's schoolbag.

"That's a couple of quarts of Shampoodle," he said. He

then reached across for a box from the shelf. "And one packet of Fabulous Fish Fin Formula. They'll shrink a jumbo jet when mixed right. Just don't be seen leaving with them or I'll lose my job."

Hugo took a moment to contemplate that possibility, knowing being sacked would be a sweet release from the doggy drudgery.

"No," he said. "I can't think about losing my job. I must plow on. It's the only way for now."

"You keep saying that, Dad, but what's changing?" said Finn, grabbing a towel and laying it over the labradoodle's sodden back. "Nothing. It's getting worse out there and you're stuck in here."

"Listen to me, Finn," Hugo said. "Do you think I want to be here? Do you think my only plan is spending my life with pets whose toenails are out of control?"

"Then what is your plan?" Finn asked, frustration building. "Because I don't see it."

"I have it under control, Finn. You just need to be patient."

"And while we wait," Finn said, "we're crammed into a small house, waiting for disaster, knowing they're scheming something but we just can't see what yet." He was getting really angry now.

His father stopped toweling the dog. "Please just go to

school, play soccer, do whatever, but I need you to let me deal with this in case things really do get out of control."

Mr. Green shouted from outside the room, "Hugo! Rabbit poo! Now!"

Hugo gritted his teeth. Took a long, calming breath. "You need to understand, Finn," he said before leaving. "The most effective way to grab victory is to first look like you've lost everything."

"That makes no sense," Finn muttered, alone now.

The labradoodle sneezed, covering Finn in flecks of water.

Wiping himself down, Finn stepped into the salty Darkmouth air. Things were definitely as bleak as they'd ever been. He could sense it. It was as if the world itself had darkened. Then Finn realized that it *had*. While he'd been in with his dad, a low, heavy cloud had dragged itself across the sky. The bright, cloudless blue of the day had given way to a near twilight.

A drop of rain splashed onto Finn's shoulder. He put his hand out and caught two more.

It wasn't supposed to rain today.

The rain fell heavier, stinging drops hopping off his head, bouncing off the road around him.

Rain meant Legends, breaking through.

Finn looked up, took a raindrop in the eye. He wiped it away, and when he did he realized that the ground around him was being lit by a growing golden glow.

Finn felt a tiny prick in his neck, like he'd been stung, smacked at his skin as he swung around to meet the chest of someone. Something. He looked up, saw an eye staring at him. One eye. No more.

"Sorry, kid," the Legend said, voice deeper than hell. "You're coming with us."

4

The gateway opened for a few seconds.

About three minutes later, four panting assistants finally arrived at the scene, carrying Desiccators awkwardly. They'd been delayed by an argument about which alley to run down. Half of them had said they should go right. Half said they should go left. They ended up going straight ahead, which, by sheer luck, was exactly where they should have gone in the first place.

They burst into the dead end near the back of Woofy Wash, where the gateway had torn its way into our world.

But there was no gateway.

There were no Legends.

Even the rain had gone, stopping so suddenly it was as if someone had turned off the shower tap.

The assistants looked at one another with some bemusement.

"There's nothing here," said one of them.

"I told you we should have gone right," said another.

"You said we should have gone left. *I* said we should go right," said a third.

A noise startled them and the assistants lifted the Desiccators they'd brought.

But it was only Hugo, throwing out a basin of dirty, rabbit-poo-filled water.

They kept their weapons raised. He paused, liquid slopping around the edge of the basin.

The assistants lowered their weapons. Hugo threw the water along the ground, so that it lapped and splashed at their gleaming shoes, then returned inside.

As if a single entity, the assistants turned to clatter and bump their way away from the dead end back toward the main street, still arguing about which direction they should have gone in.

But someone else remained unseen. Emmie had followed their movements, knowing they'd be so wrapped up in the thought of catching Legends that she could shadow them easily.

She crouched to the ground, found a patch of dust, exactly the sort created when something comes through a gateway. But there was only one smattering, as if a large foot had been placed in this world, and immediately withdrawn. Otherwise, there was no sign of scratch marks on walls, or bite marks on Dumpsters.

Nothing.

She was about to leave the scene when something else caught her eye. A small bottle of Shampoodle rolling across the ground, spilling a dull blue chemical from its open top. Emmie walked to it, rolled it with her foot, and glanced back at the door of Woofy Wash.

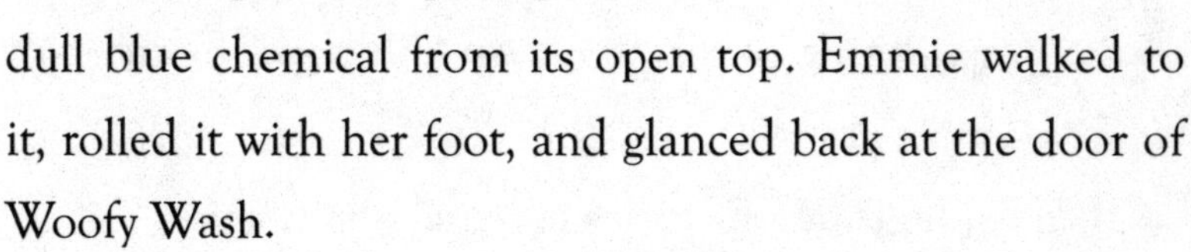

Something was wrong, although she couldn't quite figure out what it was. Finn would know what to do, she decided.

She set off to find him.

5

Finn woke.

He was trapped in a small space, so dark he could see nothing at all, not even the hand in front of his face.

Hold on, he thought, *maybe my hand is missing*.

No. He wiggled his fingers and it felt like they were all present and correct. But he still had no sight. No light. Only a sandpapery surface at his back and a gooey, ribbed roof he could feel inches from his face.

Panic grabbed him, even as his mind was slow to get moving, heavy, dopey, unable to quite fix on where he was or how he had gotten here. He tried to stay composed, to figure it out.

The sharp sting on his neck. Passing out. He must have been drugged, Finn thought, and dragged here. Wherever here was.

The smell was so deeply terrible it was invading every

pore in his body. He would need a change of skin if he ever got out of here. He tasted it on his tongue, wanted to pull his tongue out in disgust.

It would be pointless trying to find a way to describe the stench in earthly terms, because there was nothing on Earth like it. It was a smell that belonged only to one place.

The Infested Side.

Finn's breath quickened. He groped for a wall on either side of him, and found bars of some sort, surrounding him on at least three sides. And those bars were wedged into a hard but slippery surface. The fourth side was narrow and soft and his hand couldn't quite find the wall.

It made his stomach crawl. Or maybe that was the movement he now realized he was feeling in jolts. He was moving. In fact the whole *room* was moving.

Up. *Drop*.

Up. *Drop*.

A damp breeze blasted through each time it rose, heating his ears. There was also a deep, unnerving gurgle from somewhere terribly close.

Finn wriggled onto his tummy, feeling the roughness against his face giving him the chills as he reached out and pushed his hands through the bars, whose dark outlines he could just make out against the redness of the walls.

He prized open a gap in his prison, working it wider with his fingers, just enough for gray light to pour into the space and show him that the bars were, in fact, large fangs.

He was lying on a tongue.

A pink tongue, rough and pulsating with each of the breaths pushing up from the throat at which his feet dangled.

A giant tongue, in a giant mouth.

Finn allowed himself to panic some more. It had been a bad day already, but now he was something's lunch. Could this day get any worse?

Pushing his face toward the crack in the mouth of whatever creature was carrying him, Finn saw water rushing past outside, a blur of dark waves, getting closer. And closer. He retreated just before the creature hit the sea, brine leaking through the mouth as Finn breathed hard and shallow.

Yes.

His day could get worse.

Up. They were out of the water.

Drop. Whooosh. Back into it.

A few seconds later, the creature hit something hard, slid to a sudden halt. Finn gripped onto a long tooth to stop himself from being thrown back into the deep cavern of the creature's gullet.

Blurpp. A rumble was building from deep within the throat, getting louder, closer.

Oh no, thought Finn, at the precise moment a belch hit him.

The mouth opened and he was propelled into the gray light of the Infested Side.

He looked around, dazed. He was lying on a shoreline, a beach of smashed rock in the shadow of a looming mountain, chunks missing from its slopes and most of it swallowed by heavy cloud.

The sea creature retreated into the waters before Finn could even get a proper look at it. He was instead distracted by a huge figure approaching up the beach, feet stuffed into boots with three-clawed toes stabbing through. It had granite hands, muscles popping from its wide shoulders. Glancing up, Finn realized this was the single-eyed giant, the Cyclops that had grabbed him from Darkmouth in the first place. This must be one of Gantrua's goons, out for revenge.

It snarled something at him.

Finn jumped to his feet, his skin sticky with sea-creature saliva, his hair flattened and damp, his legs numb from being trapped in such a small space for . . . well, he didn't know how long. But they had enough feeling left to help him scramble across cutting stones among which were scattered splintered and broken tools—axes, knives, picks, hammers.

He stumbled, saw the nearing shadow of the Legend. He needed a plan. Perhaps he had an expert move learned over many hours at training. Maybe he could threaten to explode, just as he had done before in this world—draw himself up and stare even the mightiest of them down with his power. Even if he didn't really have it anymore.

Instead, Finn did what he had so often done best.

He ran.

He heard the roars and shouts of other Legends joining the Cyclops. He didn't look back. He needed to keep pushing along the shifting rock and broken tools of this beach, which sloped upward now, away from the sea toward the scarred mountain and, he hoped, some sort of shelter. The Legends were closing. His legs burned with adrenaline. He needed to keep climbing this slope, to get somewhere safe.

Finn reached the top of the slope and went straight over a cliff.

6

Finn held on to a blackened, blasted tree root, one foot dangling over a sheer drop that a quick and frightening glance told him went down far enough that there were dark angry waves where the ground should be.

The sea. On both sides. He was on some sort of narrow cliff jutting perilously out over the waves.

And he had come within a Manticore's whisker of falling straight off, had thrown a hand out just quick enough to save himself. For now.

He wrapped his arms around this lone root and prayed it would not break. He never wanted to let go.

Above him was dark cloud. Below him was darker sea. And behind him on the cliff, he realized, was a pair of boots bigger than his head. Three claws were sticking through one of them. The Cyclops.

"Don't be trying to fly out of here," said the deep-voiced Legend, offering a hand.

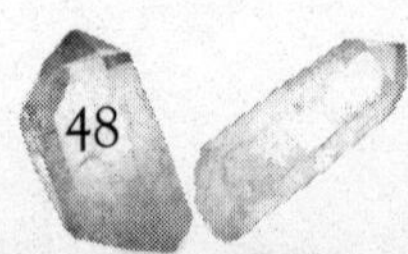

Finn's grip slipped a little on the slimy root. He grunted with the effort of holding on, but he wouldn't be able to for much longer. He felt dead either way.

Then a more familiar voice intruded.

"Accept that helping hand," it said.

Finn saw four paws on the ledge now. Beside them, the lime-green arrowhead of a snake dropped into his sight line.

"We need your help," said Hiss, "and you won't be much use if you're dead."

"T*he number you have dialed is either unavailable or–*"

Emmie didn't wait to let the message finish but ended the call, put the phone back in her pocket, and continued her search for Finn. She'd tried contacting him several times in the couple of hours since the gateway appeared. There had been no answer yet.

She had also walked a good part of the town, head up, watching out for him, ignoring the usual glares of the fearful townspeople and the curiosity of the assistants infesting Darkmouth.

She had not found Finn, nor any sign of him. Nothing about this felt right. She broke into a run, rounded a badly bent signpost, ducked around a mailbox with a dent punched in it, jumped across a puddle of rainwater, and almost knocked Lucien over as they collided at a bend in the street.

"Take it easy there, young lady," he said, stepping back and searching for something on the ground. He found his pen, picked it up, began to weave it through his fingers in a practiced fashion. "I got this pen the day I graduated as an assistant. Writes with squid ink. Don't want to lose it."

She went to pass him.

"Where's your friend?" he asked, causing her to stop.

Emmie loathed Lucien, but there was the fact of his superior rank, and she had to recognize that or it might make things far worse for her and her dad. And things were bad enough as they were.

Lucien sensed something amiss about her. "Is everything all right?" he said, pen tumbling through those long fingers. Across. Back again. "You seem in a great hurry."

"I just want to get home," she said, not wanting to look at him but hardly able to avoid seeing the swish of the pen. "In case it rains again."

"Yes, the rain," said Lucien, looking up, sniffing the air almost theatrically. "It wasn't in the forecast. Strange."

Even with her back to an open street, Emmie felt backed into a corner.

"So, no Finn? What's he up to?"

"Even if I knew I wouldn't tell you," she said, finally

looking him in the eyes. She immediately regretted it—feeling like she'd given him a small victory.

"I wouldn't expect you to tell me," said Lucien, smiling. Or, at least, using a smile to cover over whatever was really going on in his mind. "It's all part of the job to keep secrets, Emmie. Important to remain silent under questioning. To trust no one."

"What job?" she replied, trying to be as rude as possible without giving away the nervous anger she really felt. "You took all this from us when you came in here and accused everyone of being a traitor."

"I accused no one of anything," said Lucien.

Emmie *paah*ed at that idea.

"You might dismiss that, and you'd be wrong, but I don't blame you. Maybe you're a little young to appreciate the nuances of an investigation. I simply looked at the evidence and came to objective conclusions. Anyone else would have done the same. Once I saw the highly unusual events happening here, precautions were needed. After all, here we were in Darkmouth, with a boy and his family who had a habit of going to the Infested Side, fraternizing with Legends, and bringing back trouble."

"Finn was a hero," insisted Emmie. "I saw it. I went to the Infested Side too."

"So did Estravon, and like him, you surely have to admit you don't know what was really going on with Finn at all times." He let that idea sink in before continuing. "I worry you're getting dragged into whatever he's up to."

"Nobody's dragging me into anything," she said.

Lucien was still doing that thing with the pen. Through the fingers, across, and back again. It was really beginning to bother Emmie. He noticed it. Stopped. Slipped it into his suit's breast pocket.

"You've proven yourself an exceptional apprentice Legend Hunter," he said to her. "Honestly, really exceptional. Steve, your father, must be very proud."

Emmie shuffled, uncomfortable, and feeling alone now that she was reminded that her dad was stuck so far away in Liechtenstein.

"You should have been next in line for Completion after Finn," said Lucien. "You should be first in line now."

"I need to go home," she said, and tried again to move past Lucien.

He stayed where he was, simply loitering on the spot, looking skyward once again, examining the town around them as if he just hadn't noticed her desire to get going.

"You could be the next Legend Hunter, the first in many years," Lucien said, his eyes still on the surroundings. "I'm pretty sure that once the investigation is complete, you and your father will be free to get on with your lives, to claim your place among the Legend Hunters."

Emmie squeezed past him, forced him to step aside to let her past, then turned to him, feeling her nails digging into her clenched palms. "I know you're trying to turn me against Finn," she told him, voice trembling with anger. "It won't work."

Lucien remained eerily unflappable. Somehow, he had another pen in his hand, was turning it too through his fingers. "You only have to ask yourself one simple question, Emmie," he said. "Do you *really* know what Finn is up to?"

He thrust the pen into his breast pocket, turned, and walked away.

8

Cornelius was scratching. Hiss was complaining. It was exactly how Finn remembered the Orthrus, this strange hybrid of dog body and snake tail. He had met them over thirty years ago. Or only a year ago. It depended on your perspective. Time travel had been involved. Headaches had resulted.

"After all our years together, I still pray you will satisfy that itch one of these days," Hiss said to Cornelius as the canine adjusted himself and started a new round of intense scratching.

Finn had taken the hand of the one-eyed Legend and allowed himself to be hauled up to safety. He'd then been led back down the slope to the beach, huddling against the scraped rock wall at the base of the mountain. It looked like it had been hacked away, piece by piece, and its debris left to scatter the beach. Even the slope he had climbed he now saw to be a path made by hand, or claw.

And the tools littering the ground had a variety of handles and grips, to accommodate, he guessed, the variety of hands and paws and claws that had done the clearing.

The Cyclops chewed slowly on a cigar-shaped rock, rolling it across his mouth from one side to the other while he watched Finn, who couldn't quite shake off his wariness bordering on fear. He'd studied Legends, read the guidebooks. The Cyclops was not supposed to exist. It was a myth even among Legends.

On the Cyclops's shoulder perched a tiny Legend, no taller than Finn's leg, with a squashed pink nose, wide

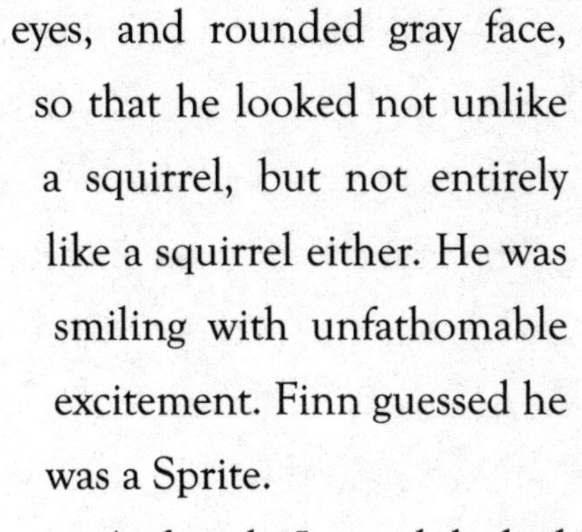

eyes, and rounded gray face, so that he looked not unlike a squirrel, but not entirely like a squirrel either. He was smiling with unfathomable excitement. Finn guessed he was a Sprite.

A fourth Legend lurked farther along in the tall grooves of the rock face. Finn could not see much of this creature but for the eyes, black slits on yellow. Finn had seen eyes like that before, but couldn't recall where. They flooded him with dread.

"What is this place?" Finn asked over the sound of the sea sucking at the stones like it was trying to steal them.

"You'll have a lot of questions, kid," said the Cyclops, "and we've very little time, so pay attention. First, you're on an island."

"Tornclaw. In the middle of the Great Ocean of the Dead," said the Sprite in a helium-high voice, smiling brightly as if delighted to see Finn. He scrambled down the Cyclops's arm and around behind Finn to get a closer look at him.

"Those tools you see? They're here because this whole island used to be a crystal quarry," continued the Cyclops. "It once stretched all the way out into the sea there, but has been hacked away until only the mountain is left. There are no crystals anymore, just the bones of those once forced to work here."

". . ." Finn started to say.

"How did you get here? We found you because the little guy"—he pointed at the Sprite lurking at Finn's legs—"traced you through an energy imprint you're leaking since you exploded in this place all those years ago. He can see you through the invisible walls separating our worlds."

"I can't see you clearly, though." The Sprite grinned. "You look more like an orange blob."

Cornelius was still scratching an itch while Hiss got out of the way.

The other, quiet Legend stayed half out of sight, except for those burning eyes.

"But most of all," the Cyclops said to Finn, "you're wondering, how are you talking to a Cyclops when they don't exist in the first place?"

"That's *not* what I was wondering," Finn said, even though it was what he was wondering. Or at least, one of the things he was wondering.

The Cyclops leaned back, grinning. "Well, you'd be right to wonder."

"If that's what you were wondering," clarified the Sprite, looking up at Finn while picking at the fabric of his jeans.

Finn swatted him away, and he backed off without complaint.

"We don't exist," said the nonexistent Cyclops. "True, I have one eye. But it wasn't always that way." He paused and gave Finn a closer look at the scar circling an eye that appeared to have been pulled over across his face; around it was a patch of crooked, raised skin that looked like it had been carved with a stone and stitched back with that same stone. "I'm a Fomorian, like Gantrua. But we had a little disagreement. This was the result. And now I work for your old pals here."

Cornelius had finally stopped scratching, and Hiss was able to lift himself, curled and steady, to meet Finn's gaze. "His name is Sulawan. Our tiny friend there is Beag. And I am sorry we had to grab you like that. It was the easiest way."

"The easiest way?" exclaimed Finn. "You put me in the mouth of a sea creature."

"A Leviathan, to be precise," Sulawan the sort-of-Cyclops said. "Which means that you, pal, got the luxury trip."

"It didn't smell like luxury," said Finn.

"The rest of us had to rely on being flown here by a Quetzalcóatl," growled Sulawan. "They don't like carrying me, and I sure as hell don't like being carried."

As if on cue, a shadow crossed the beach, a wing slicing through the cloud cover. Finn looked up and saw one of the Quetzalcóatls—a kind of enormous flying serpent that looked too broken to fly yet did so majestically. Some of them had led the resistance against Gantrua when Finn first came here, had controlled the Orthrus through some psychic trickery. But they had also been at war with serpents loyal to Gantrua. He had seen them fight in a great sky battle when rescuing his father from the Infested Side.

"Uncomfortable as it was, we are always in danger of attack in the skies, so the Leviathan was about the best way to hide you and get you here to some sort of sanctuary. There is a lot we need to keep you safe from," explained Hiss. "There is the danger of other Quetzalcóatls trying to grab you. And the Leviathan is big and tough enough to keep you hidden from some . . . other very dangerous threats."

"Why?" asked Finn over the sound of the tide grinding on stone. "Gantrua is gone. I stopped him. Me and Emmie did."

Sulawan took the rock from his mouth, worn almost to a stub. He decided there was a little more chewing in it. "Yeah, well, when you grabbed Gantrua you let loose something far worse."

Cornelius whimpered, shook his head; his ears whipped around.

Finn looked to Hiss. "I don't understand. I thought with him gone, things would be better here."

"They were," said Hiss. "For a time."

"But when you rip the head off a Hydra," said Sulawan, "you shouldn't be surprised when two more grow back."

"Don't talk to me like I'm new to this," argued Finn. "I've stared down the throats of a Hydra."

"It's a metaphor, kid," said Sulawan, amused by his spirit. "And you might want to turn down the attitude a little. My friend over there doesn't react too well to attitude."

The hidden Legend remained in the shadows of the rock, eyes yellow, silent. It bothered Finn, although he was distracted by Beag the Sprite at his leg, staring up, delight glued onto his face.

"So, why bring me here?" Finn asked.

"To answer a question," Hiss said. "Is Gantrua still alive?"

Finn considered this. They'd gone to all this trouble, and *that* was the question?

"Yes," he answered. "Sort of. He was desiccated."

A shudder ran through everyone. Finn sensed it even from the Legend in the shadows. Even the sea seemed to smack at the broken ground extra loudly.

"Where is he kept, kid?" asked Sulawan.

"In my house, I suppose. My old house. An assistant named Lucien took it from us."

"So if you had to, you could get Gantrua back?" asked Hiss. Cornelius moaned a touch, shook the muscles beneath his sleek but weathered coat.

Finn was stunned by the idea of returning the Fomorian, had to replay the sentence in his head to make sure he'd heard it correctly. Once again a shadow passed overhead, darkness crossing Finn's face and jolting him back into reality.

"Who would want to bring Gantrua back?" he asked.

No one answered.

"*You* want to bring Gantrua back?"

"Not really, kid," said Sulawan, stubby rock crunching between his chipped teeth.

"But we have no choice," said Hiss. "When he left this world, he left us a gift in case he ended up trapped in the Promised World. A sort of . . . insurance policy. To wreak devastation in the Infested Side."

"What did he leave?" Finn asked.

A Quetzalcóatl swung from the clouds, circled, and shot out across the sea. They followed its path.

"It looks like we will be able to show you," said Hiss.

With a whine, Cornelius stood and followed a narrow curve around the edge of the mountain, with Hiss swinging gently behind. Sulawan pushed up behind Finn, glaring at him with his one eye to encourage him to follow. Beag was scampering across too. Finn couldn't quite see where the other, silent Legend had gotten to.

He almost tripped on the broken tools that scattered the entire beach.

"As Sulawan said, this island was once rich with crystals, and the mines were here for many years," said Hiss sadly. "So many spent their lives here and gave their lives here. They hacked and hammered at this island in search of opportunities to open a way to the Promised World. Piece by piece, strike by strike, over so many years, so many lives, until most of the island itself was lost beneath the ocean."

Finn walked carefully after the Orthrus. A new serpent appeared above them, where the mountain met cloud, and dived straight toward a point about one hundred yards out to sea. Finn could see that out there the ocean was bubbling, foaming.

"Out there in the depths are many bones, long covered over by the encroaching water," continued Hiss. "But it turns out that Gantrua found a way to rouse the dead, wherever they lie in this world."

"You call us Legends, kid," said Sulawan, "but we have Legends in our world. And when they become real, they're far scarier than anything you humans can imagine."

Cornelius moaned, pitiful. They stopped and peered out at the frothing sea. Finn wasn't sure what exactly he was looking at.

"Wherever there are dead, this creature finds life," said Hiss. "And in this place, there are dead everywhere."

"He left a creature to ravage this world, and there is only one way to stop it," said Sulawan.

"A charm," said Beag, flat nose twitching.

"He took it with him," explained Hiss. "To Darkmouth. You see, he was wearing it. When he crossed over. When you desiccated him. We need that charm. Which means we need Gantrua too."

One of the Quetzalcóatls stopped circling, shot back toward where they stood on the beach. Hiss straightened, gripped in a psychic link with the creature, just as Finn had seen before.

"It is happening," said Hiss, in a droning voice that sounded as if it came from someone else.

"What's happening?" asked Finn.

Hiss stared ahead. "The dead are rising."

The waves came at the shore in spiteful bursts, lifting themselves only to smash down hard. But even the waves seemed to avoid the circle of boiling water out in the depths.

"That thing forming in the deep is what they call Gashadokuro, or just the Bone Creature," Hiss continued. "Millions of the tiniest of organisms come together, binding the bones so that the Gashadokuro rises and rampages anywhere in this world where there are bones to build from. The only way to stop it for good is with the emerald charm Gantrua carried with him to your world. He knew we would have to rescue him if we ever wanted to defeat the terrible creature he left behind."

Finn watched the spitting sea, which was becoming more active by the second.

"Shouldn't we . . . um . . . move?" he said.

"Don't worry," said Sulawan. "The sea is deep and the

Bone Creature not so tall. Yet. We have time. But it is growing ever stronger. If you don't find us Gantrua and his charm, then it will not be stopped until we are all dead and our bones joined with it."

The circle of water was widening, darkening. Beag the Sprite hid behind Sulawan's thick legs. Again Finn noticed the mysterious fourth Legend was still with them, but again pressed into the shadows of the rock wall. He couldn't seem to see its shape, only its yellow eyes.

"Maybe we *should* g-get out of here," stammered Beag. "You know, just in case."

Finn looked at the Orthrus to see if Cornelius and Hiss were as fearful. Hiss appeared to be whispering something calming into Cornelius's ear.

From the depths, the sound grew. It also appeared to be coming closer.

"The Gashadokuro has grown bigger with every visit, but has never reached this island," said Sulawan. "We should be safe here."

With an explosion of spray, something massive punched upward, forcing a shock wave across the water. It frightened Finn enough that he stumbled back, lost his footing on the uneven ground, and fell toward the cutting debris.

Sulawan grabbed him by the arm, held him as he dangled awkwardly, his view of the creature obscured by falling water and black seaweed. But he could make out a yellowed concoction of bones among the dark surf, a ghastly frame forming a makeshift skull with cavernous eye sockets hit by waves.

Sulawan jolted Finn back away from the sea. "That thing's bigger than before," he said to Hiss.

The Bone Creature started to push forward, forcing itself through the high waves.

"It shouldn't be able to get to us," said Hiss.

"Yet it *is* getting to us," said Beag, jittery now and backing away behind the retreating Sulawan.

Where the sea grew shallower, the Bone Creature was slowly emerging now, its skull clearing the water, followed by shoulders made up of many layers of bones. It was accompanied by the sound of scraping through the earth, its feet crunching across the seabed. The shale and broken tools at Finn's feet shifted.

"It is *much* bigger than before," Hiss said to the other Legends. "We should–"

A great bone hand reached out from the sea.

"Run!" said Beag, leaping onto Sulawan's shoulder.

Before Finn could take two steps, Sulawan swept him

up under one armpit and began to stride hard along the uncertain ground.

Behind them a hand smashed down on the shore, a thump of splintering bones that fell like shrapnel around those fleeing.

The serpents dived from above, attacked the Bone Creature, but Finn couldn't see if they were having any effect on it.

"Finn, we need to say good-bye now," Hiss said. "Sulawan will explain your mission."

Before Finn could ask anything else, the Legends broke off in different directions, Sulawan running with Finn under his arm.

The bone fist cracked the beach between them. Being shaken around half upside down, Finn made out only the blur of bone hitting rock, and the way the scattered splinters immediately swept back together and returned to the Bone Creature's hand as it lifted it free, ready for another attack.

Sulawan pounded across the shore, Finn held solidly and helplessly in the crater of his armpit—his nose less than an inch from being worn away to a nub on the rock wall. Beag was clinging on to Sulawan's shoulder with apparent ease despite the sharp turns and juddering speed.

They reached the part of the beach where Finn had first arrived on the island, the pathway running up to the cliff he'd almost fallen off. Sulawan slowed, and peering around his forearm Finn could see only glimpses of the Bone Creature swinging wildly at circling, dive-bombing serpents.

"Let go," Finn just about managed to say.

Sulawan let go, dropping Finn onto stony ground.

"I didn't mean let go *like that*," said Finn, winded.

Sulawan grunted.

Above them, more serpents were appearing through the clouds to pour toward the creature.

"Call him," Cyclops said to Beag.

The tiny Legend stuck two fingers in his mouth and whistled so loudly that the shrill, piercing sound still rang in Finn's ears after he had stopped.

Above them, a serpent reappeared with the Orthrus in its jaws, taking Cornelius and Hiss to safety.

The mountain shook with the sound of battle.

"Okay, kid, this is where you go home," said Sulawan. "Next time I see you, you'll have Gantrua in your pocket."

"I can't do that," Finn told him. "That would be crazy."

Leaning down and thrusting his single eye in Finn's face, Sulawan snarled. "I hear old Cornelius and Hiss saved your life once. *And* your father's. Maybe you should think about that before going all selfish on us."

There was a stirring in the water, a blackness moving through the waves toward them.

"So, let's say I decide to grab Gantrua," asked Finn hurriedly. "What then? I just reanimate him, tell him it's all been a big mistake, ask him for a charm, and hope he doesn't pull my head off?"

"You call us," Sulawan said, and handed him a tube, a little longer than Finn's open hand and made of some kind of thick shell, ridged and lumpy on the outside but smooth inside its rim. "In here are three of the crystals we smuggled out of this mine over the years and kept out of Gantrua's hands. You push the end of this Gatemaker, a crystal will poke out the other end. It'll be enough to punch a gateway open for a brief few seconds. We'll know you're ready then."

Finn took the thing, felt a squirming within the thick shell.

"The crystals are attached to living scaldgrubs," said Beag, "so they can survive the trip to your world."

He saw the disgust on Finn's face.

"Don't worry, they're only baby scaldgrubs," said Sulawan. "Just don't go putting your finger in there. They nibble."

"I can't steal Gantrua," said Finn.

"You will. For some reason Hiss thinks you can be trusted with this job," said Sulawan.

"Sulawan doesn't trust anyone," said Beag, smiling.

The noise from the other side of the cliff was of pure havoc, of serpents screeching, of the Bone Creature attacking.

"This is a crazy plan, you do realize that?" Finn said over the encroaching noise.

Sulawan thought about that. "Yeah," he decided. "It is."

The dark shadow in the sea rose, pushing up a humped film of water and creating a wave that raced away on either side of it.

"One last question before you go," said Sulawan. "Why have you humans been trying to open gateways into our world?"

Finn shook his head. "I didn't. We haven't been."

"Well, someone has," said Sulawan. "Someone on your side."

Then Finn remembered what he'd seen at the cliff back home. The assistants. That's what they must have been doing with the crystals, he realized. Trying to open gateways.

"Actually . . . ," he said. "I think I know who that might be." But it was madness. Why would they do that? Why would they deliberately try to open gateways to the Infested Side, in a town that had always tried desperately to protect against that very thing?

"Well, here's some free advice. They'd better stop," said Sulawan. "If they keep trying to punch a hole to our world, someday they're going to open one they won't be able to close."

"He needs to get into the Leviathan now," Beag said, watching the advancing form breaking through the churning waters.

"Back into that mouth?" asked Finn, aghast at the idea of being thrust into the slobbering jaws of a sea monster. "I can't."

"Would you prefer to be unconscious?" asked Beag. From somewhere, he had produced a needle of bone—a long serpent's tooth perhaps. A glint of liquid dripped from the end of it.

"No!" screamed Finn.

Sulawan grabbed him, held his arms down. "The Leviathan will take you away from here. It's quicker than the Bone Creature. Hopefully."

Finn felt helpless in Sulawan's grip. "You're not putting me to sleep again," he yelled over the racket.

They put him to sleep again.

Finn's last memory was of the world tumbling as the jaws of a Leviathan rose from the ocean depths to swallow him.

10

Finn woke on a stone beach, while being pecked at by a seagull.

It ate a touch of the dust that surrounded him, immediately regretted it, gagged as it flew away.

Shocked, Finn jumped to his feet, saw the outline of his body in dust on the stone. The sea lapped at his feet, washed the dust away. He slapped the rest of it from himself, felt his head to make sure his mind was still there, and briefly wondered if he had been in a dream.

But that smell couldn't be imagined. He stank very badly—the stench of the Infested Side. Of sweat. Of the breath of a belching sea monster. He briefly considered jumping into the water to be free of it, and only then realized it was raining. Heavy drops, but already easing off.

The dust was also evidence that he had been on the Infested Side. He remembered one other thing, patted around his pocket until he found the shell tube attached

to his leg. This was the Gatemaker, the way back to the Infested Side when he wanted it. Scaldgrubs squirmed inside. Finn's stomach squirmed with them.

The task they'd given him was a crazy one. Should he do it? He reckoned he *could* pull it off. After all he'd done before, everything he'd been through, he thought he'd find a way. Somehow. He just wasn't sure he should.

Finn started to move on up the beach, the loose stones giving way beneath his feet, adding to his general exhaustion. He reached the grass between the beach and the road just as, from farther up the coastline, he saw the arrival of three assistants. They must have been alerted by the brief flickering of the gateway that had released him back home.

He hid out of sight, crouched behind a wall as they passed. And once they were gone, he darted low across the road to an alleyway to start back to the house he still refused to call home.

"Where have you been all day, Finn?" said Emmie, appearing around a turn behind him. "I've been looking everywhere for you. And Lucien was acting very weird, and you know he's talking about kicking you out if there's any more trouble, and me too, and what on earth is that smell?" She wrinkled her nose in disgust.

Finn didn't quite know where to start.

The hours in the mouth of the Leviathan. The boiling sea. The mountain. Cornelius and Hiss. The Legends. The destruction. The attack. The kind-of-Cyclops. The Gatemaker hidden in his sopping jacket.

Being asked to steal Gantrua.

Any of these on their own was enough to have him banished from Darkmouth for good. And Emmie too.

"I just went for a long walk to clear my head but fell into the sea," he told her. "Seaweed. Crabs. Fish heads, and all that."

She looked at the back pocket of his pants, saw a shell sticking out from it, and seemed stuck between suspicion and trust.

"Fish heads?" she asked.

"And all that."

He walked on, the lie burning in his throat.

DO NOT PUBLISH

Report by Tiger-One-Twelve

Location: London, England

I did not expect glamour in this job, but I did not expect to find myself at a half-built high-rise, at the end of a filthy alley in the grimmest part of the city I have been in, staring at a wall. And it was, if I am going to be honest, the dullest wall I have ever looked at.

"It was more exciting yesterday," said the security guard standing behind me.

"Yesterday?" I asked.

"Oh yeah, yesterday it was sumfing else," he said. "All kinds of craziness. I've been in this job twenty years. I ain't never seen nuffin like it."

The sounds of the city, of traffic and footsteps, intruded deep into this dead end. I knew this was once the worst, most dangerous part of the city, avoided even by those who thrived in a city's underworld. They had heard the rumors. They all knew someone who knew somebody who had seen something that scared them so much they couldn't talk about it without crying.

That was a long time ago, though. Long forgotten. By most, anyway.

"The wall started . . . leaking," the security guard explained.

"Leaking?" I asked. "The wall?"

"That's the only way I can explain it," he said. "I was doing my rounds, and I did one round and nuffin' was here. Then I did another round and nuffin' was here. I did a third round and nuff—"

I looked at him in a way that clearly said, "Get to the point."

"But on my sixth round," he continued, "I snagged the leg of my uniform on sumfing small, sticking from the bottom of this wall here. It was, if you can believe it, some kind of bone."

I could believe it.

"And that's when I realized it wasn't

the only bone in the wall. There were lots of them, all kind of poking out of the brick up to about, say, here." He held his hand at chest height.

Obviously, I had looked up this part of the city before coming here. The files confirmed that many, many years ago, before the city ate it up, this spot had been a village. A Blighted Village. And in that place there had been an ancient graveyard, long since covered over.

We were standing on it right now.

"And this morning these bones were gone?" I asked.

"Gone," the guard confirmed. "Like they'd not got the energy to fight the wall, you know what I mean?" The security guard looked at his watch. Remembering something, he then took a curved piece of metal from his back pocket and handed it to me. "Anyway, you asked me to keep anyfing unusual I found. I don't know if this counts."

The metal was dulled by time, and appeared to have been burned black at the edges. If I was to guess I'd say it was the sleeve off a fighting suit, but one wide enough only to fit someone young.

"It has a drawing on it," he said. "A corner of what looks like a monster or sumfing. A kid's outfit, I'd say. But we don't get many kids down here."

The security guard's watch alarm went off. He turned it off, stretched, started to walk away.

"Where are you going?" I asked.

"For a snooze. It's my break time. I'm off duty for the next firty minutes."

"Mind if I keep this?" I asked him, holding out the metal sleeve.

"You can eat it for lunch for all I care," he said as he left. "I just want a normal life, without any bones leaking from walls."

Which, to be honest, was what I was thinking too.

II

Finn sat over his bowl of Chocky-Flakes, spoon halfway to his mouth, the crazy request from the Infested Side running around his brain like a hamster on a wheel, and watched the business of the household. He surveyed the boxes of ornaments, clothes, books, stuff brought from their old home, still scattered around the small house. Two families living together, neither really wanting to believe they'd need to stay here forever.

"Please think about Smoofyland some more," Clara said to Finn. "Slotterton isn't that far away, really. And it's better than sitting around here. We haven't been anywhere in so long."

Finn looked at her, brown milk dribbling from his spoon. If only she knew how far away he had just been. "No Smoofyland. Anywhere but Smoofyland," he groaned.

Clara turned on the tap, which spluttered and spat out

sludgy, undrinkable water into her glass. She grimaced as she held it up to the light from the window. "That keeps happening," she said. "I went to rinse Mrs. Walsh's teeth yesterday and almost made them blacker than when she came in. They were black enough to begin with."

Emmie arrived down the stairs. Finn remembered when she had first arrived in Darkmouth: she had hardly been able to contain her excitement at being in the infamous Blighted Village, fizzing like the human version of a mint dropped into a bottle of cola. She'd been so eager for the life he led, even when he hadn't wanted it. She would talk one hundred miles an hour, and rush into trouble twice as fast.

She wasn't like that so much anymore. Instead, she was more often subdued, cautious, and, he felt, suspicious.

Finn tried to shake off the idea that she was suspicious of *him*. They'd been through so much together, he wanted her to trust him. Even when he was lying to her. Even when he was holding on to a secret so big he could still smell it despite showering for so long last night that his mother had banged on the door, fearing he'd slipped and knocked himself out.

In his schoolbag, he had a half-living device that would open gateways to the Legends.

Of course Emmie should doubt him. He was beginning to doubt himself.

"Hey," he said, Chocky-Flakes milk dribbling down his chin.

"Hey," she replied, and popped two slices of bread into the toaster.

"Tell him Smoofyland will be great," Clara asked her.

"That place in Slotterton with the sparkliest roller coaster in the world?" asked Emmie.

"You'd think he doesn't want to go on a vacation," Clara said. "That he just wants to sit here waiting for whatever disaster lurks around the next corner."

Finn felt a rush of panic, a tightening of his chest, an implosion. He caught his breath, blew out, drew in air steadily, calmed himself.

"You okay?" Emmie asked him.

He nodded and kept eating, watching the goldfish picking at the stones in its bowl, the silence broken only by the sound of toast springing up.

"Gotta go," he said. "See you at school."

He didn't go straight to school, though. Instead he went to find his dad, who was already at work at Woofy Wash. Finn hurried, propelled by a rush of honesty. It was wrong to keep this secret. No matter the consequences, it would all have to come out. He should tell his dad everything. About the kidnapping. About going to the Infested Side. About the assistants being up to something strange in the remnants of the cave and what the Legends had said about people on this side trying to open gateways. About how dangerous it could be. About the flashes of light. About the Legends. About the request that he steal Gantrua. About the Orthrus. About *everything.*

"Dad—" he started as he walked into the shop.

"Good morning," said Lucien, standing by the counter.

Hugo was behind it, apparently deeply unimpressed by Lucien's mere presence.

Through the back, they could hear the sounds of cats, dogs, possibly a parrot, plus something that sounded like it was coughing up a squeaky toy.

Finn felt himself clam up again, the lid slamming shut on his honesty. He did his best to give Lucien a look that said he hated every single molecule in his body. Lucien, though, wouldn't give him the satisfaction and instead addressed Hugo.

"I don't want to delay you from whatever sort of emergency dog-washing scenario you might have going on," he said, as if he meant it sincerely. He didn't.

Finn fervently wanted to grab a bottle of Shampoodle off the shelf and make him drink it down until foam began to pour from his ears.

"Then make it quick, Lucien," Hugo said, framed by wall posters of a cat having its teeth brushed and a gerbil being taken for a walk.

"It is clear that things are getting a little . . . how best to put it? Chaotic. Yes, chaotic."

"Gateways?" guessed Hugo.

"Two of them. Only yesterday. One outside here, as it happens." He looked at Finn, who instinctively looked away.

Finn didn't want to reveal what he knew: that he had been pulled through one of those gateways, and pushed back home through the other.

"Not my place to interfere, right, Lucien?" said Hugo.

"Nothing came through that we could find," Lucien continued, "but we have to believe the Legends are poised to return. Maybe your old enemy Mr. Glad isn't quite gone yet. These are great and mysterious worlds we deal with."

Finn's secret screamed in his head. He kept his mouth shut in case it escaped. In the back room, an animal squealed, so like a child that Finn wondered if it actually *was* a child.

"We may have stirred a viper's nest," Lucien continued. "Just because we have captured one of their leaders—"

"Just because *Finn* captured one of their leaders," interjected Hugo.

Lucien barreled on regardless. ". . . It does not mean this is the end. For all we know this is only the beginning. We have grown complacent and lazy over the years, as each Blighted Village has gone quiet. What happens when the Legends come back? What if that's been their plan all along? These creatures live for many more years than us. What if they decided to use that to their advantage, to withdraw for a decade or three? That's hardly the length of a lunch break as far as they're concerned."

The general noise of upset animals from the rear of the shop grew louder. Finn wished they'd quiet down so he could properly concentrate on figuring out what Lucien was building up to. He fiddled with the bell on the desk.

"Hugo," continued Lucien, "I'm not so blind that I can't see how difficult this is for you to be stuck here, working this job, watching while all these out-of-towners come in and try and run Darkmouth for you."

"Great," said Finn. "Just give us the keys to our house and we'll get things sorted out again."

"Finn," said Hugo, with a hand out to quiet him. "Not now."

"Not *now?*" asked Finn.

"It's fine, Hugo," said Lucien. "I understand the young man's frustration. He was destined for great things and now here he is, as are you, watching while others decide when this ordeal must end."

"Others?" said Hugo, skeptical. "You're the only one making decisions."

Lucien considered his response a moment. "Hugo, I want to get you involved with us again."

Finn straightened up, wary but interested.

Hugo was silent, curious.

"It's not right to have someone of your experience sitting here on the sidelines waiting for the result of the investigation," said Lucien, "when it's clear that we could use your knowledge of Darkmouth at times of difficulty."

"Me too?" inquired Finn.

"Yes, why not?" Lucien said, like that was a fine idea. "Next time there is an invasion, or a gateway, or some enemy running through our streets, we'd like you both there."

Hugo's face lifted.

"To direct the traffic," concluded Lucien.

Hugo's face fell.

"Traffic?" spluttered Finn, red rage coming over him. How could Lucien do this? How could his father sit there and take it?

"Not *only* to direct traffic, of course," Lucien said brightly. "Crowd control too, if necessary. Reassuring the locals, the shopkeepers who own places such as"—he picked up a small clump of fur sitting on the counter, examined it before clapping it from his hands—"this establishment."

"Maybe we can give the Legends speeding tickets," said Finn. "Ask them to wait at traffic lights while we desiccate them."

Hugo didn't quiet him this time.

"*The Most Great Lives of the Legend Hunters* is such an important book," said Lucien, the change of focus abrupt and pointed. He folded his arms, ignoring the sounds of animals rising at the back of the shop. "It is the one they will look at for many generations to come. It is the book that defines a Legend Hunter's reputation. Or a traitor's. All they want to do is print a new version. Finn, you must know that if you don't act properly, if you refuse to help, suspicions will grow. The *Most Great Lives* writer is due here any day now. You don't want the black paper to fall over your family's name."

Woofy Wash's owner, Mr. Green, stuck his head from his office door. "It sounds like a zoo out back, Hugo. What's going on?"

"Think about it, Hugo," Lucien said, tapping his fingers on the counter. "That's all I ask."

"Oh, I'm thinking about it all right," said Hugo.

Lucien was enjoying this. Finn knew it. He knew his father knew it. It was as clear as the shine on Lucien's wispy-haired scalp that he had come simply to humiliate them under the guise of friendliness.

"Elektra! Tiberius!" Lucien called out.

His children appeared from the back of the shop, pushing rudely past a perplexed Mr. Green. Elektra had a parrot feather in her hair. Tiberius had a writhing lump down his sweater.

"Hand it back," Lucien ordered his son.

Tiberius reached down his sweater, pulled free a shivering gerbil, and handed it to Mr. Green before leaving with his sister and Lucien. Mr. Green shook his head, drew a whistling breath through his clenched teeth and—with a writhing, slippery gerbil in hand—returned to his office.

Hugo had his head down. He took a long breath. When he spoke, it was with enormous control.

"You might think I'm doing nothing, Finn, but you would be very wrong," he said. "I know what Lucien was up to. But I also know we have to be very careful and not give him any excuse to kick us out entirely. There's no Council of Twelve to help us. No other Legend Hunters. The Half-Hunters are gone. But I do have some friends left. And I do have a plan, son." He lifted his head. "So you're not to do anything stupid, do you understand?"

But Finn had already left.

12

It was a half day at school, because they had tests to take. Finn felt like he was sleepwalking through the hours, his mind elsewhere. They had a history test, and when it was over Finn hardly remembered taking it.

"How did you answer question seven?" a classmate, Tommy, asked him.

"Genghis Khan, I think," Finn answered.

"Genghis Khan was the first person on the moon?" said Tommy, looking pretty disturbed that he might have gotten the question wrong.

The rest of school sort of drifted by, while Finn wondered why he even needed to be there anymore. He was going to be a Legend Hunter, no matter how much Lucien tried to prevent it. That was his path, his destiny, and he'd already qualified for it through hard-earned, dangerous, explosive, unprecedented experience.

Why did it matter what year a battle took place that

involved no Legends whatsoever? Why worry about the geography of the Asian continent unless a crater had been ripped in the ground by some rampaging creature from another world? These were civilian concerns, not those of a Legend Hunter.

On the way home, Emmie nudged his arm and smiled, as if trying to break through his gloom.

"We should get fries," she declared as they walked down Broken Road. "Everything is better when you have a bag of fries in your hand. Except your breath maybe."

"Lucien asked my dad to direct traffic if any Legends invade," Finn said.

"Well, if they invade in the next half hour we'll stab them with the crunchy fries at the bottom of the bag," she said.

She hurried past him and around the corner toward the neon glare of the nearby fast-food place.

When Finn got there, Emmie was already inside, weaving through the hard plastic tables and chairs welded to the floor, her red hair aflame under the unnaturally bright light. Behind the counter stood a large man in a green short-sleeved uniform, with a hairnet gripped tight on his bald head.

"Fries please, Mario." Emmie was sorting the change in

her palm, counting how much she could afford.

"Give the money to me," said Mario.

Emmie slapped the change on the counter, and he worked through it with his thumbs.

"I'll throw in a couple of onion rings, and we'll say nothing more about it." Mario swept the money into his palm and shoveled raw slices of potato into a wide deep-fat fryer on his side of the counter. They hit the oil with a violent crackle.

"We're getting onion rings," Emmie shouted out to Finn, rubbing her hands.

"The lights in the cave under the cliff," Finn said.

"What?" she asked, no idea what he was talking about.

Finn started to explain. "The flashes we saw. It's more than just simple experiments . . ." He caught himself about to blurt something about his visit to the Infested Side, about Sulawan asking why someone was trying to open gateways, but decided against it. Not yet.

"Do you think the assistants might be trying to do something really dangerous?" he simply asked Emmie.

"Ask them yourself," she said, leaning on the silver counter.

Finn looked back over his shoulder. Across the street, coming in their direction, were Scarlett and Greyson, the two assistants they'd heard inside the cave in the cliff.

Finn ducked behind the counter, and when Emmie didn't follow he popped up, grabbed her by the shoulder, and dragged her to where he was crouched.

"Oi!" protested Mario.

"Please, Mario," Finn begged and gave him the best look of desperation he could muster. "Can we just wait here until those two go?"

At the mouth of the spitting deep fryer, Mario considered the sight of Finn and Emmie crouching behind his counter before breaking into a sunburst smile and greeting the assistants as they arrived.

"Hello, my friends," Mario announced in an overly cheerful way. "What can I get you fine visitors today?"

Emmie poked Finn in the ribs and pointed toward the corner of the ceiling above them. There was a screen relaying security camera footage of the fast-food place. Finn could see Scarlett and Greyson, fuzzy and black and white, from above. He watched them as they ordered.

"Fries," Scarlett said. "Two orders."

"The sherbet has been the only thing to work so far," they heard Greyson say to her, continuing a conversation from outside, it seemed.

Mario shook the potatoes in the fryer while quickly

catching the eye of Finn and Emmie crouched at his feet.

"But only for the briefest moment," Greyson added.

"How many times do I have to ask that we don't talk about such things in public?" Scarlett asked. "There are a lot of Half-Hunters around the world who would not be happy if they found out what we were doing."

"Come on, don't pretend it's not all you think about," said Greyson. "We're so close to a breakthrough, yet so far. And if it is going to work anywhere, it *should* be here."

On the screen, Finn saw Scarlett sit at a table, and Greyson leaned in close to her to speak lower.

"But the results we're hearing from elsewhere aren't any different," he said. "It's frustrating that we're not making progress."

"Only if you get excited by the idea of risking your limbs in a battle," Scarlett said, relaxing into the idea that no one but Mario was listening to their conversation.

"Don't tell me you don't." Greyson grinned. "Why else would you be here, doing this, if not to escape the filing and reports and having nothing more dangerous to do than sharpen a pencil?"

Emmie looked at Finn, still unsure what the assistants were talking about. Finn knew full well. The gateways opening on the Infested Side. The flashes in Darkmouth. It added up to only one thing. They were experimenting with something very dangerous. They were in danger of opening up a door for Legends to pour through.

"Slotterton might give us better results tonight," Greyson said.

Finn's eyes widened at the mention of Slotterton. What was it his mam had said? That it was an old Blighted Village? They must be planning on experimenting there too.

"We can try adding toffee there," Greyson continued. "As long as that Gantrua Legend doesn't explode or something on the way. Do you think it makes sense to carry him out of here?"

Emmie flashed Finn a look.

They're moving Gantrua out of Darkmouth, he thought.

Emmie was frowning and he knew she was worrying about what might happen if Gantrua got loose or fell into the wrong hands. Finn wondered how she'd react if she knew Finn had been asked to steal the desiccated Legend himself. That he could be those wrong hands.

"Since the reports that gateways opened yesterday, Lucien has been nervous," said Scarlett. "He just wants that Legend out of here and taken to Liechtenstein where it can be studied more."

"Do you want ketchup on your fries?" Mario called out to them.

"Just on one," said Scarlett, steadying herself, suddenly reminded they weren't alone. "Not on the other."

"We'll do some preparation in the Dead House later, so we'll be ready to just get straight to it at Slotterton," Greyson said.

Mario dropped the two orders of fries on their table.

"Could we have two glasses of water to go with these?" Scarlett asked Mario.

"I wish you could," Mario said to her, "but at the moment the water is all black and tarry. You'd be better off surfacing a road with it than drinking the stuff."

Mario returned behind the counter, where he gave just the quickest of glances at Finn and Emmie hiding low.

"The water problem again," Scarlett said to Greyson, as if she had asked for the drinks only to test a theory.

"Just like the sap coming out of the trees during the experiments," said Greyson.

They were silent for a moment, munching their fries, until Greyson spoke up. "Right, to more important matters," he announced, turning to Mario. "Where's your bathroom, sir?"

The bathroom was along a narrow hallway that would

take Greyson past the countertop, behind which Emmie and Finn were still hiding. Mario had no choice but to point the assistant in that direction.

Realizing this, Finn and Emmie scuttled low through the kitchen, past the dishwasher, around a couple of large blue plastic tubs of peeled, cut potatoes, and out the back door. It brought them to the yard, and through a door into an alleyway. Once safely away, they pressed tightly against the high stone wall to stay out of sight.

"What was all that about?" Emmie asked.

Finn was thinking through what he had heard. "They're opening gateways," he said. "I think they're using crystals or dust or whatever from the cave to *try* and open them anyway. And they're experimenting with sherbet and stuff because, I don't know, they might help activate the crystals?"

"So, that would explain the flashes," said Emmie. "And all those poor birds stuck in the trees. It sounds like they think their experiments are causing that. Bad water too."

"And who knows what other problems they might be creating," said Finn.

"There's the Gantrua thing as well," said Emmie. "They're taking him out of Darkmouth. That could be dangerous, couldn't it? What's going on?"

"At least we know where to find some answers," said Finn. "The Dead House. It's a ruin on the edge of Darkmouth that my family used to use for storage of desiccated Legends. I haven't been in it for years. No one has. Or they hadn't."

He started to walk away.

"You're going there now?" Emmie asked him.

"I'll go on my own," said Finn. "I don't want to get you into trouble."

Emmie walked after him without hesitation. "Just promise me that if we find anything we'll tell your dad and not do anything crazy."

"Okay," said Finn.

"Besides," added Emmie, "how can I resist going to a place called the Dead House?"

Finn waited, crouched among brambles, finger pushing in his earphone. He could see the front of the house, with its scuzz-covered windows and remnants of the boards that had run across them, the moss creeping up from the base of its walls. This was the very edge of Darkmouth, a few fields stretching between the Dead House and the rest of the town. Behind it, the Black Hills sloped up steeply, a barrier protecting the world beyond from the Blighted Village.

They had watched from a distance, observed the two assistants guarding the supposedly empty house. They were doing rounds of the exterior, and had separated four minutes ago. He checked the time. They would pass again soon.

"Five seconds," said Emmie in his earpiece.

"Okay," he whispered into his phone.

The guards met and loitered at the front of the house.

One was so bald the skin of his scalp gleamed in the daylight, while the other had a lush beard that spread across his whole neck. Instead of suit jackets, they wore awkward-fitting armor over their shirts to indicate their new role as security guards. Each was armed with a Desiccator.

"Why do we have to walk around in circles like this anyway?" said the bearded one. Finn couldn't place the accent. Hungarian maybe. Or Welsh.

"We're walking around in circles because those are our orders," said the bald guard, his accent definitely Australian. Or possibly Dutch.

"If you were ordered to put your head in a bag of custard, would you do it?" asked the beard.

The bald guard just stared back.

"Great," said the beard. "I'm on duty with someone who'd happily turn his scalp into dessert if there was the chance of a promotion."

They turned and walked away from each other, resuming their rounds of the house's perimeter.

"I'm going for it," whispered Finn into the phone.

"Roger," said Emmie. "I'll keep an eye out."

As the two guards rounded opposite corners, Finn broke from cover, running stealthily through the drooping weeds and uncut grass at the front of the Dead House, and straight for the front door.

It was locked.

He fished for his dad's spare keys, a bunch of which he'd grabbed on the way over, held them up, and had a flush of panic as he realized he had no idea if any of these was the right one.

He tried a key. It didn't fit. Another, this time with the keys jingling too loudly for his liking.

"Finn," said Emmie in his ear, with alarm. "The guards will be back around in thirty seconds."

He fumbled through the keys, found one that looked right, and tried it. It wasn't right.

"I can see them coming back. The baldy one is almost there."

Finn hesitated, tried to decide if he should run for cover again or try another key.

"Don't run—they'll see you," Emmie told him.

Seeing a foot appear around the corner to his left, Finn threw himself flat against the door.

The bald guard appeared. Finn sucked in his belly in order to not be seen. There was a plonking noise in the grass, something solid hitting the ground. The guard stopped, looked to his right, away from Finn, and wandered off toward the source of the disturbance. From the grass, he picked up a can of orange soda, looked around and up in search of its origin.

While he was distracted, Finn tried another key in the lock.

Please, please, please.

The guard popped open the can while he turned back around toward the Dead House. The bearded man appeared from the side he had been patrolling.

They met at the front door.

"Where'd you get that, Olaf?" the bearded assistant asked.

"Not sure, Ricardo," Olaf said, and swigged from the can.

The beard reached out in anticipation of having a sip.

"Uh-uh, Ricardo. I found it on the ground," said Olaf, pulling back and chugging from the can, a dribble of orange running down his chin. "It's probably riddled with disease."

He took a final, long, satisfying gulp from the can before wiping his mouth with the back of his hand and walking away from his unimpressed colleague.

On the other side of the door from them, inside the Dead House, Finn was pressed against the wall, not daring to move a muscle.

He had *just* opened the door in time, but felt anything but calm. He waited until he heard the second guard walk away, muttering complaints, before allowing himself to breathe again.

"I'm inside," Finn whispered into the phone to Emmie.

"I distracted the guards by throwing a can of orange soda," she said, pleased with herself. "I'm thirsty now, though."

"Thanks," Finn said, stepping forward carefully.

The floorboard creaked, so he stopped again in the near dark, waiting for Emmie to give him a warning should the guards be on their way back. No warning came, so he moved through the hall again.

Even though he hadn't been in the Dead House for some years, it was still familiar to him. He had played in it as a kid, running from room to room, pretending to hide from spies, roaring like a Legend, acting the Legend Hunter, all the things he thought were fun once but which turned out to be very different when there were real spies, Legends, and Legend Hunters involved.

The Dead House was pretty much the same now, its floors scattered with papers, abandoned tools, some collapsing chairs, and a couple of picnic tables brought in years ago as a temporary measure but which had never left. There was graffiti on the walls: some of it blobs of artistic swirls, some names scrawled on plaster by passing Legend Hunters long dead (Timothy the Strong, Emrid Latecomer, Ingrid of Boneford).

Finn used his phone for extra light in the dim hallway, careful to avoid the curtained and boarded windows. A shadow crossed a gap in the window. He paused. Let the guard pass outside.

He leaned his head into a small room, in which there was nothing but a warped wooden floor, dust, and a few rusted bolts left over from some device or other, then moved on toward the largest room of the house.

"The guards are on the far side of the building," said Emmie in his ear.

The door to the largest room didn't open at first, but Finn remembered it used to require a bit of help. He lifted it at the handle, turning it and pushing the door with his shoulder. It swung stiffly inward, revealing a room with a sense of life that was absent from the rest of the Dead House. It was clean, swept, and polished so that even in the low light the old surfaces gleamed.

The first thing he saw was a bell-shaped cage standing empty, its door unlocked. It was a couple of heads taller than him, and he recognized it as having come from the library in his house.

At the center of the room was a large modern table on which sat four heavy, transparent cylinders, with thick metal handles at the top. Housed within each of them was something Finn knew all too well.

Crystals.

"The guards are turning around now," said Emmie over the phone. "Be careful."

The crystals in the canisters didn't have the clarity of those from the Infested Side, nor the bloodred color of those that had been found in Darkmouth. They were yellowish, bordering on orange, and uneven, as if dust had been squashed and glued into an unnatural shape. They looked unwell, impure. But he knew for sure they were using these to try and open gateways in Darkmouth. Why would they do something so reckless?

"The guards are on their way back," said Emmie in his ear.

On the desk was a small neat pile of papers. Scanning through them he found that most held little but sequences of words and numbers, some crossed out in red pen, others circled in green. None of it made any sense to him until, buried farther down the pile, he found a note.

Gantrua is to be moved from Darkmouth to Liechtenstein HQ by road, via our Site One headquarters in Slotterton. While there, the opportunity should be taken to carry out tests at Site Two.

Lucien

Attached to the note was a black-and-white printout of a map, with parts of it numbered by hand. In the veiled light, Finn couldn't quite read the small print on it, but he folded the letter and map and put them in his jacket anyway, opposite a pocket containing the Gatemaker he'd brought with him.

The documents confirmed that the assistants were not only trying to open gateways in Darkmouth, but that they planned to do the same elsewhere. But given how it was doing strange things to the trees, turning the water sludgy, and attracting Legends' attention on the Infested Side, Finn knew it was a bad idea.

Now he had the vital proof to bring back to his father. He would share it with the rest of the Half-Hunter world. He would stop the assistants before it was too late.

Putting his hand on the desk, Finn accidentally knocked a computer screen into action. He got a shock when he saw himself staring back from the screen.

It was a picture taken with his father a couple of years ago, in full armor, crouched and smiling in the house. This was the day he finished making his first fighting suit. The picture was on the computer because this laptop had been theirs at home. They had stolen *his* memories.

Anger swelled inside him, hardened his determination to stop Lucien and the assistants from getting what they wanted.

Finn hovered a moment, trying to decide what to do next. It couldn't be stealing if it was yours in the first place, could it? Besides, the computer would have evidence in it, surely. Everything he needed to reveal the conspiracy against his family.

A bag sat on the floor, square and rigid, with a drawstring

at the top. He shut the computer's screen, placed the device in the bag.

A shadow passed the window, the guard circling.

Finn then noticed a narrow rectangle of light forming a long strip along the base of a wide cabinet taking up the far wall of the room. It was a drawer of some sort. He opened it, felt the sting of the light on his eyes. Inside was a long white container; a faint wisp of blue smoke rose from it.

It held a row of five spaces for desiccated Legends, in jars nestled in foam hollows, ordered in size, from one hardly bigger than a walnut to the largest, about the size of a soccer ball.

Through the glass jar, he recognized the middle Legend as Broonie, knew it by his green and rough-skinned exterior. Finn had seen his Hogboon friend in this form a few times before. The poor guy had been desiccated more often than he had eaten hot scaldgrubs. It broke Finn's heart a little to see him there, all wrapped up in a drawer like this. He considered lifting him, hesitated.

Farther along was the Legend in the largest jar. A dark sphere, its surface was broken by what seemed to be the shrunken, petrified veins of wings.

Gantrua had been sporting wings when Finn desiccated

him. They weren't actually *his* wings, but shrunken up like this, who could tell? Was this Gantrua?

Finn reached out his hand, hesitated. He hadn't come to steal this. He hadn't agreed to the Legends' request. Although if the assistants were going to take Gantrua away for good, then this might be his only chance.

"The guards are about to reach the front of the house, Finn," Emmie whispered in his ear. "Will you be much longer?"

Finn knew he couldn't leave yet. He would have to wait while they had their brief chat before starting their lap of the house again.

"The guards are at the front door again," Emmie told him.

It could be Gantrua, ready to be brought to Slotterton and then onward. Stealing him would look very bad, though. Still, the desiccated ball could contain the charm that would stop the Bone Creature from ravaging the Infested Side. Finn just wanted to know. To be sure. A look wouldn't do any harm.

He reached in and carefully removed the jar containing the shrunken Legend.

An alarm screamed.

Wailed.

Clanged.

Clattered.

It gave Finn such a fright he didn't react for a second, was rooted to the spot when he should have been running. His brain gradually got that message through to his legs. He didn't even think about it after that. The desiccated Legend was in the bag, along with the computer, the bag was on his back, and he was leaving whichever way he could.

And it was then, finally, that he heard Emmie shouting in his earpiece.

"The guards are in the house, Finn! *Get out!*"

He pulled open the room's door to find the two guards pointing Desiccators at him.

It was a competition between Finn and the guards as to who was most shocked by the encounter.

Thankfully for Finn, the guards won.

Taking advantage of their surprise, he barreled between them, knocking the bearded one against the wall. He felt like he was strong and fast enough to get clear.

Then something hit him on the back of the leg and he stumbled, looked down. A book. One of them had thrown a book at him.

"Stop!" Olaf, the bald guard, shouted, raising a paperweight.

Finn didn't. He slammed the door shut behind him and ran to the empty kitchen. Faded cans were scattered on the floor, with a rusted teapot, a broken chair. There was a large window jammed shut with age, so after a brief and futile attempt to open it, he picked up the three-legged chair and chucked it through the thin glass. It exploded outward, releasing a burst of fresh air into the stale house.

A few moments later, the guards crashed through the door into the kitchen, ran to the window, the bearded guard thrusting a head out.

"I don't see him," Ricardo said.

"Climb out the window and see."

"I will not. There's broken glass."

Just then, Finn dashed out of the tall, musty cabinet he'd hidden in, ran across to the kitchen door, pulled it closed, and turned the lock.

The guards slammed their shoulders against it, kicked at it, while Olaf shouted into a radio about "The boy! The boy!"

Finn didn't hear the rest because he was already at the door out of the house, half falling through it, bag over his shoulder, desiccated Legend bumping around with the rest of the stolen evidence.

"Come on!" he shouted, running in the general direction of where he thought Emmie was.

"I hope that was worth it," Emmie answered, appearing right in front of him. Her voice was in his ear too, adding to the strangeness of the moment.

He pulled the earpiece free, allowed her to help him stand properly.

"I got . . . some stuff," he said, deciding it wasn't exactly the time or place for an argument about the rights and wrongs of what he'd grabbed.

They started to run across a field toward the town. Finn held the new bag tight, while Emmie had his backpack flopping around on her shoulders.

"They're doing things, Emmie. They're definitely carrying out experiments elsewhere too, in Slotterton. We've got to get the evidence back home before they stop us. Come on, this way."

Several assistants appeared about fifty yards ahead, directly in their path. Lucien and Estravon were at the head of them.

"No, not that way," said Finn, reversing direction. They had to make for the hill behind the Dead House, the punishing climb that he used to go up as a kid just so he could slide back down.

"We've got to hurry," he said to Emmie. But she was already gaining ground.

Finn still had the bag, and felt like dropping it to make running easier, but he couldn't let himself do it. The computer was in there, and it was his family's. It would have evidence on it too, he was sure of it.

Below them, the two guards had freed themselves from

the Dead House and had joined Lucien, Estravon, and the assistants in scrambling at a good pace up the hill after them.

"We know too much," Finn said to Emmie. "They won't let us go this time."

Behind them, one assistant slipped on the stones littering the bank, and his tumble took out two assistants following behind him. It bought Finn and Emmie an extra few seconds as they pushed on up the slope, pain spreading in their legs, effort squeezing their lungs. They hit the brow of the hill, after which there were only fields, stretching ahead toward the world beyond.

"Maybe we should just show them what you found in there," Emmie panted. "Maybe they won't be so tough on you after all."

A spit of Desiccator fluid arced over their heads, a fizzing ball of blue fire hardly a couple of yards off target. Landing with a sickening *scrunch* ahead of them, it chomped up the ground, left only a crater and a small ball of stone rolling in it.

"You think?" said Finn.

Looking back to see if another was coming, he could see Estravon again. The careful, pedantic man who had once accompanied them to the Infested Side had slowed, dropping behind Lucien's choppy stride. He looked as shocked by the use of the Desiccator as Finn and Emmie were.

The rest of the posse of assistants kept striding up the hill after them.

Finn and Emmie left the brow of the hill, dropping out of view on the other side.

Above them, the assistants appeared, piling over the crest of the hill to slide after them.

"I can't believe they fired," said Emmie as they began to scramble down the slope. "They could have *desiccated* us."

"I think it was just a warning shot," said Finn, feet in a delicate balance somewhere between falling and skidding. "I hope it was anyway. We don't want to give them a chance to fire another. They could hit us."

Finn and Emmie were quicker down the slope than their pursuers, more agile and reactive, seeing where to place their feet on ground that was determined to trip them up. But they were heading for open fields—no buildings, no shelter. Just a train track cutting through the land.

"There's our way out," said Finn.

"Where?" asked Emmie, breathless.

Finn pointed.

Making its way serenely through the countryside beyond Darkmouth was a train.

There is no train station in Darkmouth.

The crest of hills that squeeze the town against the coastline always made it difficult to get into the heart of the town. A long tunnel would have been needed. A lot of planning and engineering and effort. Not that it wasn't suggested at various times in the town's history. It would be good to have a train platform, people said, from which passengers could alight and enjoy the salty air, stroll the promenade, and slurp on an ice cream while gazing out at the waves smacking the steep slopes of the rocky island called Doom's Perch.

For very obvious reasons, the idea never got very far. It was generally thought best not to direct busy locomotives through a town that, at any given moment, might see a passenger pop their ticket into a machine before themselves being popped into the jaws of a passing Legend.

So the train track did not go through the town. Instead, in a long, tranquil valley on the far side of those Black Hills that separate Darkmouth from the rest of the world, there is a track along which a train passes a couple of times a day. It has stopped only once in fifty-six years, during a period of Darkmouth's history sometimes referred to as the Brief Lull.

The Brief Lull was just that: a few months during Gerald the Disappointed's time when, for reasons never explained, Darkmouth had no Legend invasions. It was the summer, and a glorious one at that, when families took walks along the beach and kids frolicked in the shallows and everyone dared believe that this freedom might last forever.

The government decided to send an inspector, someone to examine this unusual state of affairs, but he didn't drive, so made arrangements for the train to stop at a convenient field outside Darkmouth, where he would take the short stroll into the then-tranquil Blighted Village. Sure enough, the train stopped, the official climbed down, and the train chugged up the line again with an agreement to pick up the official when returning in four hours.

The appointed time came. In the cool of an evening that had been spectacularly sunny all along the coast but then turned strangely wet, the train's driver noticed three things:

1. Smoke rising from not one but five separate locations on the town side of the hills.
2. Something framed against the smoke that he could have sworn was a dragon.
3. The official. Sitting on the tracks. Eyes fixed, clothes tattered, his briefcase sporting a long diagonal tear that revealed his uneaten sandwiches.

The official was shivering and incoherent with shock, so all the driver could do was bundle him onto the train, take him home–and help himself to a sandwich while he was at it. And that was the last time the train was asked to stop at the field outside Darkmouth.

Until now.

The driver of the train passing the fringes of Darkmouth was sucking on a strawberry milk while wondering what he might have for his dinner tonight when he spotted two people running crazily in the direction of the tracks. Instinct caused him to pull hard on the brake lever, so that the train screeched and whined, while its passengers gripped tight to their seats.

He watched the two youngsters running toward him, waving. It was a girl and a boy. The boy had a bag in his arms; she had one on her back. The girl's hair bounced like it was barely hanging on. The driver had heard rumors about Darkmouth, had heard that it was a strange town. This wasn't dispelling those rumors. But these two young people seemed very eager to get on board, so he kept pulling at the brake until the train was almost at a complete stop.

Then he saw a gang of people–all in gray suits, two with what looked like armor over their shirts–appear at the far end of the field. They were shouting and waving, and at least one of them was sporting something that looked like a vacuum cleaner.

He looked at the girl and boy.

He looked at the chasing pack.

One of the people in armor lifted the vacuum cleaner and sent something shooting from it. But normal vacuum cleaners did not spit some kind of liquid fire that ate up the ground.

The driver released the brake, pushed down the accelerator lever.

The girl slapped on the side of a rear car, calling at him to stop.

Another arcing, glowing spit hit the ground beside them.

If it had hit the train, a passenger or three might have been lost. The driver pushed harder on the accelerator, and the train began to match the speed of the two kids running alongside. The gang of suited people were almost there now too, only a few seconds away from reaching them.

As the train picked up speed and moved on past the hills beyond which lay Darkmouth, the driver kept his head out of the window until the train had pulled away and the running kids were lost behind it.

He felt a little guilty, and discomfited, but more than anything he felt relieved that he wouldn't have to explain all this to his boss. He would, he decided, tell no one about how he had left a girl and a boy behind to be chased down by people with highly dangerous vacuum cleaners.

Finn had often watched this train pass, wondering what it would be like to stop it, to step on board, let it carry him somewhere distant and exotic. Or just anywhere. Close and boring would do.

Now they were waving and calling and running after it with a frenzied appearance that had clearly freaked out the driver. But the train began to scream and brake anyway. Until a spit of Desiccator fire landed not too far off their heels, quickening Finn's pulse and legs, and encouraging the driver to speed up the engine and get out of there.

Still they ran, and Finn felt carried along in Emmie's slipstream. Her determination to make it brought them to the train while it was still slow enough to run alongside, Emmie battering the car exterior while passengers watched, bemused, from inside.

A head appeared.

"You okay?" a woman asked. "Did you miss the train?"

"Open the doors!" shouted Finn.

"I can't. I'll get into trouble."

A second Desiccator shot almost took a corner off the car. The train juddered as it accelerated further and began to ease away past the chasing duo, the passenger shrugging her shoulders in a "Well, this is all a bit weird for me so I'm going back to my seat" sort of gesture.

There was a door at the back of the rear car. A narrow step to it that could be jumped. If they were willing to take the risk.

"Come on," Emmie encouraged Finn, and somehow—to Finn's growing astonishment—she caught up with the back of the train, reached for the rail, and hauled herself up in one fluid movement.

Emmie held out a hand to him.

He glanced over his shoulder and saw Olaf, the bald guard, with his weapon raised, a final warning shot that might hit him this time.

He wanted to tell her that he couldn't make it, that his legs wouldn't get him there, the bag was heavy, the ground uneven, and his lungs burning. But he saw a look in her eye when she focused on him again that told him she would not take no for an answer. Finn found one last reserve of energy, somewhere in the very depths of his panic. He

reached out, grabbed her hand, and allowed himself to half jump, half be pulled onto the rear of the train.

Emmie yanked open the door and threw herself into the car.

He stumbled in after her, turning to kick the door shut.

Suddenly, the chaos of engine noise and shouting and firing Desiccators was replaced by the relative peace of the train's interior.

They couldn't hear the assistants shouting in anger as they gave up the chase, but they could see them falling away, slowing, Olaf deciding against one last shot at the departing train and instead shooting in anger at the ground, gobbling up a hole in the field with unheard violence.

Lucien watched from the center of the tracks, chest heaving with the effort, thin hair wild, cleaning his glasses with his sleeve.

Estravon was there too, eyes wide, mouth open as he watched them disappear down the track.

Emmie and Finn turned. A handful of people stared back from their seats, their books drooping unread, earphones in their hands so they could hear what this was all about.

At the far end of the car, a door opened. A large man in a dark uniform stepped through. Everyone swiveled in his direction. He examined this unusual sight, narrowed his eyes, pulled at the collar of his jacket.

Finally, snapping the tension like a karate chop, the man spoke.

"Tickets please."

Emmie paid for the tickets, rummaging through the pockets of a school uniform now stained with grass, dirt, and diesel fumes.

The ticket inspector stared at them, unsure of what was going on.

The smattering of passengers in the car watched him punch the details into his ticket machine, wind it, pull a ticket out, and hand it to Emmie. No one mentioned how she and Finn had ended up on the train. It was as if the passengers had collectively decided to pretend it hadn't happened.

When the inspector finally turned and left to walk up the rest of the train, Finn and Emmie sank into a pair of seats, saying nothing for a couple of minutes while they got their breath back, calmed their heart rates, and let the weight of their new situation settle. Finn stared upward, watched an abandoned umbrella roll around the luggage rack above him, while he tried to comprehend what kind of mess he'd ended up in this time.

He was lost in his warring thoughts as the train pulled into a station out in the countryside, where a couple of the car's passengers disembarked. Finn glanced around, nervous about who might be waiting for them at the stop. But the only person to get on was a man with a briefcase in one hand and a newspaper under his arm. He sat behind them.

"What do we do now?" Emmie asked as the train slowly pulled out of the station. "And what were we *thinking* in the first place?"

"I didn't expect everything to go so wrong," said Finn.

"We should always expect everything to go wrong," she said. "Everything *always* goes wrong."

"I told you that you didn't have to come."

"I couldn't let you go it alone."

"We're going to have to explain all this to my dad," said Finn.

"We're going to have to explain all this to *everyone* when we get back."

Finn said nothing.

Emmie turned in her seat to glare at him. "We *are* going back, aren't we? I mean, we'll figure out what to do, but we can't just stay on this train forever."

"We can't go back," said Finn, fields passing by outside the window, opening up into a glistening estuary. "They could have desiccated us. They'll catch us before we get to my dad or to anyone we can trust."

"Finn, I like getting into trouble as much as you, but only if it's worth it. What's this going to do but get us all kicked out of Darkmouth?"

"Which is why there's no point in going back," concluded Finn.

"So, where are we going?" she asked.

"Slotterton."

"Slotterton?"

"We know Lucien is ordering experiments in Slotterton as well as Darkmouth. That's dangerous. The opposite of what Legend Hunters are meant to do. We're supposed to guard against gateways, stop Legends from coming through. Not go around trying to open them ourselves. Who knows what could happen? They could trigger another all-out invasion. If we can't stop them, at least we can catch them in the act in Slotterton, show the rest of the world what's happening. Everyone will have to believe us. We will get Darkmouth back."

Frustrated, Emmie ran her hands roughly through her hair, shook her head.

"Finn, they nearly caught us," she said. "We're in trouble. Your dad's in trouble. I'm in trouble. Which means *my* dad's in trouble. Which means I'm in trouble with my dad when he gets back. Basically it's just trouble. Huge trouble. We're better going back and sorting this out now."

"What's wrong with you, Emmie?" Finn asked, genuinely irked. "You used to be the one pushing me on."

"What's wrong with me? I haven't gone crazy, that's what's wrong with me."

"There's so much going on . . ." Finn clammed up again, trying desperately to keep quiet about what had happened to him on the Infested Side.

The train had picked up a lot of speed already, swaying and juddering through the countryside.

"Something else is happening, and you won't tell me what it is," said Emmie.

"Just trust me," said Finn. "I'm coming up with a plan."

"And stealing whatever you stole is part of this brilliant plan, is it?" Emmie asked.

Finn lifted the bag onto the wide table in front of them and began to pull out objects. First out was the computer.

"You stole a computer," she said, not impressed.

"I didn't steal it," he replied, offended. "It was mine in

the first place. Well, my family's. It had pictures of us on it. Nice pictures of how things used to be. It's not theirs. It's *ours*. Besides, there must be a lot of evidence of Lucien's conspiracy on it."

She pulled something else from the bag. "A nice-smelling candle?"

"That was already in there, I guess."

"Some Scotch tape," she said, going through pockets.

"I just grabbed the nearest bag," explained Finn, defensive. "I didn't know what was in it."

"Is that half a bar of chocolate?"

"I *said* I didn't have time to be picky."

Emmie took the chocolate out, snapped off a piece of it, and put it in her mouth as she rummaged in the bottom of the bag.

"What is this?" she asked, pulling a large object free.

The jar had a crack in it, running from base to rim, but had remained otherwise intact. Inside the jar was a hairy ball. With wings.

Emmie looked aghast. "Is this a Legend?"

"It could be," he said. "Yeah, I suppose so."

"What were you thinking?"

Finn needed an answer. "There was a cage in the Dead House and some desiccated Legends. I thought they might be reanimating them and maybe this could be Broonie. That we could rescue him."

"This doesn't look *at all* like Broonie did when he was desiccated and we've seen him that way enough times." She examined it. "You sure it's him? You took it without really knowing, didn't you? We are in such big trouble now."

"Look, I panicked," Finn said, and he was being truthful now. "I lifted it and it set the alarm off. I just kind of ran after that."

"Ugh," she said, reaching the bottom of the bag. "Something broke in here. A bottle of juice or something. It's all sticky." She wiped her hand on her skirt, wrinkled her nose in disgust. "Look, Finn, we can get out of this situation. We've been in worse."

Finn pulled the map from his pocket, opened it up on the table, flattening out its creases. The corner of the map told them this was Slotterton, the town shown at detailed scale, with crisscrossing streets, highlighted buildings, and landmarks.

A *1* was written in red ink over one spot beside a place marked as *Old Hall.*

A *2* sat beside three small crosses—a graveyard, Finn presumed. Next to that was written *8 p.m.*

"This is Slotterton," he said, pointing a finger at it.

“The letter said they’d experiment at Site Two, which must be . . . here. And in the fast-food place one of those scientist assistants said they’d be doing it tonight. That must be what the eight p.m. means, only a few hours from now. The other one must be the headquarters Lucien mentioned in a note that I found.”

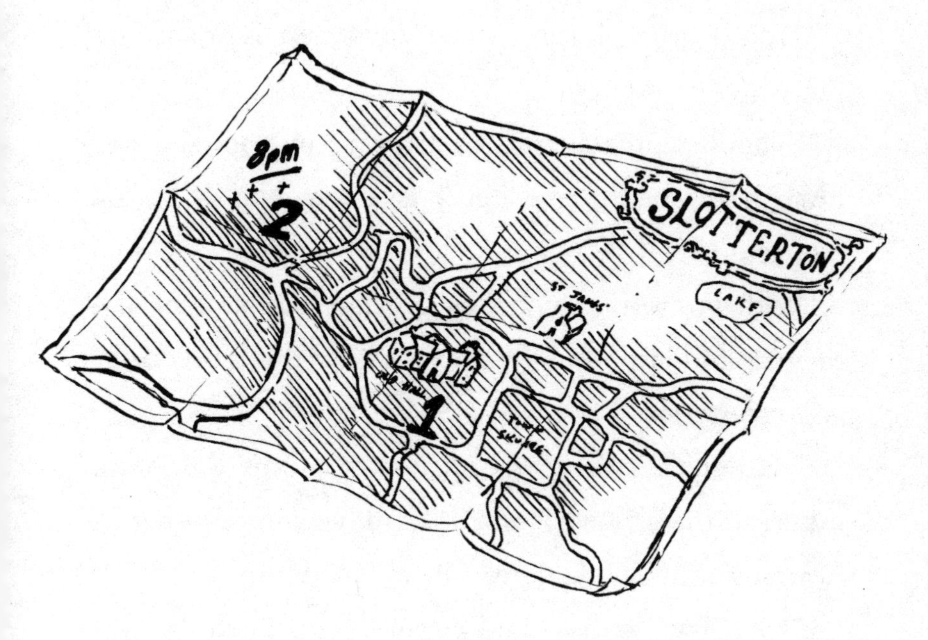

Emmie lifted the map to examine it, and for the first time Finn noticed that on the back of the page was a series of pictures. One was of an old building, set back behind a wall and foreboding gates. The other took Finn a moment to figure out. “Does that look like a roller coaster to you?”

“Maybe,” said Emmie with a shrug, taking a quick look

at the images. "Anyway, now that we know all of this we'll call your dad, get him to pick us up, and we'll tell him everything."

"We're fugitives," said Finn. "There's no way he can leave Darkmouth on his own without Lucien using it as an excuse to get rid of him."

"You're giving Lucien a pretty good excuse right now, Finn."

"They'll send assistants to arrest us instead, and we'll never hold on to the evidence that way. No, we'll go to Slotterton."

With the world zipping by outside, Emmie looked at the map of stations on the car wall. "But this train doesn't go to Slotterton."

"No, and that's good, because it means they won't expect us there," said Finn. "Instead, we can get off at the nearest station and look for a bus to Slotterton."

"Even if we do that," said Emmie, exasperated, "we have to call your dad and let him know what's happening in case he can help us somehow. He's going to find out about this pretty soon anyway."

Finn conceded that was a good idea, but there was one problem. "I think I dropped my phone running for the train," he said, patting his jacket.

"We'll use mine," she sighed, taking it out to make a call.

"Excuse me," said a thin voice behind them.

Finn and Emmie knelt over the back of their seats, peering over them to see a man in a blazer, reading a newspaper, fingers to his lips.

He pointed at the sticker on the window. "This is a quiet car," he said. "You're not allowed to use phones in it."

"We won't be on it for long," explained Emmie.

"It's the rule," said the man. "You can't break the rules."

Finn didn't need to look at Emmie to know she was on the verge of throwing the phone at the man's head.

Finn motioned to the end of the car and together they walked up the aisle to the door between cars so they could make their call in peace.

Emmie held out her phone. "Let's be honest, Finn. We can't stay on this train forever."

Finn looked at the phone for a little longer, eventually took it from her. "I'll call him, but it doesn't mean we're running straight back to Darkmouth. I'll tell him we're going to Slotterton. He'll know what to do."

Then, from where they had been sitting in the car, there came the sound of glass cracking.

That caught Finn and Emmie's attention. The man with the newspaper noticed too. He craned his neck around the back of their seats to see what was making the noise.

"Shush," he said.

There was some creaking. Growling too, perhaps.

"*Shush*," insisted the passenger.

"Finn," said Emmie, an idea dawning on her. "That stuff in the bottom of the bag, *was* it juice?"

"Not sure," he admitted.

"Finn," Emmie said. "You saw a cage in the Dead House. Maybe they're bringing Legends back to life for some reason. So is there any chance that the leaky stuff could be Reanimation fluid?"

Slowly, Finn nodded.

"Oh no," said Emmie, resigned.

"Oh no," echoed Finn.

"And the crack in the jar . . . ?" said Emmie.

"Not good," said Finn. "Not good at all."

"What about the Legend? Do you really think it's Broonie?"

Finn shook his head. "It could be. Or it could be . . . something else."

Glass smashed.

"It had *better* be Broonie," said Emmie.

Then a Griffin burst into life in the car.

The man who had *shush*ed at them screamed. He screamed very, very loudly.

Half eagle, half lion, the Griffin glared at him as he scrambled away on hands and knees, then turned back to Finn and Emmie while sniffing the air, calculating who to attack first. Its front legs had talons that looked like they could shred the car itself. Its back legs were those of a lion, a shiver running up through its muscles, through its feathers,

to a quick shake of its curling beak. Its eyes opened, black pupils narrowing against the white of the iris.

The shushy man screamed again.

The Legend opened its beak and gave a long, brain-rattling *scree* to match the screech of the train's wheels as it plunged into the blackness of a tunnel. In strobing light, the Legend spread its wings, punching the windows on either side with an ugly thud.

It decided to go for the man, lunging at him as he scrabbled away.

Finn wanted to get out of there, to run the length of the train. But if he did that the man would be the Griffin's appetizer. And the rest of the passengers would be the main course.

Beside him was an emergency ax behind clear plastic. He punched the cover, took the ax, and, with no time to aim, flung the tool at the Griffin. The ax's blunt wedge hit its shoulder and simply bounced off the layers of feather, muscle, bone, and fur.

The train left the tunnel, daylight flooding the car again.

Emmie held a fire extinguisher. Unloading it, she almost lost her balance as it sprayed foam at the Griffin's neck, until she switched tack and just smashed it across its back instead.

But still the Griffin kept on going, heading for the cowering shushy man.

The man held up his briefcase, as if it had any hope whatsoever of stopping the claws from tearing his head from his shoulders. As if the flimsy leather case full of papers and lunch would be enough to stop this furious, hungry, living weapon. He pushed himself backward and squeezed himself into the luggage rack.

The train threw itself along the tracks, shunting, shifting, seeming like it might topple over at any moment.

Suddenly it braked.

The train screamed, then jolted violently, skidding along on suddenly static wheels.

The Griffin was thrown back off its claws, sliding along the aisle, while Finn and Emmie clung hard to the door in an effort to stay standing against the sudden force of the stop.

The Griffin was briefly stranded, on its back, stuck between seats, struggling to get upright again.

Finn had an idea, grabbed his backpack, and took a bottle from it. "The Shampoodle," he shouted, handing it to her, followed by more bottles. "Mix it with this Flea-Be-Gone."

He started to make his way up the car. "Then add three

drops of Fabulous Fish Fin Formula—only three drops—and a splash of Pet Poop Hardener. My dad showed me the recipe. It had better work."

Emmie was at it right away, trying to mix the bottles as the train began to move, the driver speeding up the train to hurtle again along the track.

"Throw it to me when you're done," said Finn, edging forward.

The Griffin righted itself as Finn got close.

"Finn," Emmie called, closing the lid on the mixture and raising a hand to toss it to him.

The train jolted again, and she stumbled, dropping the makeshift Desiccator fluid.

It rolled away under a seat as she dived for it and missed.

"I dropped it!" she shouted from the floor, worried that the fluid might desiccate nothing but upholstery and discarded potato-chip bags.

The Griffin loomed over Finn, screeched so loudly he felt like his eardrums would split.

Oh no, Finn thought.

Behind the creature, the man with the briefcase was trapped at the far end of the car, his eyes shot through with fear. There was nothing either of them could do now.

The train curved sharply at a bend, sending the Legend

and humans falling to the right. Emmie's Desiccator bomb rolled back across the aisle, nestled under the far seat.

The Griffin was lifting itself up again, clawing at the floor, gouging marks across it, and seemed to decide it was time to attack Finn now.

"This had better work," Finn said as he climbed up the back of a seat, clambered into the luggage rail above it. Pushing himself along the tight space as the Griffin tried to claw him out, he found the umbrella loose there. The Griffin roared. He thrust the umbrella into its beak, pressing the button at the last moment so that it opened suddenly, jamming open the creature's mouth. Spokes snapped, metal bent, but the umbrella stayed in place, wedged in tight.

The Griffin stopped, fought with it. Finn pushed himself back out of the luggage rack.

"You," Finn said to the businessman, "stay there if you don't want to become a human football."

The train lurched sharply to his left, throwing him off the rack. He landed painfully on the ground, elbow pushed hard into his ribs, just as the Desiccator bomb rolled across the aisle, by his head. He reached out and caught it.

The Griffin stretched down.

Finn impaled the bottle on an umbrella spoke in the Griffin's open mouth, then tumbled backward, clipping his head on a table upon leaping up. He had no time to feel the pain, and instead followed Emmie through the open car door, shutting it closed before the Griffin got to them.

The Legend bit down on the umbrella, bottle, spokes, everything.

"Any moment now," said Finn.

The Griffin had blood running through its feathers, umbrella spokes sticking out from its beak.

"Any moment now?" asked Emmie.

The Griffin turned around toward the horrified man at the back of the train.

"I hope so," said Finn.

The passenger screamed again.

"I really, really hope so."

The Griffin raised its wings and imploded in a spectacular moment, like a bubble popping, into a hard sphere, rolling to the passenger's feet.

The man screamed again. And screamed. And didn't stop screaming.

"Told you it would work," said Finn.

Emmie sighed.

Behind them, an entire car full of people was watching them.

"Pet," said Finn, pointing unconvincingly toward the rear car and the panicked man in there. "Someone in there brought a pet. On board."

"A dog," said Emmie.

"A really big dog," agreed Finn.

The train pulled into a station. Even if it wasn't their stop, it was time to get off.

20

Before they left the train, they grabbed the computer from the floor where it had fallen, quickly put it in Finn's bag with the desiccated Griffin, the stolen map, and the letter. They then jumped onto the platform, eager to get away before they were grabbed, questioned, lectured, fired, jailed, or all those things.

With a walk that they hoped looked casual but that was really just short of breaking into a sweaty run, they made their way toward the exit of the small station while ignoring the calls of the train conductor, the shouts of the ticket inspector, and the continued screaming of the businessman.

They ducked under the turnstiles of the unstaffed station. Outside was a recycling bin, a large metal container with a small round hole into which bottles could be pushed.

Finn went to shove the desiccated Griffin into it.

Emmie looked at him, unsure.

"Do you have a better idea?"

Emmie didn't have a better idea.

He dropped the Griffin into the bin, the *clank* and *crack* of bottles echoing inside as it rolled its way down the dark, unseen glass slope within.

The train conductor had appeared out of the station door and there was nothing to do but to run away from the building before any questions were asked. They charged up a short slope of asphalt, out through the open gates, and onto a country road.

"Which way?" Finn asked.

"Right," said Emmie, as Finn went left.

They stopped, waiting for someone to make a decision, and then, realizing Emmie had already made one, Finn followed her. They were on a country lane, a long curving stretch of road with a sliver of footpath on the train station side. Weeds grew through cracks in the concrete, dangling briars reaching out to snag them as they ran past.

As they turned out of sight of the station, they heard a siren coming from the unseen road ahead of them. They dropped back into the bushes, let a police car flash by. Finn had no doubt as to its destination.

Once sure that the vehicle was gone, they popped out onto the path again, Finn pulling a thorny branch from his sweater and moving fast in the opposite direction.

"That man on the train was very, very lucky," Finn said, as they ran. "If he'd been closer to that bomb, he'd have been a ball in a tiny, shiny suit."

Emmie stopped, forcing Finn to double back to her.

"He's lucky?" she said, aghast. "Finn, *we're* lucky. No, sorry. We're *not* lucky. Not really. After all, we've just reanimated a Legend on a moving train with civilians on it. We're on the run with stolen property. We have a math project to do, which I had *completely* forgotten about until now. So, we're not really lucky. But if there's even a tiny, tiny, tiny bit of luck for us it's that we didn't kill that man. That's what we would have done, without that glimmer of luck. Killed him. We're lucky that didn't happen. But as for the rest of it, no luck. No luck at all. We're in huge trouble."

"Are you finished?" asked Finn.

She stared at him, incredulous.

At a nearby gate, a curious cow wandered over.

"What's happening to you, Finn?" she asked. "I know we've done some incredible things before, but you've never been this reckless."

"I'm not being reckless," he said, wounded–and conscious that a cow was staring at him.

"What else is this but reckless?" Emmie said, waving a

hand around at the countryside. The cow flinched.

"You wouldn't understand," said Finn, walking on again.

"What? That's . . ." She struggled to find a word to do her feelings justice.

Finn had gone walking around the bend, and she was forced to follow him.

"That's just . . . you know that's not true. This is my problem too."

"Okay, sorry. You do understand," said Finn. "Which means you understand the only way to get Darkmouth back is to uncover the experiments in Slotterton, to reveal what's been going on."

"This plan isn't working, though," said Emmie. "We know they're trying to open the gateways. They're experimenting. They're causing havoc. We have that proof—the papers you took, maybe the computer too. Let's just go back to Darkmouth and show them."

"We don't have any real proof," said Finn. "Just our word against theirs. A scrap of a map, a few things written down, that's all," he said, marching farther up the thin path.

"We still have to call your dad for help," she said, scrolling through her phone.

"Okay," he conceded, "but only to tell him the time and place of the experiment. Maybe we shouldn't mention the whole escaped-Griffin thing just yet."

"We *have to*," she said.

"No, we *don't*," he said.

The phone rang. They looked at it like it was the strangest object in the world.

Private number.

She answered it, putting it on speaker.

They heard only breathing. Calm. Unremarkable. Patient.

"Let me guess," Lucien's voice said eventually. "Birdsong. Quiet." The cow mooed. "You're in the countryside."

"We're not coming back," said Finn, and Emmie stared at him in disgust for being so quick to crack.

"I believe there was a little problem on the train. An unwanted passenger."

They did not respond.

"The police were called," continued Lucien. "Naturally, the first thing the police did was to contact us. They don't want to deal with any of this, trust me. They want *us* to deal with it. To quietly *neutralize* the problem."

Finn did not like that word: "neutralize." It sent a shiver through him even in the afternoon warmth.

"It is not too late to come back to Darkmouth," Lucien

said, his voice turning soft. Finn knew it was an act. "Finn, you're young. You are allowed to make mistakes. This does not have to go any further."

Finn didn't want to believe him, but he felt the tug of home, the promise of this all being over by dinnertime. But he knew it wouldn't be. Just *knew*. A sense, a warning signal pulsed strongly in his mind. He had to finish what he'd started. Reveal the plot. Get Darkmouth back. He looked up and down the stretch of road. One way was back. One way was forward. He couldn't be sure either would end well, but he had to choose.

"And, Emmie," said Lucien, "you got wrapped up in all this. We've talked about that already. You know I understand it's not your fault."

Finn shot Emmie a glance. She refused to look back, but he could see her face tighten, that she felt trapped.

"You should come home," continued Lucien over the phone. "Even if Finn doesn't. You're in no trouble at all."

Finn grabbed the phone from her hand. "We're not coming back. We're going to tell everyone what you're up to."

"Then it will not end well for—"

Finn lobbed the phone high and away into the field, where it *plunk*ed and sank into a cow pat.

Emmie stood, openmouthed. "My phone!"

"Look, Emmie," said Finn, stepping up so close to her he practically knocked her back off the path. "I'm sorry. I'm sorry for dragging you into all of this. I'm sorry that we're now out here, in the middle of nowhere, with half the world looking for us. And I'm actually sorry I threw your phone into cow poo like that—it was kind of stupid."

He stepped back, allowing her some space on the path.

"But I'm begging you," he continued, "this one last time, to trust me. Please. They have taken Darkmouth from us. They're doing something really dangerous with dust and gateways, and we don't know what else might be happening that we haven't even seen yet."

The cow wandered off to see what had plopped in the field.

They heard a car approach from the direction of the station and stepped off the path, crouching down at the entrance to the field.

"What they're doing is going to get people killed unless we stop them, Emmie. Maybe a lot of people. Maybe the whole world. We have to stop them. *I* have to stop them. But I can't do it alone. I need your help. Please."

The warm breeze pushed and pulled at the briars. A few insects hopped around between colorful weeds. Emmie looked blank. Finn tried to guess what was going on in her mind. Wondered if she'd push him over. Walk away. Scream.

"So what now, O chosen one?" she asked, unimpressed—but Finn knew he'd convinced her. For the time being.

He stood, stepped back onto the path. "I'm going to have to do something I've never done before . . . ," he said.

They could hear the sound of a car approaching from the other direction, the high rattle of an old engine.

"What's that?"

"Hitchhike." Finn stuck his thumb out.

Emmie threw her eyes up, shook her head, and pulled him away from the road, then took his place, thumb out as the car came closer. "You look like you've been in a fight with, well, a Griffin, as it happens."

The car passed them in a spray of dust.

"Great," said Emmie with full sarcasm.

There was the sound of brakes and of the car reversing. It reappeared, slowing to a halt beside them. Inside was a woman looking unsure of whether she should pick them up. Finn didn't give her any choice, just opened the passenger door and hopped in.

"Oh . . . ," said the woman. "I . . ."

Emmie climbed into the seat behind them.

The woman started up the car again. "Where are you going?"

"Slotterton," said Finn, hopeful. "Any chance you're going in that general direction?"

The driver appeared cautious, unsure. "Actually, that's exactly where I'm going," she said after a moment.

They passed the train station. The blue of rotating police-car lights was dancing on its walls. The train was still there, passengers on the platform, conductor and inspector explaining all to the police officers. Finn and Emmie sank in their seats as they passed, hands covering their faces, suddenly aware they had no idea where they were.

Their destination set, Finn glanced behind at the train station, wanting to feel relief as he lost sight of it. But he couldn't. Even on this long stretch of empty country road, he felt like the walls were closing in.

DO NOT PUBLISH

Report by Tiger-One-Twelve

Location: A storage facility, undisclosed location

It was the same story, spread across the world.

The dead were easing their way out of the ground like moles, bones pushing through the earth into daylight and then lying, scattered and crumbled, to be found by puzzled and often frightened locals.

The thing was that—more and more—other things would come with the bones. Truly strange things.

And when they were picked up and handed over to us, they ended up here. In a storage unit, in an industrial park, with a door that only half opened so we had to bend to get in.

And inside, on a table with a spotlight

perched at its corner, was a selection of items. The schoolbag. The piece of armor. A slice of a belt with a biting mouth as its buckle. A couple of pens.

Those pens had been found along the edge of a mighty lake in the middle of a forest so thick it took me four days to trek there. I have been in more welcoming places. At this lake, there were big animals that would drag you below, small animals that could crawl under your skin, and, like at every site where these items were discovered, there were the unseen dangers. A Blighted Village stood there long ago.

Of course, the items on the table might have been nothing important. Even in this remote place people used pens. Even in this place where half-revealed bones protruded from the lakeshore. They just didn't usually have the words *Tails and Snails—Darkmouth Pet Shop* on them.

What else was on the table?

A scrap of a sweater with a Darkmouth school crest on it, found in a Finnish village once called Hell-Sinki.

A bit of a shoe that had appeared in long-drowned wetlands in the Czech Republic.

And there was a box. Plastic. Rectangular. Blue, but transparent. And inside was a shriveled fossil of an apple, mummified almost. The plastic had been melted, flattened in parts, but was otherwise in pretty good condition for a school lunchbox that had somehow made its way into an abandoned settlement at the edge of New Zealand's third smelliest volcano.

We knew who these belonged to. Each object had once been owned by Finn and Emmie, a pair we had been investigating for some time now. Banal accessories of their daily life had turned up all over the globe, singed and torn as if they'd been scattered by an explosion.

No, the mystery was: How were they getting there?

What was causing this strange activity? And how many more places did I need to visit to put the pieces together?

I got the answer far more quickly than I expected when my phone rang and a voice at the other end said one word.

"*Disaster.*"

Finn and Emmie sat in the car, silent for the most part. Finn was in the front, Emmie in the back. Even after several miles, the driver still seemed unsure whether she should have picked them up.

"So, where are you two from then?" she asked with forced cheerfulness.

"Nowhere," said Finn.

"Darkmouth," said Emmie at exactly the same time.

The driver looked at Emmie through the rearview mirror. "Oh," she said. "Darkmouth. That's supposed to be a nice little place?" It was very much a question, a hint that she had heard Darkmouth wasn't that nice a place at all.

Neither of her hitchhikers said anything.

"My name's Anne, by the way," she said. "And you are . . . ?"

"Emmie," said Finn. "I mean, I'm not Emmie. She is.

I'm Finn." He felt like he was giving away far too much information already.

"And what has you two out on that road at this time of day?"

"We got lost," said Finn.

At the same time as Emmie said, "The train broke down."

"The train broke down and when we came out of the station we went the wrong way," Finn said, knowing how contrived it all sounded. This time he caught Emmie's eye in the rearview mirror. She looked away.

"So why are you going to Slotterton?"

"Just a day out," he said. Emmie didn't contradict him. "We thought we'd go to see the sights."

They passed a factory belching smoke from a tall chimney.

The woman seemed to be appraising them, although she had probably made up her mind at this stage, no doubt deciding that there was more to all of this than met the eye.

"It's fifty miles from Darkmouth to Slotterton," she said quizzically. "That's a long way just to see the sights."

They didn't answer that, just sank a little lower in their seats.

"Smoofyland is in Slotterton," pressed Anne. "Are you going there?"

"No," said Finn, definite.

"It has the sparkliest roller coaster in the world."

"Yeah, I heard that," said Finn.

"So what happened with the train back there?" Anne asked.

"Nothing," said Finn, defensive. He could sense Emmie's apprehension behind him. "Why do you think anything happened on the train? Nothing happened."

"I just noticed the police car," she said. "That's all. You said the train broke down. I was wondering if something had happened to cause it."

Finn didn't answer and the silence in the car lasted several miles more. To distract himself from how uncomfortable this all was, Finn concentrated on the swinging fluffy dice hanging from the mirror, quietly berating himself for showing less calm than he should have.

The driver eventually put the radio on to fill the silence. At first, she found only static, the words of a DJ lost beneath hiss and squall. She pressed the button to scan for a station.

Finn could almost feel the heat of Emmie's growing annoyance behind him.

The radio crackled.

"... extensive damage to the train ..."

Anne turned up the volume.

"... wild animal ..."

Finn talked over the presenter. "It's lovely around here," he said, as they drove by an abandoned building, its walls covered in graffiti. "Were you out shopping?" Any question would do.

"Shopping?" asked Anne.

"Yeah, shopping," Finn pressed, looking for a topic, any topic, to distract her.

"Yeah," Anne replied. "I was shopping." It was almost like she'd just remembered this herself.

After a while, Finn noticed they were entering the edge of a town. The fields were giving way to houses, lining the road on either side, and people on footpaths were heading one way or the other, walking their dogs.

A sign read:

It did not mention anything about monsters, or the town's population, or its bloody decline. Yet Finn knew a couple of truths about the place. Its original name was Slaughtertown and many centuries ago it had been a Blighted Village of such renown that whenever it was mentioned to Legend Hunters in other Blighted Villages, they would suck air through their teeth and screw up their faces in the internationally recognized expression meaning, "Whoa, that place is a *mess*."

Not anymore. It had become dormant. No Legends had bothered it in a very long time. Slotterton had become dormant so long ago that even its Legend Hunter family had gradually vanished.

That was not the only thing that was different from Darkmouth. Something seemed not quite right about this place. Something was off with the people he saw going about their business. Finn couldn't quite figure out what it was.

"I just need to grab gas," Anne said, turning off the road at a garage with a gas station, "and then I'll drop you wherever you need to go. You okay to wait here?"

Finn agreed. Emmie didn't answer, appearing to have taken a vow of silence in protest against this entire escapade.

"I'll take you the rest of the way," Anne said as she stepped out. "I'll just be a moment."

Finn observed Slotterton and its people through his window. There were wide attractive streets, with busy shops painted brightly. Flowers hung from baskets, sprouted from window boxes. The people going about their day were enjoying the afternoon sunshine, the warmth.

He had an uneasy feeling about it all, as if it wasn't real. That everyone he could see was pretending. He shuffled in his seat, unable to shake a queasiness about this place.

"Something is not normal here," he said.

"Tell me about it," said Emmie, sunk in her thoughts. "Why did we stop anyway?"

"For gas," said Finn.

"Then why hasn't she bothered getting any?"

Finn looked out and saw Anne just inside the door of the shop, on the phone. She seemed agitated, glancing over at them repeatedly.

"We have to go," said Finn immediately, almost out of the car before he had said it, awkwardly pulling his bag behind him.

Anne's back was turned as she kept talking on the phone.

Emmie was flustered as she stepped out after him. "Why the rush?" she asked.

Finn jogged away from the car, Emmie following, only

looking back very quickly to see Anne realize they were no longer there. She left the shop, scratching her head, looking around.

"She said she'd been shopping," Finn said. "Did you see any shopping bags in her car?"

22

A horrible realization dawned on Finn as he sat on a doorstep at the edge of the town square, watching the residents of Slotterton greet one another with friendly waves, stop to chat on the street while their kids ran freely around the town square.

None of this seemed real to Finn. Or the way it should be. He'd spent his life in Darkmouth, where everyone had their heads down. Where invasion and destruction and rain were always just around the corner.

"Everyone seems, I don't know, so . . ." Finn couldn't even find the words to describe it. He had his hood up, jacket pulled tight over it. Hiding from anyone looking for him. Hiding the lies he was keeping from Emmie. Hiding the Gatemaker he'd been given on the Infested Side and that might now be of no use given he was all this way away.

"Normal," Emmie said, finding the word for him. "This is how normal people live, Finn. This is how I used to live

before I came to Darkmouth." She was still very annoyed about how everything was turning out, and how her phone was now fertilizing a field many miles away.

"These people just have no idea, though," Finn continued, watching the shoppers, strollers, talkers, cyclists, skipping kids. All of them moved like they had nothing to weigh them down. He'd never seen the likes of it. "They have no idea of what could burst into their world at any moment. They have no idea what's been going on in Darkmouth, of what we've done to save them all, over and over and over."

"Thankfully they have no idea you released a Legend on a train either," Emmie reminded him.

"That wasn't on purpose," he protested.

"I'm not really sure that matters."

Two men pushed strollers past them. The men were in bright T-shirts, wearing sunglasses. It was like they were on vacation. Finn could hardly cope with this levity. He felt claustrophobic, trapped among such general happiness.

"Why did you steal the Legend in the first place, though?" Emmie asked. "You must have known it wasn't Broonie. We've seen him desiccated. He doesn't look like that—he looks more like an angry cabbage or something."

"I had it in my hand when the alarm went off. I just ran.

I didn't have time to think."

"Is that really all it was?" she asked him, and he wondered if he could crawl any further into his hoodie, to disappear forever.

It was time for a distraction. "Come on," Finn said. "We'll be seen if we stay much longer here."

He stood up and walked to a shaded corner of the street, a table under a café awning. Taking a seat, he removed the computer from his bag and opened it. Emmie sat with him, her weariness beginning to drag significantly on her every gesture.

"If there is something else going on, you have to tell me," she said to him, as he pressed close to the screen while it blinked into life. "We're in this together."

"The assistants make notes of everything," Finn said. "They don't put their shoes on without writing down what foot they started with. They'll have everything on here. Every experiment. Every failure. Every problem. I'm sure of it."

"Lucien has been trying to persuade me you're acting very strangely," said Emmie.

A waitress put menus in front of them, and then went off to clean up another table.

"Now we're in an old Blighted Village, after a Griffin fight, trying to stop gateway experiments because you stole lots of stuff from them, all while you're holding back something," Emmie continued. "You're not exactly doing anything to prove Lucien wrong."

"It'll all be here," he said, this time doing his best to ignore the emotional pull of the family picture on the screen and pressing a key to clear it and get to business. "The gateways. The experiments. The cave. The cage." He scratched his chin. "All this messing around causes problems. I'm going to find the proof. This is how we tell the world. I'm getting Darkmouth back."

ENTER PASSWORD came up on the screen.

He typed in the old one his family used.

BUBBLES.

It didn't work.

"What password do you think Lucien would use?" he asked.

Emmie looked incredulous. "Do you know how desperate you sound, Finn?"

He watched a couple across the street, stopping at a florist to pick up a bunch of lilies. "Did they look over at us?"

"You're getting paranoid," said Emmie, her tone caring rather than critical. "I know why you're worried, and we *are* on the run obviously, but you're seeing trouble everywhere and that's not good for you."

“Of course I’m paranoid, Emmie. They shot at us. They’re after us. They want to stop us. They want to stop *me.*” He thumped his chest.

The waitress was standing over them, notepad poised for an order but scrutinizing Finn after his outburst.

“Can we get two glasses of tap water, please?” Emmie asked her.

The waitress rolled her eyes, shoved the notepad in her back pocket, and went away, shaking her head.

“There’s something else going on with you. Tell me now, Finn,” Emmie demanded. “Tell me exactly what you’re keeping from me.”

Finn looked around, tugged at the strings of his jacket hood, sat forward so he didn’t have to shout. He was cornered, he knew that. Silence wasn’t an option anymore.

“They asked me to help them,” he said. “They told me I need to do it.”

“Who told you?” asked Emmie.

He had been told time and again that he had a destiny. Whatever that was, he couldn’t do it alone.

So Finn told Emmie everything. It was the only thing he could do.

It did not go well.

By the time the waitress brought the glasses of water, a couple of straws, and a loud *tut* for having to bother doing it at all, Finn was a decent way through telling Emmie about the kidnapping, the Cyclops that wasn't a Cyclops, the mine in the middle of an ocean, Cornelius and Hiss.

He went on to tell her about the destruction Gantrua had left behind on the Infested Side, the request to steal the desiccated remains of the ghastly Fomorian in order to get a charm from him and use it to save the Legends over there, the Gatemaker device for opening gateways.

And for a good chunk of the story, he felt it was going quite well. Emmie did not speak. Not an interruption. Not a question. She hardly even blinked, so absorbed was she in what he realized was an incredible tale of adventure and survival, of near-death and rescue, of an impossible mission from an unlikely source.

He finished his story and waited eagerly for her response.

"What a load of rubbish!" Emmie said, standing up.

"No, it's all true," Finn insisted. "It's exactly how it happened."

"Oh, I believe all that all right," she said, shoving the chair in so that it rattled the table, then walking away.

He was forced to follow, almost falling over the café furniture as he tried to keep up.

"So, what is it?" he asked, puzzled. "What's wrong?"

Emmie stopped in the middle of the sidewalk, forcing a couple of people to walk around them. TVs flickered in the window of an electronics shop.

"What's *wrong*?" she asked. "Where do I start? You traveled to the Infested Side, for ages, met half the Legends there, got given a secret mission—"

"Okay, I should have told you earlier—"

She refused to slow. "Or maybe what's wrong is that you were handed a device they said would open gateways but could be a bomb for all you know. Or maybe the problem is that you stole a Legend and now I know why. You wanted Gantrua."

"No, Emmie," he stressed. "It wasn't that way. Not really."

A shopper walked between Finn and Emmie, forcing

them to step back. But Emmie wasn't finished and quickly closed the gap, causing Finn to retreat further into his hoodie. He could feel the heat of her annoyance.

"That Legend you stole that ended up escaping on the train," she said. "It could have killed people. And do you know what the worst thing is?" she asked. "That the Griffin is not even the worst thing. What really hurts me is that I defended you to Lucien. I didn't let him get to me. I didn't let him convince me that you could, despite everything we've been through, actually be a *traitor*."

That word hit Finn as hard as any kick. He felt the wind knocked out of him just as strongly. The flicker of the TVs in the window needled him. The whole world felt painful.

"I'm not," he said.

"Then why are you acting like one? Everything you're doing, everything you've just told me. How am I supposed to tell anyone that it's all fine?" She stopped, took a breath, tried to steady herself. "How am I supposed to convince *myself?*"

The world moved around them in this town where the people didn't worry about Legends or gateways or rain that brought chaos and carnage. It was sunny and bright and probably quite a lovely day. It didn't feel like that to Finn. Everything felt broken.

"Emmie . . . ," Finn started, then wasn't entirely sure what to say next. A part of him was urging him to fight her, tell her how wrong she was. Another to apologize. In the end there was only really one thing he could say. "I just need you to help me. Please."

She shook her head, sad as much as dismissive, caught between emotions, trying to find a path through her confusion.

"The Infested Side doesn't matter," Finn said. "It can wait. First we just have to expose Lucien's conspiracy. We can still get Darkmouth back. That's all that matters now. I know you will find it hard to trust me. I should have told you about everything that happened, but I didn't because I didn't want to get you in trouble. I didn't want to drag you into it."

"You dragged me so far into it I don't know if we'll ever get out of this mess," she said. "I didn't think I'd say this, but I wish my dad was here."

"Steve would just hold us back. We need to move forward."

Emmie lit up with anger. "Don't talk about my dad like that. He's bailed Darkmouth out—no, *you* out—when it's not even his Blighted Village. He got trapped between worlds, which was really horrible. But still everyone thinks it's your dad who's so heroic. So don't you dare talk about him like that again." She turned her face away from him, toward the shop window and winking TVs.

"I'm sorry," Finn said. "Really, I shouldn't have said that. But I just mean that we're here and we have a chance to sort out this problem. We have to take that chance before it's too late."

In the window, three shelves of TVs of various sizes all flashed up one thing: pictures of Finn and Emmie. Finn's photo was a couple of years old, his hair stuck in a cowlick, one eye not yet finished blinking. Emmie's picture was more recent, her smile contrasting with the words on the screen below.

TRAIN ATTACK: YOUNG SUSPECTS ON THE RUN.

Finn looked around cautiously. A couple of shoppers were already eyeing them a touch suspiciously. Across the street a woman was standing with a policeman, pointing in their direction. The policeman picked up the radio at his shoulder, said something into it.

A bus along the road blocked the view between them before slowly rumbling away again.

When the policeman crossed the street to find them, Finn and Emmie were gone.

24

"I can't run," Emmie protested, even as she followed Finn, reluctantly, down a side street.

"You can," he insisted. "According to the map there should be a bus station this way. We can reach that and get out of here for a while, make it look like we've left Slotterton for good."

"That's not what I mean, Finn."

She stepped after him as he hid in a bookshop, where he picked up the first thing within reach and peeked over its spine to see if they were being followed.

"Hello, can I help you?" asked the bookseller. "If you're interested in yoga for babies we have other titles available too."

Finn looked at the cover of the book, with its picture of a baby doing a handstand. "Thanks," he said. "Just browsing." He picked up a book about cheese and pretended to read that instead. The bookseller wandered off.

"It's obvious they're going to catch us eventually," said Emmie. "They must be able to call in the police when needed. They could probably use the army if they wanted to. And when they catch us, they'll pack us off back to Lucien in no time. It would be hard to blame them."

Finn put the book down, took out the creased map of Slotterton, and examined it quickly. Holding it, he left the shop, hugged the walls, with his hood so tight on his head it was in danger of cutting off the blood supply to his shoulders.

"Finn," Emmie called, her face fully visible to the world as she tried to keep pace. "I'm not doing this anymore."

"The map tells us where they're going to experiment," he said. "We know it's at eight p.m. It's almost five p.m. now. We'll get there, wait for them to do it, and send the evidence to everyone. Every last bit of it. They'll see how dangerous it is."

"You're not listening to me," said Emmie, slowing. "I'm not going with you."

She stopped on the street, forcing him to backtrack.

"I've told you everything, Emmie," he said, anxious to keep moving. "I promise I haven't held anything back. You have to trust me." He kept glancing around, looking for the police officer.

"I want to," said Emmie. "But after everything you've told me–"

"I am not a traitor," he said, the desperation clear in his words. He had hung off the edge of an abyss or two in his life. This felt too similar for comfort.

"This can't be the only way out," Emmie said, staying where she was even as Finn tried to start moving again.

They were at an intersection, people and cars coming from four directions. Finn felt horribly exposed.

"Emmie, you have to believe me," said Finn. "There's a huge conspiracy going on here."

"There has to be a better way," she said.

"The worst thing is that I think they *want* it to happen," Finn continued. "Lucien wants Legends invading again so he and the other assistants can stop sitting around doing nothing but reports and jobs and whatever they've been doing. They're trying to make it look like it's the Legends coming after us again. They can then step up to protect us. It's crazy. We're going to stop it. We're going to let every Half-Hunter know what's really going on."

She bowed her head, shook it.

Finn saw someone watching them across the road. "It's that woman," he said. "Anne. The one who gave us the ride."

Emmie didn't look up, simply let her hair hang heavy over her eyes.

"Seriously, she's over there, watching us," said Finn.

Across the street, Anne caught his gaze, held it for a few moments. It wasn't a look of friendliness, but Finn couldn't detect any malice either. Her true intent was difficult to make out.

"Finn–" Emmie started.

"Look," he said, "I know you hate me right now. I know you think I'm paranoid and a liar and can't be trusted and probably loads of other things as well."

"We can't–"

"And I'll admit some of those things are probably true, but some are not. So you have to come with me, because she is watching us for a reason and we need to move."

Anne started to walk across the road toward them, and Finn's instinct was to run–but Emmie did not move. Anne hesitated as she left the sidewalk, her attention apparently drawn to something else to her right. Finn followed her sight line, down the street, saw the police officer spot them and break into a sprint in their direction. He slowed momentarily to wave to someone on the road to *his* right.

Gray suits. Assistants. Homing in on Finn and Emmie.

Among them, his legs moving at twice their speed just to keep up, was Lucien.

It meant they were being converged on from three directions now.

"Let's go," Finn said.

Emmie shook her head. "I'm not running," she said.

The police officer was about to cross the road to get to them. Lucien and the assistants would reach them at about the same time. Anne was still watching, but hanging back now, hesitating for whatever reason.

"It's over," said Emmie.

Finn looked at her, saw the determination hardening on her face.

The clock in the town square chimed five times.

"In three hours they're going to try and open a gateway in this town," said Finn. "I still plan to be there. This won't be over for me until I get Darkmouth back for my family."

He turned and ran across the street, through the pedestrians, in front of a truck that had to brake suddenly to avoid hitting him. He feinted to go one way but instead went another. And when he thought he had a sliver of a moment, he glanced back, still expecting to see Emmie alongside him, having decided to trust him after all, to fight with him, to blow the conspiracy apart.

She wasn't there.

He saw her being swallowed up by chasing assistants. Lucien put a hand on Emmie's shoulder, looked up, met Finn's gaze, and grinned as the other assistants resumed their chase.

Finn turned away and kept running.

Alone.

Finn didn't know Slotterton like he knew Darkmouth. Didn't know its shortcuts, its alleys, its gaps and cracks. So he ran in the general direction of the bus station, but with only half an idea how to get there.

People jumped aside as he sprinted past, shouted at him to be careful. Drivers punched their car horns as he jumped off the narrow sidewalks to get around obstacles, people, pets.

He ignored every yell but couldn't ignore the sound of the siren, its rising wail echoing off walls so that it sounded like it was coming from everywhere at once.

The whole world seemed to be closing in on him, streets narrowing, pavements becoming busier with people.

He found a side street, ran into it, stopped to get his breath and his bearings. He was standing in a small square of old, low houses, a couple of them with overhanging thatched roofs.

Hearing footsteps and further shouts approaching, Finn looked again for a way out and this time spied a very narrow gap between houses, just enough to squeeze through sideways. He fled down it as a police car screeched to a stop at the entrance to the square.

His shoulders scraped against the walls; his bag bumped against the stone. Through the gap, he could see two police officers leaving the car to chase after him.

Exiting the gap, he found himself on a quiet street of empty buildings, stone warehouses, and what seemed to be small abandoned factories. It was as if the street had been hidden here to crumble alone. Finn stepped onto the sidewalk at the exact same moment the assistants arrived from a road a few yards to his right. He almost stumbled in an effort to get away from them, just as the police squeezed through the gap behind him.

A full gang was on his tail now. Police. Assistants. He still wasn't sure that Anne, the woman who'd given them the ride, wasn't about to pop up out of a drain and grab his ankle. It was clear that no one was going to stop until he was in handcuffs. Or a jar.

But Finn was far more accustomed to running from trouble than they were to chasing it. He opened some distance between himself and the chasing pack while seeking a building to hide in or escape through. He checked doors as he passed, but they were all locked up or boarded over, some with empty windows too high to clamber into. He ran across the street to another door, pulled at it while still moving. No luck. Dashed back across the road to try another. It didn't budge either.

More assistants appeared around a corner ahead of him, getting into a pincer formation with those behind him. He realized that one of them was the bearded assistant Ricardo, now trussed awkwardly in an overcoat because his armor would have been too conspicuous.

But bulging beneath his coat was the unmistakable form of a Desiccator.

Finn pulled hard at another rusted steel door into one of the street's empty, blank-stoned buildings. This time it opened just a touch, a sliver for him to squeeze in under the heavy chains securing it.

Inside it was muggy, a smell of mold in the air, and bare but for blackened brick and the long-cold ashes in an old fireplace filled with burned cans. There was a second story above, but the stairs were gone, leaving only a square hole in the ceiling through which thin streams of daylight mixed with dust. Otherwise, the back wall was a solid stretch of stone. No doors. No windows.

Unless he could walk through walls, there was no way out but the way he had come in.

He was trapped.

Outside, the footsteps reached the door. There was the sound of the chains being pulled, then hacked at. Voices, shouting together so Finn couldn't make out what they were saying, only that it wasn't anything pleasant. Fingers pulled at the gap at the door, trying to open it fully.

Unless he could walk through walls . . .

Finn patted his jacket, felt the object within. The Gatemaker.

He went to the fireplace, shoved the bag with the computer as far up the chimney as possible, so as to be out of sight. He still had faith it contained vital evidence of Lucien's wrongdoing so it might be useful later on, but it would have to stay there for now, because he couldn't be sure it would survive the trip he was about to take.

"Stand back," he heard Ricardo say. "I'll desiccate this door and if you're standing behind it I won't be responsible for turning you into a doorstop."

Finn went to the farthest wall while fumbling for the Gatemaker, pulled it free from his jacket, gave it the quickest of examinations to figure out how to use it. It had a rounded piece at its base, about the width of his thumb.

He pushed it, felt the strange sensation of something wriggle inside. A small crystal peeked out of the top. It was clear, beautifully so.

Outside, there was the click and wheeze of a Desiccator being armed.

"Right," said the assistant's voice. "You've been warned."

Gripping the Gatemaker in his palm, Finn was relieved to find a snag on the air quickly. The crystal sparked instantaneously, like a match finding a flame. There was what he thought might be the brief, tormented squeal of a dying scaldgrub—he really, really hoped it wasn't that—before a golden, sparkling gateway sliced down the wall.

The Desiccator fired outside.

The door crumpled violently, its hinges ripping from the brick, and the assistants poured into the space within.

It was empty.

26

Finn was already in the portal to the Infested Side, experiencing a sensation he had not forgotten, no matter how much he had tried. There was nausea, of course, like a punch in the stomach, but this was also accompanied by a sense that every single cell in his body had been separated, washed, scrubbed, pecked at by birds, then put back in the wrong order.

It only lasted a moment.

Forever.

Both.

All he knew was that almost as soon as he stepped into it, the gateway shut behind him with a crunchy snap and he was in the gloom of the Infested Side, doubled over, searching for breath, relieved he hadn't exploded but half wishing he could so that it would blast away this terrible feeling.

He looked up to find he'd landed in the middle of a

horde of Legends, teeth upon teeth, eyes upon eyes, claws upon claws.

Gasping.

Roaring.

Reaching for him.

27

Finn dived to the ashen ground, scuttling between at least two legs of a Legend that had an abundance of them, until he was clear enough to jump to his feet. He registered some kind of village of muddy huts, heated by meek fires leaking smoke into the low gray cloud he knew all too well as an oppressive feature of the Infested Side.

Nausea heavy in the deepest part of his stomach, he still managed to get a head start on the Legends and dodged between huts, before arriving at a clearing and glimpsing something strange, causing him to stop dead in his tracks for a moment, a mud-formed figure sticking up from the burned ground.

Is that . . . ? he thought.

But there was no time to think.

The Legends were seeking him out, their snarling breath closing behind him. There was nothing for it but to dash

inside the nearest hut. He was relieved to find it empty of Legends, but somewhat concerned to see its floor covered with sharp spears and jagged knives instead.

How many crystals had Sulawan the sort-of-Cyclops told him were in this thing? Three? Four? Then he should be able to open another gateway, escape the Legends, and return to his world—far enough from the assistants and police in Slotterton that he could flee from them too.

He pushed his thumb into the base of the Gatemaker again, revealing another crystal. He searched for a snag, struggled to find it this time as the ground shuddered under the pounding of approaching Legends, their growls and cries growing so loud he could hardly hear himself think.

The crystal hooked on empty air. Finn breathed again in relief.

Sparks. A scaldgrub scream. Gateway.

He threw himself back into Slotterton.

The journey was hell, as always.

The gateway closed. Finn was back in the town, in the middle of a road, as a car bore down on him blaring its horn. He rolled out of the way just before it flattened him.

Up the street, outside the building he'd first disappeared into—and from—the assistants were alerted by the squeal of brakes and quickly abandoned the warehouse to come and grab him.

He forced himself up, every step a feat of superhuman effort over the gateway's uniquely awful travel sickness, calculating how far he needed to get from his pursuers in both worlds.

An assistant appeared from his right, surprising him with a tackle that sent him sprawling to the ground, the Gatemaker rolling away toward a drain. The assistant followed him to the asphalt with a winding thump, letting go just enough for Finn to rise and use his assailant's chest as a launchpad to jump after the Gatemaker.

He grabbed the device as it was about to drop from the street into the drain, stood, took flight again.

His sense of direction skewed by tackles and gateways and cars, he realized he'd run straight into a dead end, the alley hemmed in by a tall building, completely boarded up, metal door riveted shut, wood nailed over windows.

He pulled at the door anyway, searched for a rotten section in the windows. Nothing gave.

The Gatemaker holds how many crystals now? He pushed,

and one emerged. Was it the last one? He couldn't tell. He didn't want to put a finger in there and lose it to a snarky scaldgrub.

"Finn," said Lucien.

Turning his head at the entrance to the cul-de-sac, Finn saw the man who had taken everything from his family.

Lucien pushed his glasses up his nose, held a hand out. "This can end now," he said. "No more running. No more trouble. You can be home in Darkmouth with your mother and father in a couple of hours. This will all be over."

Finn faced the wall again. Solid brick. Nowhere left to go. He'd lost Emmie. He couldn't get into the computer, but he figured that was safely hidden away for now in the warehouse. If he was captured, though, he wouldn't be able to produce the evidence to condemn Lucien. Every decision he had made had ended in near disaster. Total disaster, really.

But he couldn't give up. Not now.

Behind Lucien, a group of sweating, panting assistants arrived, as well as the two guards with Desiccators, fingers on triggers, pointing at him. Finn saw them from the corner of his eye as he turned his head again. But he did not turn fully, instead kept himself facing the wall of the locked-up building.

"What do you say, Finn?" Lucien asked. "We don't want any accidents."

Finn had seen something over on the Infested Side. Something that had caused him to stop, but that he couldn't forget and that hinted at other, stranger things going on over there.

But if he opened a gateway now, he might be lost there. For good. No guarantee he would ever get back again.

Finn put his hands at the back of his head, a show of surrender. He left the crystal snagged on the air.

"Good choice," he heard Lucien say.

"My dad said something before that made no sense to me, but does now," Finn said, hands raised, his back still to Lucien.

A snarl of satisfaction played on Lucien's lips.

Then came the explosion of the gateway opening.

"The best way to grab victory is to first look like you've lost everything."

Lucien screamed, glasses dropping from his face, all composure lost. "I am going to desiccate you and bury you where no one will find you."

Finn heard the protests, heard the Desiccator shot too, as he threw himself into the gateway, hoping he'd made the right decision, persuading himself he had nothing left to lose. But he had a lot to lose. Fingers. Toes. Family. Home.

Infinity. Scrambling. Sickness. Stomach somewhere between worlds.

The blue Desiccator fire hitting the air as a damp squib.

The gateway biting shut.

The Infested Side.

The nausea felt normal now, not so crippling. The first thing he did as he lay on the blackened ground was to check the Gatemaker, pushing at its tube in the hope of a final crystal.

It was empty. No way home.

Rolling onto his back, he was greeted by a terrifying sight.

A mass of Legends, a legion of different shapes and sizes and limbs and teeth and limbs that looked like teeth. They surrounded him.

But the most surprising thing happened.

One by one, they dropped to their knees, heads bowed.

Finn stood up, suddenly taller than them all, and saw a second strange sight, the same one that had stopped him in his tracks only minutes before.

The lumpen object jutted from the ground. A little shorter than Finn, it had been fashioned from the clay of the dark ashes but had a distinct shape to it. Two arms perhaps. Something that might be roughly hewn legs. A ball on top that was some approximation of a head. And covering the top bit of the upper part of the sculpture was a pieced-together fighting suit. *Finn's* fighting suit. The one he had worn and left behind after exploding on his previous visit to the Infested Side.

This was a statue.

A statue of him.

Finn circled the strange sculpture. It stood in the mud, glistening. He ran his fingers along its armor, the ragged and burned edges. The rust of the hinges, the dust on the leather. He couldn't believe it. It looked like it had been dragged from the depths of hell. Which, in a way, it had. Last time he'd seen this armor, it had been in a crater of his making.

The rest of the object was largely bare, its surface shining a little. Finn touched it, guessed it was made of clay fashioned from the dry ground.

A Legend stepped forward, some kind of upright goat with feathers. Finn felt no menace from it. Instead, the Legend was approaching him with something like trepidation.

"We are sorry. We had no water," explained the Legend, gesturing to the statue. "So we had to create clay using the dirt and whatever we could get from the sulfuric rivers

without dying. And because that wasn't enough, we added our own spit."

Finn withdrew his hand quickly, wiped it on his leg, but knew he would not feel clean again until he'd showered for about a week.

He stood back and assessed the strange sight of this tall lump of clay half dressed in his ruined fighting suit, and from a short distance began to see its form a little more clearly.

"It's meant to be me, isn't it?"

The goat creature's face fell. "We didn't have anything but memories to work from. Only the half-remembered descriptions of sometimes reluctant or half-alive eyewitnesses. But I hope you like it." He looked at Finn, needy.

"Oh yes," Finn said eventually, his feelings now about one-third embarrassment at having been so rude, and two-thirds horror that *this* was supposed to look like *him*.

"I admit, now that we see you in the flesh, that the nostrils could be narrower," said the goat creature, "and the ears could stick out a bit more."

"The ears?"

"They're obsessed with your ears, kid," said Sulawan the sort-of-Cyclops, arriving through the throng, Legends moving aside for him. Beag the Sprite zipped along the ground beside him, excitement on his wide gray face. "And I've since told them that your legs are much punier than this," Sulawan added, "which is why in real life your head looks so outsize."

The eye of every Legend fell on Finn's legs. He felt horribly self-conscious.

"But we did our best to present you in the most dignified manner possible," said the goat creature.

Finn looked around at the assembled Legends, still stooped in some kind of display of reverence, but looking up at him. He saw many things on those faces: various types and sizes and numbers of eyes, long fangs and stubby teeth, various degrees of hairiness, but each had one thing in common. A clear desire for him to like this statue.

Finn wanted to please them. "No, no, that's really good how you used a torn bag around my waist as underpants. Really."

"They didn't always succeed in the dignity part, kid," said Sulawan, enjoying every single moment of this.

"I hope you're not disappointed," said Beag.

"No," said Finn, unconvincing. "I just . . . why did they do this?"

"Why do you think, kid?" asked Sulawan. "They worship you."

Finn struggled with that sentence, not because it was complicated or any such thing but simply because it made no sense to him. "*Me?*"

"I guess they just haven't gotten to know you yet," said Sulawan.

Finn cast an eye on the Legends. Some had what he assumed were children, either clinging to their legs or held up at their shoulders. One Legend had a row of them in a pouch in its belly. Another had a single, furry youngling sticking out from its mouth like a rogue fang. Finn looked at it and it ducked quickly back inside its mother's mouth. Or maybe it was its father. Finn didn't know. He just knew there were so many of them, and that they appeared utterly transfixed by his presence.

"They even have a name for you," said Beag, picking up the remnants of a notebook from the base of the statue. "Finnagetwelveandthreequarters."

Finn's silence told them he was really stumped at that.

Beag held up the cover of the notebook, where Finn's writing spelled out his name and his age when he had done it.

"No, you don't understand," Finn said, taking it and flicking through history homework he'd forgotten he'd ever done. "That was just my age when I used it."

"It is only a shame we could not bring Red Warrior here too," said Beag, wrinkling his flat, flesh-pink nose.

"Red who?" asked Finn.

"He means the female," said Sulawan. "The one who talks and fights and talks. But never backs down. That's how the story goes anyway."

Finn caught on. "You mean Emmie? *She's* Red Warrior? How come she gets a great name like the Red Warrior and I get Finn the Blah-Blah-Blah Whatever?"

"Finnagetwelveandthreequarters," said the goat creature, trying to be helpful.

"*That*," he said, genuinely irked. "By the way, I'm way over thirteen now. And I don't do the quarters thing anyway—that's for kids."

"Finnagetwelveandthreequarters," said the goat creature, regardless. "You did incredible things all those years ago. You destroyed half an army with your extraordinary power."

"I didn't even know I was doing it at the time," mumbled Finn, unable to hold these stares. The intensity was uncomfortable.

"You need to understand that no one but the human called Niall has come here and done what you did," continued Beag. "And he turned to the dark side, became a servant of Gantrua."

"He was my grandfather and thought I would destroy the world, our world," Finn tried to explain. "He was just trying to stop me from doing it."

"His prophecy also said that you would save *our* world," said the goat creature, "because if you were the humans' destroyer then you would be our savior. We tried to spread this message."

"They really did," said Sulawan. "They yap on about it all the time. Always trying to convert me."

"And in that time, so many of your relics have been passed between them, through their claws and paws and wings," said Beag cheerfuly. "Now they're using them as offerings to appease the Gashadokuro, burying them with the bones in the ground all over this world."

"They're burying my old stuff because they think it might stop the Bone Creature?"

"Yes," said Beag, as if this was a perfectly logical solution to the crisis.

"The problem is that the Bone Creature seems about as interested in your belongings as I am," said Sulawan.

A large catlike but scaly Legend stepped forward, cautious, but with an edge of excitement Finn did not normally see in Legends. It hesitated, then moved forward again. With surprising strength for one so small, Beag gave

Finn a gentle push on the leg as encouragement.

The Legend touched Finn's hand, its eyes not leaving his, and turned his palm upward. Finn glanced at Sulawan, who was chewing his rock nonchalantly, yet with a glint of curiosity he couldn't quite conceal beneath his cool veneer. Finn looked back at the Legend, gaze still locked on him, and tried not to jump out of his skin when it flicked its tongue at his palm.

Finn had closed his hand, an instinctive reaction to the tongue flicking at it. But he felt something in his grip, left behind after this strange gesture. He opened his palm to reveal a stubby pencil. Tooth marks where it had been chewed at the top. The tip blunt. The words *Darkmouth Bookshop* were embossed in faded golden lettering on the side.

"This is mine," he told them. "Thank you."

The Legend nodded, delight spreading across its face, eyes not leaving him, before backing away until it was in among the crowd again.

"Where did they get this?" he asked Beag. "Where did they get *any* of it?"

"You left it here," said the Sprite. "The day you went all . . ." Unable to quite find the words, he instead mimed an explosion, fingers spread wide. "*Booccckkccchh!* You left these objects behind. Inside a container. And you also left many pages of your human manuscripts. Like this one . . ."

Another Legend came from the crowd, holding a square of shiny paper, faded and yellowing but still with neat creases. It was a page from his schoolbook *Let's Do Math 4*, his answers still legible beside the questions.

"They believe these are your ancient scrolls," said Sulawan with a heavy edge of sarcasm. "Great wisdom from Finnagetwelveandthreequarters."

"It's not wise—it's my homework," said Finn. "I got a C-minus for that. Look, my teacher Mrs. McDaid said it there in red pen. 'You can do better.'"

"*You can do better*," the Legends repeated in a chant.

Finn's lip curled in surprise.

"We can all do better," said the goat creature. "That is what we learned from this."

Finn had been confused enough already by his presence here. This was making his brain do somersaults in his skull.

"We do not have all of your relics and teachings here anymore. They have spread across the land, been buried with the dead to calm the Gashadokuro, but we memorized many of them before they went," said the goat creature. "My favorite is the Great Scroll of the Jam Tart."

"The Jam Tart?" asked Finn.

"One cup of sugar," intoned the Legend.

"*Six circles of mighty pastry*," responded the entire throng.

"But that's just a recipe," Finn told them. "Something we made at school."

"Six blobs of the jam of raspberry," concluded the goat creature solemnly.

"It wasn't even that great when I baked it," insisted Finn. "The pastry was really soggy."

A Hogboon stepped forward. "If you might so indulge us, we beg answers to an important question. Does Emmie smell?"

"What?" asked Finn, flummoxed.

"We once had an object—now lost to us—that claimed 'Emmie Smells,'" said the Hogboon. "But it was followed by a message that contradicted it, saying, 'No, I Don't.' It has caused a few arguments among your worshippers." The Legend looked at a neighbor, a glance that betrayed some kind of rocky history between them. "In fact, we are now split largely into two factions. The SmellyEmmies and the NoIDon't-ists." He leaned forward. "The NoIDon't-ists are a strange bunch. They think that washing is the way to purity. We, of course, know that stench is the path to glory." He sniffed at Finn. "I can immediately tell that you agree."

They continued to stare at him with an admiration that made him utterly uncomfortable. "I'm not some kind of god," he said.

"Oh lord, no," said Sulawan, pulling the stone from his mouth to see how much chewing was left in it. "Don't get ahead of yourself there, kid. No, they don't think you're a god. Gods abandoned this world aeons ago. They just think you're the savior of their entire world. Big difference."

"How you will do this remains a mystery to us," said Beag, perky as ever. "But you will have plenty of time to explain it to us once you have helped us defeat the cruel and terrifying Gashadokuro."

"The Bone Creature is getting worse," said Hiss, emerging from among the Legends, the Orthrus unseen by Finn until now. How long had they been there? "It gets bigger with each attack. And something more dangerous is occurring because of what you humans are doing in your world. We cannot stop it without your help. Come in—we will more fully show you the reason why you are here."

"Show me?" asked Finn.

He looked around. There was a hut, hardly able to support the weight of its own roof. With a moan and a nod of the head, Cornelius motioned Finn toward its entrance. He heard the breathing before he got there, the rattling breathing of someone, or something, near death. Finn had seen his grandfather die. He could not forget that sound.

In the gloom of the hut, he made out a serpent, crumpled on the ground, one wing bent back at a horrible angle, the other folding messily along its back, a long fang snapped in half.

Finn entered, reluctant—not because he feared this Legend but because of the pall that hung over it, the impending death.

The Orthrus followed, Sulawan and Beag too. Hiss almost immediately went into a trancelike state, his eyes widening as if gazing upon a whole other reality. Finn recognized it as a psychic state he'd witnessed before, when he was on the Infested Side long ago. The serpents had been in charge and communicated telepathically through Hiss. This time, though, Hiss did not speak the Legend's words. Instead, he relaxed again, dropped as if temporarily weary, then rose toward Finn.

"We must be honest," said Hiss. "This will not be pleasant for you."

"What won't be pleasant?" asked Finn.

Sulawan grabbed Finn around the chest, pinning his arms tight, and lifted him over to the prone serpent. Finn fought, kicked, wriggled. It was useless. A tongue–wet and rough–emerged from the Quetzalcóatl's mouth and, despite Finn's strong attempts to turn away, its tip found his ear.

Finn's entire world was filled with death.

Finn was flying in a sky thick with Quetzalcóatls.

The air pulsed with the beating of wings, churning the clouds. He felt he was one of them, but only as a passenger in its mind. He had no control over the movement, was a prisoner to the jarring of a swift maneuver, a surge of acceleration, the sickening, stomach-emptying plunge as his serpent rocketed toward the ground far below.

He knew that his body was back in the hut, this experience just a vision being planted in his mind, yet it all felt so gut-lurchingly real.

The serpent swept across a landscape of Legends, so many he couldn't focus, only a speedy blur of swinging weapons, swiping claws, giants wading among dwarves, four-legged monsters pouring past those with two.

All of them moving in one direction: toward a field divided into mounds of clay in neat rows, each and every one with a shard of petrified tree sticking straight up from it.

The serpent kept going. Gaining speed as the ground came nearer and nearer, and Finn tried to scream but was voiceless, helpless, as they reached the hard earth . . .

. . . and passed straight into it without resistance, without impact, and now Finn was in the ground, still, as if lying among the bones heaped within, no longer in the Quetzalcóatl's mind but viewing the earth from inside.

Bones.

He wanted to kick against the claustrophobia, claw his way out, but had no power, no movement.

Beside him in the burned earth a long bone moved. Just a quiver at first. Shaking itself, waking. He watched it wriggle, trying to find space amid heavy, dead clay. It jolted, earned a gap, pushed into it, moved higher toward the surface.

As it shifted, it snagged a piece of fabric. Finn recognized it. It was his old football-shaped pencil case from school.

Another bone squirmed through the clay to meet with it, the two forming a joint. Finn followed them as together they moved upward, forcing their way through topsoil, into the light, where these white, pocked bones lay on the ground as if exhausted from the effort.

Finn rose with them, arriving on the surface as if he too was some long-buried bone, to lie there, suddenly released into the world again. Around him other bones began to appear, worming their way through the earth, shaking off the dirt, the sound like hailstones striking the ground. Until bones were scattered all over, a strange crop carpeting the earth.

Lying still, as if wasted by the effort.

But they weren't on the Infested Side.

There was grass. There were trees. There was blue sky and butterflies, the hum of insects and the chirping of birds. There were people. Talking. Laughing. Unseen but near. This was home. Not Darkmouth, as far as Finn could tell, but somewhere in his world.

Then he was sucked back down, dragged again through the dirt, darkening, blackening, until seeping back onto the surface of the Infested Side of deathly gray and poisoned soil. There were bones here too, but these were not still. They possessed energy; almost as one they were shuddering into life, joining up, latching onto other bones, dragging along the ground until they attached to an ivory lattice that began to lift, to rise, as if finding its feet.

Legs formed now. From skulls, wing bones, antlers, claws, bones usually hidden so deep within a Legend that they are only ever seen by the earth in which they eventually crumble. All moved into the crude form of a creature, growing, gaining height. Great clods of dirt fell from it, splatting to the ground, pushed aside by the last few bones rising to join the behemoth. Until a creature stood tall, a rain of earth shaking from its rough torso, its horribly concocted head.

The dead had come together to create something living. Something terrible.

The Legends arrived to fight it. From across the land. From the sky. Wielding flaming torches to burn it back to the ground. The Bone Creature went to meet them, clawing serpents from the air, scooping Legends from the earth. Where its bones were broken by the attack, they simply re-formed elsewhere so that it was a constantly shifting shape. Already dead, it was impossible to kill.

Finn watched all this, helpless, trapped in the vision. He saw the arrival of a Quetzalcóatl, diving toward the creature, fearless, determined, mouth wide in attack.

The Bone Creature swung for it, struck it hard.

With a shock, Finn found himself back in the hut, cowered, arms raised as he protected himself from an attack he had only imagined.

The building was unused, dull, an old hall down a Slotterton side street that had none of the surprising fun and scale of Finn's house. Yet this was the Legend Hunters' hub. A building they would have used frequently many years ago but which had long since been handed over to the public. Now they'd taken it back.

Emmie scanned its walls, seeing the evidence of the hall's civilian use. There were torn posters for long-finished festivals, a bulletin board on which someone had stuck an old newspaper headline–*SLOTTERTON: VILLAGE OF THE YEAR AGAIN*–and a dusty, green rosette with *Fourth Place–Battle of the Bands, 1986* fading at its center.

"Doesn't look like a place where Legend Hunters once operated, does it?" asked Lucien, sitting on a wheeled office chair at a bare wooden desk. He stretched back, hands behind his head, looked at the wall too. "But that was a long time ago, and time has moved on in Slotterton. They haven't had a Legend invade here for many, many decades. We never forgot, though, and we always had this place on standby in case it was needed. It was only supposed to be a stopover today, but your friend decided to make it a longer visit for everyone."

Emmie didn't respond, just stood with her hands in her pockets.

Lucien got up, pulled his chair over to her, and sat on the corner of the desk, his short legs just barely reaching the floor.

"Sit," he said. "Please. You must be tired."

She placed her jacket on the back of the chair and sat, hands pressed beneath her.

"They gave you a phone to call your father?" Lucien asked.

"Yes, thanks," answered Emmie. "My phone is in a field somewhere. Finn threw it there."

"His behavior is very erratic. Did you see what he has done now?" asked Lucien, matter-of-fact. "After that stunt on the train, disappearing into the Infested Side sort of caps it off. Although, given he started the day off by raiding the Dead House, where he stole a Legend, dangerous chemicals and"—he lifted a page on his desk, noted what was underneath—"a small aromatic candle, he has turned this into quite an adventure. And I just have a sense there is more to come from him yet."

He waited for her response. None was forthcoming, so he resumed.

"You didn't come to Slotterton by coincidence. Can you tell me why you're here?"

Emmie looked at her feet. "He thinks you're experimenting, trying to open gateways here. Like you've done in Darkmouth."

Lucien shuffled on the corner of the desk, pushed his glasses up his nose. "Listen to me," he said. "If there were experiments taking place I would know about it. I would be the one ordering them. There are no experiments. He is the only one opening gateways. Okay?"

Emmie nodded, still not looking up.

Lucien continued. "Finn says and does a lot of very strange things. We think he disappeared for a few hours in Darkmouth yesterday too—did he tell you anything about that?" Lucien seemed content to not push her for an answer. "Of course he didn't. No matter. I don't blame you. It coincided with a gateway opening in Darkmouth but, as far as we can tell, something only stepped out of it for a moment. And his return happened to be around the same time as another gateway opened, but for hardly long enough to do much other than throw something through it." He stood. "Or some*one*."

Lucien stood in the light that fell in through the grubby windows of the hall, ran a hand across the wisps of hair trying to drift from his scalp. "Emmie, I am so glad you have seen for yourself how Finn has behaved in ways that look, at the very least, suspicious. I know how much you like him, and I believe he is a good young man. He's just misguided; lost. He needs help. I know he won't listen to me. I'm not sure he listens to his own father anymore. His mother is . . . well, I know you are fond of her, but this is not her business and that is something we must be very firm on unless we want to hand over the whole thing to civilians and just let the world go to hell."

Emmie shifted on the seat. Its rusty creak echoed across the hall. She felt tired, scared, terribly guilty—yet certain she had done the right thing.

Lucien sipped from his tea. "And he doesn't even listen to you now—his best friend. If he doesn't start to pay attention, the consequences will go beyond anything we have seen in my lifetime. In any lifetime perhaps."

"He thinks you've set all of this up," she said, looking upward cautiously, gauging Lucien's reaction. "He thinks you've tried to frame his family so you can take Darkmouth from them."

She thought she saw the hint of a smirk on his face. That was not the response she expected.

"Does he think I set it up so that the entire Council of Twelve would be desiccated as one?" asked Lucien, regaining his serious expression. "Or that I arranged for a Fomorian invader to drag his army into this world? Was all that my doing?"

Emmie realized she was gripping hard onto the chair, pushing herself back into it as if willing it to swallow her up.

Lucien relaxed, smiling now in a way that unnerved her deeply.

"That would have been some trick," he said. "No. This is all Finn's doing. He contacted Legends. He worked with them. I simply came to investigate. No more. No less. And it was a good thing I did, because who knows what might have happened if I wasn't here to take control?"

"He *didn't* help the Legends," Emmie blurted.

"We know that's not true," said Lucien. "*You* know that more than anyone."

He let that sit in the silence for a moment, before once

again taking his place at the edge of the table.

"What we cannot doubt is that he is out there, on the run, causing mayhem by releasing Legends among people just trying to get to work in the morning. We don't know if he has plans for more carnage, whether he's escaped into the Infested Side for good, or if he's involved in something truly huge that could make everything that has gone before seem like a face-painting party."

Emmie couldn't say anything.

"You do have face-painting parties here, right?" asked Lucien. "Elektra and Tiberius love face-painting, although they like to use permanent marker when possible. I've had to bring them to Slotterton. I promised their mother I'd look after them. They're off with an assistant somewhere, causing trouble no doubt."

Emmie frowned, struggling to keep up.

"But that's not important." Lucien shrugged. "You've always wanted to be a Legend Hunter. So has your father. Right now, Darkmouth needs a Legend Hunter. I don't think we have to look too far to find one, Emmie. You have been courageous, strong, smart."

"I need you to tell me the truth," she said, letting her gut instincts push her forward. "Are you experimenting with crystals so you can open your own gateways?"

"No," Lucien said, as if mildly offended. "Of course not."

She did not reply. He must have sensed the conflict racking her, because he lowered his voice to sound as comforting as possible.

"We both have the same goal in mind. We both want Finn to be safe. We both want him to come back to Darkmouth. We both want this to be over. And we both want you to get your chance to be a true Legend Hunter."

He allowed that idea to settle in before speaking again.

"To do this, I will need your help, Emmie."

Finn lay collapsed in the hut, on his side, the ashes on the floor pushed aside by his breath, gently clawing the dirt with his fingernails. The Quetzalcóatl was silent, the rise and fall of its breathing barely perceptible now.

Beag helped Finn sit up, no matter that he was hardly tall enough to match even Finn's seated height.

"You saw it?" Beag asked.

Finn nodded. "That thing—"

"The Gashadokuro," said Hiss.

"The Bone Creature, yes. It's leaking into my world."

"I am not surprised," said Hiss. "You humans have been scratching at the barrier between our worlds and are weakening it."

"But it's not yet fully formed like it is here," said Finn, rubbing a palm along his sweaty brow.

"Oh, just you wait, kid," said Sulawan, rolling the long

rock across his mouth. "It started like that here. Just a few bones here and there, peeking out of the ground for a look-see. In a dead world, you don't always notice a little more death."

"But it got worse," said Beag. "It grew. And formed what you've seen. And now it won't stop. Can't be stopped."

"Without Gantrua's charm," concluded Finn, voice still weak. He rubbed at his ear, where he still felt the roughness of the serpent's tongue.

Beside him, a low rattle emanated from the serpent's throat. These were its last breaths.

Cornelius whimpered sadly.

"These organisms that mass to form the Bone Creature are something ancient and were contained for centuries, but live again by binding together the dead to add more to their number," explained Hiss. "They become one. It gains strength, multiplying with each appearance, until—"

"Wham," said Sulawan, but quietly.

"Because they are small, they can get through the gaps between our worlds so much easier," said Beag as he stayed sitting, exhausted, against the hut wall.

"In your world, it will eventually become what you saw," continued Hiss, "and what this Quetzalcóatl tried in vain to stop. And once fully formed, it grows, destroys, disintegrates, returns somewhere else to repeat the cycle."

Finn took the empty Gatemaker from his pocket and frowned at it. "Is it going into my world because of me? Because I'm using this device?"

"No," said Hiss. "Something else is happening. Because the other humans are trying to open gateways so clumsily, with what seems to be impure dust, they are causing damage. They cannot open pure gateways like this Gatemaker will, but they are still causing leaks between the worlds—and, increasingly, the Bone Creature is leaking into your world too. They must stop."

"Well . . . ," said Finn. "They're planning another experiment tonight, trying to open gateways. I have a map of where they're carrying it out." He took out the map and glanced at it. Then he sat up straighter, realization coursing through him. "It's in an old graveyard. They're going to experiment in a place filled with bones."

"Well, that is just dandy," said Sulawan.

"If we don't stop Lucien and the others before they carry out that experiment . . ."

"Then our very big problem will be your very big problem too," said Beag.

Finn found the strength to get up. For the first time, he noticed the mysterious Legend he'd seen on the beach, now sitting in the dark corner of the hut, eyes ablaze, watchful and silent.

Finn approached the Orthrus. Drool pooling at the corner of his mouth, Cornelius grunted as Finn reached for the collar around the dog's neck. The collar was tight against the fur of his still-sleek coat; it was put there a long time ago, and a layer or two of fat had since grown and now threatened to swallow the collar.

On its tag, a simple message: *My name is Yappy. If you find me, you can keep me.*

Finn knew what it said, but just wanted to see it. Yappy was a dog that had once lived in Darkmouth, had delivered a pair of false teeth to Finn's feet that set him off on a journey to find his father. Yappy had ended up in the Infested Side, wandering into a gateway from Darkmouth. He'd been the one who never came back.

"The canine survived after you left us," said Hiss, hovering at Finn's level. "He lived with us in a place of great stench which, to a dog who loved sniffing everything and everyone, seemed to be some kind of paradise. Cornelius honors Yappy's memory by wearing his collar."

Finn gently relaxed his hold, so that the pendant sat proud on the graying fur around Cornelius's neck. Through the door of the hut, Finn could see the silhouettes of Legends crowding outside, pensive, watchful, waiting for guidance on what might happen next. When he had first met these creatures, Finn didn't believe he could ever trust them. Now he was beginning to trust these Legends from another world as much as anyone from his own.

The serpent's breath came in irregular spasms. Finn placed his hand on its head, and it reacted a little to his touch, settling a bit as if comforted.

"The Bone Creature hasn't formed fully in my world yet, so there might still be time," Finn said. "I have to get that charm from Gantrua. They're bringing him to Slotterton on their way out of the country. If I get him and that charm, I can use another Gatemaker to bring him to you. You can stop the Bone Creature before it comes into my world. If not, then we're in big trouble."

Sulawan tutted, a little theatrically.

Beag moved away from Finn too, heading for the door of the hut, where Finn saw the crowd of Legends was waiting, anticipating.

Cornelius simply snorted.

"That is true, Cornelius," Hiss said to his dog companion. "Finn does not believe that this world is worth saving as much as his own."

"That's not–" Finn began, but Hiss continued to talk.

"He does not know that this was not always a bleak, barren world. You may not believe this, Finn, but the Infested Side was once as green as your world. It was once as fertile. The trees you see only as lifeless fossils once spread their roots through damp, welcoming soil. The sky now choked by cloud was as blue as yours. Our sulfuric rivers were as pristine as yours. Why was it this way? Because our world *was* your world. We did not come from this place. We were cut off from yours and abandoned to it."

Finn blinked. Was this true? If it was, it was a very different history from the one taught in Legend Hunter books. He had always been told the Legends had grown envious of humans and used violence to try and take the human world for themselves.

Cornelius stirred again, used a front paw to scratch behind his ragged ear.

"We are old enough to have seen this world as it could have been," said Hiss. "A flower in the Snarling Desert. A bud on a branch in the Dead Forest. A shaft of light piercing the clouds. It wasn't always winter here. But it has not been spring for such a long time."

"Maybe it can change again," Finn said weakly.

"There are some who believe that," said Hiss. "Not

many, but a few. As for myself and Cornelius here, we believe that envy is destructive, pointless. We have thrown Legends to their doom for hundreds of years—for what? Occasional victories eventually drowned by inevitable defeat. We are no further along now than when we were born. We grew to believe that we must accept where we are, learn to live here in peace. But those souls out there, they believe differently. They believe a bright dawn is coming. They found something to believe in. Someone. A savior of this world."

Finn took a moment to realize who he was referring to. "Me?" he said, almost resigned to it.

Cornelius stirred, stood with a creak in his joints, his paws clacking against the stone floor as he pushed himself up.

"I do not know the answers any better than you do," Hiss said, his head floating high over Cornelius's shoulder. "But I have to admit that there are certain signs. You came here—you and the girl and that other human with the shiny shoes."

"Estravon," said Finn.

"You survived," said Hiss. "You defeated those who tried to kill you. And when they came into your world to do it, you defeated them again. And out there, they believe in you in a way I have never seen. They believe the prophecy when it says you will 'end the war and open up the Promised Land.' The time has come for you to ask what that means, Finn."

The snake paused, coiling slowly while allowing Finn to absorb that thought.

"You will try and get that charm in order to save *your* world, Finn. We understand that," said Hiss, straightening again. "But you should ask yourself if maybe this world is the one you are truly meant to save."

Finn had never felt such scrutiny in all his life. Every eye—from the one in Sulawan's face to all those Legends outside the hut—was on him. In the corner of the hut, the serpent's breaths had grown shallower and shallower. The spaces between them growing longer each time. It was dying, and sadness almost overwhelmed Finn.

"Listen, small fry," said Sulawan. "We are putting our lives at risk for this because someone will have to take that charm and carry it right inside the bony guts of that giant. And it will probably be me because I made the mistake of being tall enough to do it. I'll have to slam it right against the part where the Gashadokuro's neck meets its back because that's where those little organism things are of greatest concentration." He mimed the action, lifting his hands over his head and swinging down as if preparing himself for that task. "And then I will hope to get clear before it all gets messy. Which it most definitely will. So, you have the easy end of this, trust me. Get Gantrua. Give him to us. We'll stop your world from getting destroyed too. You get the glory. Job done."

The serpent had stopped breathing, was utterly still. It had given its life to save others.

"You have to save the world," said Hiss, with a flick of his snake tongue that nearly brushed Finn's face. "The question is: *Which* world?"

Finn looked at the many eyes staring at him. The yellow eyes of the Legend hiding in the darkest shadow of the hut boring into him. The expectation of those outside who worshipped him. He felt hemmed in, claustrophobic under the pressure.

He gestured at the gathering. "I want to do this, but just because I know where Gantrua and the charm might be, it's not like we can just walk in there and take it."

"Actually, kid," said Sulawan, looking toward the shadows, "you might be wrong there . . ."

The Legend with the yellow eyes stepped out of the dark.

In Slotterton, Emmie loitered outside the hall, steadying herself. She felt like she had been hit by a wave. Her emotions swung between shame and fortitude. She had done what she needed to do. Finn would have to understand someday. She hoped he would anyway. She knew it depended on her doing the right thing.

An assistant walked down the corridor toward her, an apple in his mouth. He held a thick folder in one hand and a large bag in the other.

Emmie tried not to look awkward.

"Hello," she said.

Uninterested, the assistant walked past her and through the door.

Emmie hung back, heard the assistant being greeted.

"Yes, Axel," said Lucien. "What is it?"

The door slowly closed between her and Lucien, a small square window offering a view inside.

She watched Axel approach Lucien and place the folder on the table, take the apple from his mouth. He unzipped the large bag and together they peered inside it. Emmie couldn't see what they were looking at, and as they half turned away from the door she could only guess at their response to it.

It seemed to her that the assistant was serious, but Lucien? He had been so calm with her, a calm bordering on cheerfulness that she had found creepy for reasons she couldn't quite figure out. Now, he seemed more animated. His narrow shoulders moved up and down. She saw a hand close into a clenched fist—not of aggression but of frustration.

She could have sworn she saw a speckle of spit fly from his mouth. Axel stepped back at this point, closing over the bag as he did.

Lucien noticed Emmie's jacket still draped across the back of the chair she had sat on.

She opened the door, quickly.

"My jacket!" she announced. "I left it behind, sorry."

Axel zipped up the large bag, back turned to her.

Lucien picked up her jacket and held it by the collar as he watched her cross the floor. The few steps felt like an endless journey to her. He kept it outstretched, ready for her to take it. When she got to him, he withdrew it, just enough to make her hesitate.

"This is going to work out really well for you," he said. "Are you happy with your mission?"

"Oh yes," she said.

"Babysitting Elektra and Tiberius can be an exhausting job."

Emmie tried not to look as reluctant as she felt. "They'll be great fun," she said, her tone falsely cheerful.

Finally, Lucien gave her the jacket.

"Thanks," said Emmie, before walking away as fast as she could without looking like she was running.

33

Emmie walked through Old Hall, jacket over her shoulder. Suddenly, behind her, she heard an alarm.

In fact, alarms were going off all through the building.

Across the hall, assistants were checking phones, which had gone off with a mix of chirps, beeps, wails, bird noises, pop songs—at least one that was the theme song from the TV show *Smoofy the Magic Unicorn.*

For a moment, Emmie was afraid the alarm had something to do with her, but as she looked around, she saw that the assistants were ignoring her.

"Gateway!" one of them said. "Gateway alert. Here. In Slotterton."

Haphazardly, they began to mobilize. Emmie watched as they ran about the place, some picking up the few weapons lying around, others bits and pieces of armor. They were nervous, giddy with excitement and fear. They'd spent their careers so far behind desks, organizing schedules, looking after their superiors, making tea, whatever was needed. Everything that had happened in the last few hours had been a most unexpected turn of events.

But not as unexpected as what they saw next.

Emmie followed them to the hall's front door, but her view was blocked by assistants watching something outside.

"Well, would you look at that," one assistant said.

Emmie squeezed through and saw a hooded figure approaching up the road, walking steadily toward them, hands raised in a show of peace. Or surrender.

Assistants poured out the door. A handful were armed with Desiccators—far more of them than might seem necessary for a single target with its arms raised.

The figure stopped outside, slowly lowered its hood, and then raised its hands again.

Finn spoke only two words.

"I surrender."

DO NOT PUBLISH

Report by Tiger-One-Twelve

Location: Darkmouth

I'm not sure exactly what is happening. I have an idea that there are strange experiments going on across the world, but why are bones appearing? Why are Finn and Emmie's items popping up too? How did they travel all that way from Darkmouth?

This report is being written with one of Finn's pens. *Tails and Snails- Darkmouth Pet Shop,* it says on it. I can see the pet shop from where I sit now, on a bench in the center of a town more normal—yet at the same time even stranger—than I had ever imagined. So, how did this item go from here to there? Did it cross oceans—or worlds? If it crossed worlds, then what else might have traveled back with it?

I took on this mission thinking it would lead to the truth about what is going on with the one who wanted to call himself Finn the Defiant.

Really, I have no idea.

There is someone here who might be able to help me. Someone I am not supposed to meet with—but I'm not sure I can avoid it any longer . . .

34

Finn was in handcuffs. This was not a pleasant sensation at all. The metal digging into his wrists as his hands rested on his lap, the helplessness, the itchy back he couldn't scratch.

Nevertheless, it was a better sensation than that of Lucien's breath, which was filled with garlic and annoyance and was currently about an inch from Finn's nose.

"You have made things very difficult," he was saying. "Very difficult indeed."

Surrounding them were maybe two dozen assistants, the two guards Finn had met at the Dead House, and a few Desiccators pointing at Finn's head. They were all really quite nervous. One trembled a little. Finn knew they were worried he might explode. He felt like sneezing loudly just to freak them out a bit, but that would risk one of his captors turning him into something resembling a cabbage in clothes.

Lucien withdrew, his agitation clear. He had his hands behind his back, then at the front, then at the back again. He pulled his glasses from his face, pinched the bridge of his nose. "I've had to drag all of these good people here to find you."

"And now you've found me," said Finn, trying to mirror how confident and unflappable he imagined his father would be in this situation.

"Oh, the *Most Great Lives* writer is going to have a field day with this, though," said Lucien. "You think you're worthy of a mere entry? Oh, you are going to get a whole *book* written about you. They'll run out of ink just trying to describe the scale of your duplicity. They'll level whole forests to find enough paper."

Finn sat, as impassively as he could for a person whose hammering heart must have been visible in his chest. He sought out anyone familiar among the crowd, caught Estravon's eye. He was standing away from the main body of assistants, as if uncomfortable. Finn couldn't see anyone else he recognized.

"Where's Emmie?" he asked.

Lucien gave an exaggerated look of surprise. "You're not the one asking questions," he said. "You answer mine, and then we can talk."

He walked behind Finn. "Why did you come back?" he asked, reappearing at his right, arms folded now, the fingers of his left hand tapping away at his bony shoulder. "A gateway opened in Slotterton. Which showed up on our scanners. And, lo and behold, you walk in here and surrender. Why?"

"Because I had nowhere left to run," said Finn, resigned. "Where am I going to go?"

"The Infested Side seems to like you paying a visit," suggested Lucien. "Maybe you should stay with them. Open a pet hotel or something." He appeared pleased with his joke, even if no one in the room laughed at it.

"It's more dangerous over there than ever," said Finn. "This is my world. This is where I belong. Whatever you think I've done."

Lucien continued tapping his shoulder, trying to figure out the puzzle.

The jittery assistants watched, waited for an order.

"I want to talk to my mam and dad," Finn said. He really did.

"You don't get to make demands," Lucien said. "How did you get so easily to the Infested Side in the first place? Where did your crystals come from?"

Finn considered his answer, decided to be bold. "Have

you told the others here what you're doing with your experiments?" he asked.

Lucien allowed a half smile to creep across his face as if he was finally seeing the behavior he had hoped for. "They all know what I'm doing. They know I'm keeping us safe."

"You are putting everyone in danger just so you can feel like a real Legend Hunter."

"That is quite an accusation coming from someone doing exactly the same thing," said Lucien.

Finn spoke to the crowd again. "He is using dangerous techniques to open gateways in Darkmouth. And here too. If you carry out those experiments here tonight, in the place you're planning, and with crystals you don't understand, it's going to be disastrous. You could open a portal to a creature bigger than anything you've ever imagined." Finn addressed the gathered assistants, but with an eye on Estravon, who looked away while picking at his cuff links.

Finn's claims caused a ripple among those present, but they did not step forward to confront Lucien. This made sense. If Lucien was up to something, he would have the most loyal assistants with him to ensure it was carried out without question. Besides, they saw Finn as the enemy now. As untrustworthy and dangerous as any Legend.

Lucien had calmed somewhat, the anger having ebbed

a little to be replaced by curiosity. "You say it's dangerous to open gateways, yet you just entered this world through one," he said, smiling.

"I know what I'm doing," said Finn. "I have pure crystals."

"Given to you by who?" asked Lucien.

"I know you don't know what you're doing with your experiments, and your attempts have already caused leaks in the barrier between the worlds. And I know you're planning more experiments in a place where there are bones, and—"

"And you know this how? The Legends told you?" said Lucien.

Finn sighed. Whatever he said, Lucien would twist it.

"I'm not sure you realize what kind of trouble you're in," Lucien said. "You have your own private revolving door into the Infested Side. There is no precedent for this, is there, Estravon?"

The distracted Estravon took a moment to register that he was being talked to. "Yes," he said. "I mean, no. There's no precedent. I'm looking for anything that comes close to all of this. There was that time the Isle of Wight was rumored to have disappeared for a whole day. Or the occasion in Italy when a Legend pushed over the Tower of Pisa. Or–"

"I think Estravon has made his point, don't you?" said Lucien, leaning heavily toward Finn. He stood again, ran his hand across his thin hair. "No matter. You are back. And no sooner are you here than you will be gone again. Tell me, have you ever wanted to visit Liechtenstein?"

Finn hadn't known what to expect when deciding to hand himself over, but he had presumed Lucien might want to cart him off to Liechtenstein rather than send him home to Darkmouth. At least they hadn't desiccated him.

"I didn't bring my passport," Finn replied.

"No need to worry about that," Lucien said. "We can arrange anything."

"Swimsuit?" asked Finn, warming to the challenge of winding Lucien up. "Sunscreen?"

Lucien pressed in, arrogant. "Why would you need sunscreen in a windowless cell twenty yards below ground?"

That quieted Finn.

Tension crackled in the room.

Estravon approached. "Lucien, can I have a word?"

Lucien looked irked but agreed to Estravon's request to walk away from the group for a quiet conversation.

Estravon's unintelligible muttering was backed up with chopping hand movements. Lucien was shaking his head, with occasional replies that only seemed to spur Estravon into becoming more forceful.

Until Lucien shouted him down.

"We're not taking him back to Darkmouth, so stop saying it!" he snapped. "Who cares about any report now? We have him. We can do what we want with him now. And we will. And if you don't like it, there's a lovely job in the Liechtenstein laundry room that I'll be very happy to transfer you to."

Estravon kept his back to everyone, unwilling to show his response.

Lucien returned to the center of the room, where Finn was still seated, handcuffed, and looking around the room in the hope of spying an ally.

Lucien stepped across his sight line. "These assistants will accompany you."

The shiny-headed Olaf, wild-bearded Ricardo, and two other Desiccator-wielding assistants stepped forward from the group.

"They will be with you every step of the way," said Lucien. "They will be armed every step of the way. You will be safe with them," he concluded, as if any of this was for

Finn's safety. He leaned in to Finn's ear, bringing again that smell of garlic. "I just wouldn't blow your nose, if I were you. These guys might get a little bit jumpy with their trigger fingers."

Lucien stood and motioned for him to be taken away.

Finn rose, shook off Olaf's attempts to grab his elbow, and instead made his own way toward the door at the end of the hall.

Taking a last look over his shoulder, he caught sight of a face in the window of the door at the opposite end of the hall. It was Emmie.

He nodded to show her he didn't hold a grudge.

She lifted her hand to her ear in an urgent "I'll call you" motion.

Then the door closed, and Finn was alone with four armed assistants and his own growing fears that he'd made a terrible, terrible mistake.

35

The four assistants formed a square around Finn as they walked him down a corridor brightened by the sunshine splashing through windows. Hemmed in, keeping pace while his cuffed hands bounced at his belly, Finn felt small among them. They blocked the world from him, giving him only glimpses at the windows, and at the faded wood-panel walls with yellowed, frail notices pinned along them, occasional scraps of graffiti, scrawled names of people and rock bands.

Finn took a deep breath to find his focus, almost lost pace with the assistants ahead of him. Between their shoulders he saw fire doors open, and a short, boxy truck backed up to the exit. This would be his next stop.

He looked around again, searching for a face he might recognize. A look in the eyes that might tell him he would be safe.

The assistants stopped a few yards from the end of the hallway, the squeaking of their shoes ceasing suddenly. To Finn's front right-hand side, Olaf opened a door into a new room, turned, and beckoned him inside. Finn looked at him, saw cold eyes over a crooked, broken nose and tried to figure out what was going on.

"Aren't we leaving?" Finn asked.

The guard repeated the gesture and this time Finn complied, finding himself in a tiny room, with a small tower of chairs in the corner, a dried-out mop and bucket beside them. Nothing else.

Finn turned to ask again what was happening, and found all the assistants had followed him in, facing him in ominous silence.

"What's going on?" asked Finn. "Lucien said I was being taken away."

"Change of plan," said Ricardo, radiating threat.

Finn's unease was beginning to show in the sweat coating his forehead.

"Lucien won't like it if you don't follow the rules," Finn said. "Especially *his* rules."

"The change of plan is his idea," said Olaf, impassive, almost robotic. He was particularly cold and hard-edged, his neck pouring out of his collar, his head like a bullet.

Finn looked to the other assistants for some indication they might be softer. He didn't see it.

"All we know is that when we were taking the traitor to the storage room, he tried to escape again," Olaf said ominously.

"What are you talking about?" asked Finn, incredulous. "I haven't tried to escape."

"And when we cornered him he was on the verge of exploding with that weird trick of his," continued Ricardo, scratching his beard with the nozzle of his Desiccator. "And it would have wiped out everyone in this building and, for sure, a few innocent passersby too."

Finn's stomach somersaulted, and the room seemed to shrink.

The assistants took a step away from him, creating some distance in the small space.

"You can't do this," Finn said, trying to close that distance up again.

One of them pushed him back.

"Actually, we've been told exactly what we can do," said Olaf, raising his Desiccator at Finn, finger on the trigger.

"Wait!" Finn shouted, cuffed hands raised. "I know something."

Olaf hesitated, finger still on the trigger, but eyes narrowing with curiosity.

Finn decided the only way to keep them from shooting was to tell them the truth. Hold nothing back.

"When I came back from the Infested Side I didn't come alone," he said. "I brought a Legend with me."

The assistants glanced at each other, as if wondering if this was the truth or a stalling tactic.

"It's true. It came with me but it's been hidden among us since you captured me."

"Hidden?" asked the Desiccator-wielding Ricardo, his lips lost within the heavy beard.

"Really close," confirmed Finn, nodding with exaggerated enthusiasm. With the back of a wrist, he wiped the sweat from his brow, felt the damp hair of his bangs, the handcuffs chafing his skin.

"I don't think so," said Olaf. "If a Legend was sneaking around, I'm pretty sure we would have noticed it." He lifted the weapon again to get on with the business of desiccating Finn.

"No, you wouldn't," said Finn. "And I can prove it."

"How?" asked Olaf.

"Five of us walked down that corridor into this room, right?" asked Finn.

"What of it?"

"Then how come there are six of us in the room?"

The four assistants looked at one another, then around.

A fifth assistant was in the room.

Gray hair. Gray suit. Gray skin.

Silent, watchful, a fly landed on his forehead and he didn't so much as flinch. Nothing. It was as if he wasn't human.

His eyes burned yellow.

All hell broke loose.

One hour *before* all hell broke loose, Finn walked through a gateway with the yellow-eyed Legend, having finally learned that it was a Skin-Walker. A Shapeshifter. A creature capable of taking on the form of anything it touched.

Shapeshifter as Orthrus

At that moment it was shaped as a dog, though, so it was never going to have much to say. More specifically, because it had never met a real dog, it was in the form of the closest reference it had to one—the Orthrus, only with the snake-tail tucked between its legs so as not to be obvious. This was at least better than its natural shape of a large bottle-green monster of the kind that would have stopped traffic.

The Skin-Walker didn't say much. As a Shapeshifter, its speech was always limited to whatever words it had heard the individual it was imitating say anyway. But this one took it further: it was silent. It could have spoken like Hiss or Cornelius, but not so much as a "sausages" passed its lips. Maybe it couldn't say anything. Maybe it just didn't want to.

In the last moments on the Infested Side, before they had traveled together through the gateway, Finn had tried to engage it in conversation. He'd seen a Skin-Walker once before, in a cave many years ago. That poor Legend had ended up dead, something that gave Finn an abiding sense of guilt, and that worried him now he was about to travel on a mission with its cousin.

"I didn't mean it," he said, just before the gateway opened.

The Skin-Walker looked at him, so like Cornelius that Finn felt like grabbing his ears and giving him a big cuddle.

"If you know about what happened, that is," Finn said. "If you don't, then forget I said anything." He had no idea whether that made sense or not. He guessed not.

The first thing they did when they arrived in Slotterton was to find a new form, because there was only so long the Skin-Walker could hide a snake out of sight. Finn pointed at a café, told it to hurry before the assistants came for him, so the Skin-Walker trotted off in there.

Finn heard some kind of commotion and shouting, plus maybe the breaking of crockery.

A few seconds later a waitress was jogging from the scene and, with a flash of yellow eyes, she indicated for Finn to follow.

"We'll use that as a signal," he said, when he caught up. "I might have no idea who you are and when, so you're going to have to use the eyes to tell me. Otherwise I could end up dragging the wrong person into a lot of trouble. Deal?"

Another flash of those yellow eyes. *Deal.*

They'd parted before Finn walked into the arms of those trying to find him, and he had to trust that the Shape-shifter would hide in plain sight.

He was relieved when it finally showed itself in that small room. Then he ducked out of the way as the Legend became a blur of action, a controlled frenzy of hands and feet and shape changes, knocking out assistants swiftly, each touch giving it a new form to take.

The Skin-Walker morphed almost as quickly as it moved, until, one by one, it incapacitated them, and it was the double of the now unconscious Ricardo.

It left only Olaf conscious, under its powerful grip, pressed against the corner of the wall and floor, trembling with fear as the Skin-Walker—in the guise of an unconscious colleague—stared at him.

"What are you?" asked the assistant.

The Skin-Walker showed him. Slowly shrinking in size, turning into the lead guard, as if wanting to taunt him with this unveiling of his doppelgänger. The nose rearranged itself, eyes shifted position on the face, face turning like water running down a drain, hair disappearing, shoulders sinking, chest rising, until the assistant was looking at a clone.

Olaf tried to faint.

"Don't faint," Finn ordered him, and the Skin-Walker gripped Olaf tighter to keep him conscious.

"Unlock these," Finn said, holding out his hands.

Woozily, Olaf did as requested, and the cuffs fell away.

"You have the desiccated Fomorian here," Finn said, rubbing his wrists. "Where is he being kept?"

Outside they heard the sound of the truck spluttering into life. The low revving of an engine.

"Not here," Olaf said, strained, his own clone pressing against him.

"Don't lie," Finn said. "We know he was being brought here."

The truck's engine revved again, followed by the sound of it jolting and pulling away from the door outside the room.

"T-t-truck," stuttered Olaf, still doing his utmost to pass out with shock.

"The truck doesn't matter," said Finn. "Let it go without us. Where are the Legends?"

"Truck," repeated Olaf before finally passing out.

Finn looked through the blinds of the room's window, the large vehicle visible through smudged glass as it waited to pull out onto the road out of Slotterton.

"The truck," said Finn to himself. "The truck!"

It angled onto the road and drove away, with Gantrua on board.

39

Finn was first out of the room, checking down the corridor to see if anyone had followed. They hadn't. No one was in this part of the building. There was only the open door swinging a little in the breeze, and the sight of the truck's trailer moving past the trees at the edge of the building. The revving of its engine was fading into the distance already.

The Skin-Walker stood beside him, in the guise of the finally unconscious lead assistant.

"We need to get after that truck," Finn said, darting outside. "Maybe you can turn into a car or something and chase it?"

The Skin-Walker looked at him, eyes pulsing, face blank.

"Oh, so you can only turn into living creatures?" Finn asked.

Just a nod from the Skin-Walker.

"It would help if you were a bit chattier," Finn

complained. "Look, that truck is heading away quickly. Unless we move now, our chance to get Gantrua is gone, and we won't stop that Bone Creature from destroying your world and then leveling mine. So you'd better be able to turn into a horse or something that'll help us chase down that truck, or we are all finished."

The Skin-Walker nodded again, took several big steps from the door into the parking lot while stretching out its arms.

"Whatever you're about to turn into, just make sure it's something that doesn't stand out too much."

The Skin-Walker pulsed. Jerked its shoulders. A welt grew from one side of its back, while a hollow dug into the other. Hair sprouted. Teeth grew. Ears lengthened. From the welt on its back, something rounded emerged. The other head retracted below, to create a belly, while the legs split, each strand developing hooves.

"It's a horse!" said Finn, delighted.

But the legs kept splitting, four at each end.

"It's *not* a horse," sighed Finn.

A handsome, muscular, and sleek Sleipnir stood ready on its eight legs, hooves clopping at the ground, head tossing back, eager to get going.

"I have no choice, do I?" asked Finn, but he wasn't really looking for an answer.

He climbed on the back of the Sleipnir, wrapped the mane around his wrist, and prepared for the acceleration.

When the Legend charged after the truck, Finn felt like he would be flung off immediately. He was reminded of when someone in Darkmouth had thought it was a bright idea to organize a sheep race down the main street, complete with teddy-bear jockeys flopping around helplessly on the woolly backs.

In the rush of wind as they hit the road, Finn's neck was being whipped, his hands burned, his brain bounced around inside his skull so much he could almost hear his head rattle. But at least they were gaining on the truck. And gaining attention.

The people of Slotterton stopped dead as Finn and the Sleipnir passed, gawped, dropped their shopping bags. A couple of them pointed dumbly. The only ones who seemed to know how to react appropriately were the kids.

"No way!" Finn heard a boy shout.

"Yeah!" screamed a pair of teenage girls. "Yeeesssssss!"

Then they jumped out of the way, because four of the Sleipnir's hooves almost took their heads off. Instead,

OPEN

however, the Legend cut a mailbox in half as it swung around a corner, leaving behind a blizzard of letters and enough stories to keep the people of Slotterton talking for generations.

Finn had begun to get his equilibrium on the back of this great beast, to get a good grasp of the mane and steady himself. The Skin-Walker had managed to get a handle on its current body, to pick up rhythm and speed.

Gradually, they kept gaining on the truck.

The vehicle reached an intersection, slowed as traffic lights turned red. Finn's ride swerved to the center of the road to skirt the traffic. He heard the crack and tinkle of a side mirror being broken off the car.

"Sorry," he shouted back, but kept looking ahead.

Another side mirror was swiped.

"Sorry!"

Ahead, the driver of the truck, wearing the standard gray suit of the assistants, was reflected in its side mirror. He was squinting at the commotion behind, his eyes widening as he realized the horse bolting loose down the road behind him wasn't the *usual* type of horse. And wasn't too loose either. It had a rider, and it was heading straight for the truck.

The vehicle accelerated through the red light, forcing

cars to brake and swerve in either direction. Two met side-on at the center of the road, just as Finn and the Sleipnir caught up. Finn gripped hard as the Legend leaped high over the cars, landing clear, its sharp rear hooves scraping the hood of one so that it crumpled and sprang open.

"Sorry!" called Finn.

At which point he decided that if he apologized for every bad thing that was about to happen, he'd never stop saying sorry. Instead, he needed to concentrate on holding on to the Legend, and to figure out just what he was going to do when he reached the truck.

They emerged into a square, busy with market stalls, lines of them under awnings, shoppers and salespeople turning as one to see what the screech of brakes was and, more importantly, where that great clatter of hooves was coming from.

The truck turned sharply, almost tipping over with the effort and sending the Sleipnir careening into the corner of a market stall, Finn hugging its back to avoid being clobbered by poles. When he looked up again a dress and a hat were hanging from the Sleipnir's ears. He pulled them away, sent them flying high behind them.

"Quicker," he told the Sleipnir. "We're almost there."

The truck swerved around a traffic island. The Sleipnir vaulted it.

The vehicle swung right, mounting the sidewalk to curve through a gas station. The Sleipnir was now far more agile, and cut the corner efficiently.

An ache throbbed in Finn's arms, where he clung on for dear life.

In the blur of the chase, he saw the truck's driver on his radio. Hailing someone. Lucien, no doubt.

As the truck straightened up again along a stretch of road leading away from the town, Finn and the Shape-shifter reached it, managed to draw alongside its trailer. The rear door was locked.

"Bridge!" shouted Finn, as the truck bounced over the narrow arched structure spanning the river ahead, forcing the Sleipnir to slow suddenly, throwing Finn forward. He ducked just in time to avoid a road sign, before fighting his way back onto the broad back of the Legend.

A narrow road made it difficult to get alongside the truck, driving recklessly in its attempts to get away.

The Shape-shifter's neck began to morph and stretch, most of it staying as a Sleipnir, but its head becoming something far more serpentine and horrible. Under Finn's hands, the Sleipnir's silky coat became hard and scaly, and he had to wrap his arms around the neck as it thinned and carried him forward.

A second head sprouted, stretching forward to keep an eye on the road, while the long neck Finn clung on to carried him to the link between the truck's cab and its trailer. He hung on desperately to the now part-Sleipnir, part-Hydra, hovering over the asphalt whipping past below them, certain to break every bone in his body should he hit it.

The space between the truck's cab and its trailer was a mass of coiling cables and wires, obscuring the actual joining mechanism, forcing Finn to shout at the Skin-Walker, "I don't know what to do."

They were running out of time.

The half-Sleipnir, half-Hydra Skin-Walker was tiring, panting. It stumbled, just a step, and Finn almost fell from it, until it pushed itself to catch up again.

As Finn swung out from behind the cab, he saw trouble ahead. A steep hill out of the town, a tunnel through which the truck might fit, but which would force the Skin-Walker Sleipnir-Hydra amalgam to drop back. If it did that, there was no way they'd catch up again. The exhaustion of the creature was palpable, its sweat greasing the neck Finn tried to keep a hold on.

"I can't do it," he said, pulling at the wires and seeing a large heavy pin locked into place below. "I need to stop him some other way."

Abruptly, the Skin-Walker lifted its long neck—Finn just barely clinging on—and rammed its head against the window of the truck.

Safety glass shattered.

And Finn found himself half through the smashed window, inside the cab.

"Hi," he said to the driver, almost apologetically.

Then he did the only thing he knew how to do with a car, and turned the key in the ignition, switching off the engine.

He flung the keys away over his shoulder.

"Sorry."

As the truck began to slow, the assistant's face was a mask of pure rage. It blinded him from seeing that he was about to drive straight into a wall until the last second. He swerved, spun the steering wheel one way, then the other, until—through some miracle of physics—the truck cab stayed upright.

Behind it came a groan. A creak. The sound of snapping as wires pulled free, and of metal bending as the trailer tipped at an angle. The Skin-Walker jumped away, Finn thrown from its back to land in a hedge. The trailer kept tipping over, crashing and rolling across the road in a spray of glass and metal.

Its rear door clanged open, revealing only a wall of plain brown boxes.

Finn's heart sank.

Slowly the boxes tipped forward as one, scattering apart as they hit the ground. They revealed a large bell-shaped cage rolling out from the jackknifed trailer and onto the road.

It rolled a little farther toward Finn, stopping as its broken door swung open and a case popped out. Its lid sprang unlocked, and a large hard ball rolled to where Finn lay half buried in the hedge. Streaks of leather and metal, with stolen serpent wings folded up like a chrysalis along its back. Gantrua.

Finn picked it up.

At the center, almost like an eye, was a small hint of emerald green. This was the charm.

In time for the Legends to stop the Bone Creature in their world before it reached Finn's.

In time for him to return it and then intercept the experiments and prove that Lucien was trying to open gateways outside of Darkmouth that would endanger everyone.

Yet what there *wasn't* time for was to enjoy the victory. Finn heard the sound of engines heralding the arrival of the chasing pack of assistants.

The Skin-Walker responded by shifting from its freakish form to become an assistant again. But the chase had exhausted it and it was struggling to maintain the form, face shifting a little, eyes bright yellow, hair bottle green, and lumpy skin crawling around its body. It wouldn't be able to pass as anything human if examined too closely.

"We need to get out of here now," Finn told the Legend. "If we open a gateway we can save them."

But the Skin-Walker did not move. Instead, it watched the arriving assistants as they screeched to a halt, jumped from their cars, and began to run toward the crash scene. Several of them were armed with Desiccators.

The Skin-Walker simply put a hand on Finn's shoulder. Starting at the arm, the change traveling up to the swirling skin and features of its face, it morphed into a new form.

"Me?" Finn said, looking at himself. "You're going to be me?"

Finn felt queasy. He had seen this before, in the cave in the Infested Side when that Shapeshifter wanted to eat him for breakfast. He really never wanted to have to see that again. But this time was different.

Now in the guise of Finn, even as it struggled to maintain its shape, the Shapeshifter smiled. It wasn't the most convincing smile ever, but it got the message across.

"Save us," it said–in a mechanical version of Finn's voice, the first thing Finn had heard it say–then it turned and ran toward the road where the assistants and police were about to arrive.

Finn watched himself run across the road–a surreal experience, but dragging attention away from the real him.

The assistants followed the Shapeshifter immediately, chasing down what they thought was the boy they'd been searching for.

Finn ran across the field, away from the scene, hiding among the thorns of a high, unruly hedge. He pulled the map of Slotterton from his back pocket, found his bearings, and started trying to figure out how to get to the 2 marked on the map. The site of the experiment. Smack in the middle of the crosses of the "ancient graveyard."

His watch told him it was seven thirty p.m. The experiment was due to start at eight p.m. He needed to get the charm to the Infested Side and hoped they could stop the Bone Creature before Lucien's experiments opened up a way for it to come through to Slotterton.

The map told him that a short distance ahead there was a small park, hidden within trees. That's where he'd open the gateway. That's where he'd hand the charm over.

As he ran on again, he heard the sound of Desiccators firing on the road behind him.

There was a stifled *whhoooooppppp.*

Finn knew it was the sound of the Shapeshifter sacrificing itself.

On the road, the wheels of the jackknifed truck were still slowly spinning to a stop. Lucien peered into the newly empty container, his fingers tight with anger as he pulled the glasses from his face to wipe them clean.

Around him, it was mayhem.

"We got him," the assistant said.

Lucien rolled the green fur-lined ball beneath his feet.

"Do you really think this is the boy?" Lucien asked the assistant.

"It was him when we shot him," replied the assistant, uncertain.

"And do you remember ever seeing that boy walking around Darkmouth with a coating of bottle-green fur?"

The assistant gave that some thought until Lucien interrupted to yell, "No, because he never did! So you did not get him. You got whatever was masquerading as one of us—as *several* of us—and which then tore through this town as a horse with too many legs. So let me ask you one more time: Do you really think this is the boy?"

"Probably not," admitted the assistant.

"Probably not," echoed Lucien pointedly, wiping his forehead. "So maybe instead of standing around here with that clipboard you should be off finding him."

He heard the sound of children. Bickering, screeching children. Recognized those voices all too well.

Turning, he greeted the unmarked black car that rolled up to him.

Estravon was driving, although he looked like he might burst with the stress of the noise from the back seats, where Elektra and Tiberius appeared to be having some kind of punching competition with each other. Emmie was in the passenger seat, more anxious about what she saw outside the car.

"You see what he's done now?" asked Lucien.

She nodded, as if it might be possible to miss the carnage. "Where is Finn now?" she asked.

"Out there somewhere," Lucien said, sweeping the area with a hand.

Emmie breathed a sigh of relief. "So that's not—"

"No, it is not him," said Lucien. "That would appear to

be a Legend he rode through town on. Can you believe it?"

Emmie could believe anything at this point. Still, she shook her head sadly. "No. I can't."

"Well, it has happened," said Lucien. "He has stolen the desiccated Gantrua, and we can only guess at what he plans to do with it. Unleash it here. Or maybe send it back to the Infested Side so he can plan a new invasion."

Emmie knew Finn's real plan, considered sharing it. It would make no difference. Finn was on his own path now. She needed to intersect with that path before it was too late for him.

"So, Emmie, it is best if you return to Darkmouth at this stage," said Lucien. "Take Elektra and Tiberius with you." He addressed Estravon. "You can start planning their return to Liechtenstein."

Elektra and Tiberius had moved on to a competition to see who could kick the other hardest.

"I would really be better off helping you here," Estravon said. "I could guide you on the correct procedures for capturing Finn without causing any harm to—"

"Actually," said Lucien, cutting him off. "I want you to accompany Elektra and Tiberius all the way back to Liechtenstein, Estravon. I think that's best for everyone."

"You can't desiccate the boy," insisted Estravon. "It's

not the correct procedure. Worse than that, it's not—"

"That's an order, Estravon," said Lucien, walking away. "Good-bye."

Emmie watched him go, the noise of the children getting louder and louder in her head. Beside her, Estravon's knuckles were white on the steering wheel.

He slowly reversed, turned the car.

They drove away.

They would find him soon. Finn knew it was inevitable.

The assistants were not as expert as his father, but there were enough of them, and they were determined. They could also enlist the help of local police eager to get rid of this problem before it got out of control. More out of control than it already was anyway.

Finn presumed they also had Emmie on their side. Would she help them? The thought froze Finn. He didn't want to believe it. But he had seen too much now to rule anything out.

He had reached the park, which was empty save for a gently swaying swing and a helicopter-shaped jungle gym. A breeze rustled the trees, the leaves working up a soft crescendo. It was calm. He was safe. It was green and leafy and lovely. If he could hold a moment forever, he decided this was as good as any.

Right now it felt as if he had never known anything other than being the hunted rather than the hunter. But he was about to reach the end, and wanted to savor the peace of this moment for as long as possible.

Once he sent Gantrua to the Infested Side, to help Cornelius and Hiss destroy the Bone Creature, he was still determined to expose Lucien's experiments before the deranged assistants captured him. To reveal his plans to the world.

He remembered he still had the bag containing the computer, stuffed into the chimney of the abandoned warehouse. That might hold backup proof if he could get it into the hands of someone who could unlock the password.

All that would mean running more, of course. A lot more. Yet he had no choice. He had nowhere else to go now, nothing else to do. Judging by what had happened back at the hall, he'd end up a small ball of hard skin in a Liechtenstein filing cabinet if Lucien got his way.

When he was gone, they would spit his name, call him traitor, would delight in the shock and horror as they turned over the black page to read about him in *The Most Great Lives of the Legend Hunters*.

He breathed in the fresh Slotterton air. Maybe this

wasn't such a bad place after all. It had color and life and the people seemed happy—or at least they had been happy until he rode a shapeshifting eight-legged horse through their town. That would give the local kids a story to tell for the rest of their lives anyway.

The breeze ran through the park again, the branches above Finn waving in response. He took a deep breath, a last lungful of freedom. It was time.

He held the remains of Gantrua. He had handled desiccated Legends so many times. He'd seen them used as paperweights, to hold open doors, as bookends. But this one really creeped him out.

Finn was sure now that this *was* Gantrua, and he felt foolish for thinking that Griffin was the Fomorian. The veins of the shrunken, stolen wings were clear, like a chrysalis, an insect wrapped tight ready to reemerge. The streaks of white that had been stolen fangs and teeth.

And there, so clear, was a bright emerald bump glinting at the ball's surface. It was shrunken and crushed in there, but there was no doubt in Finn's mind this must be the charm that would stop the Bone Creature.

With his free hand he pulled the Gatemaker from where it had been tied uncomfortably to his calf, beneath his pant leg, since he'd last been in the Infested Side, hidden there in case the assistants went through his pockets. He pulled the conical device out and without delay pressed it against the air. He stood back as it sparked a portal into existence.

The trees shook. Birds whistled and called. The streaming light of the gateway was a sudden and blinding intrusion in the world.

Nothing came through. No hands in search of Gantrua. No one-eyed Legends. They said they'd follow him using Beag the Sprite's power to track his signature across worlds. But there was no sign of them.

He checked his watch. Seven forty-five p.m. They needed to do this now. He wondered if he should step in, or just throw Gantrua in there.

"Finally," said Sulawan, stooping eye-first through the gateway. He looked at the surroundings. "Nice place you got here," he said, an edge of bitterness just detectable below the sound of the rock he was chewing.

Beag was on his shoulder, looking anxious. "You're becoming harder to track," he told Finn. "Your signal is fading with time. It's a good thing you've got the charm, because I'm not sure how much longer I can keep following you. You *have* got the charm, right?"

Finn nodded, tapped the desiccated ball.

"Great job, kid," said Sulawan, staying close to the gateway so he could duck in before it closed. "Now hand it over and we'll finally get some sleep without worrying about the dead waking up."

Finn lifted the Gantrua ball and held it toward Sulawan. Above him he heard the sound of birds, a growing chorus of their chirping. He looked up at the trees, saw the beating of wings fighting to clear branches.

"Hurry," urged Sulawan, gruff, impatient.

Finn reached a hand out and touched the bark of the nearest tree. It was terribly sticky.

"What are you waiting for?" asked Beag.

Fresh sap coated Finn's finger, pulled at his skin. Looking up, he saw that in every tree lining this corner of the park, birds were fighting to get clear.

"They've started the experiments already," realized Finn, moving away from the gateway. "They're messing with the gateways earlier than they're supposed to."

"Cut the craziness and give me Gantrua," Sulawan insisted, leaning forward but keeping a leg in the gateway as it began to creak. "*Now.*"

Finn stood back farther, Gantrua tucked tight under his arm. "They're using the crystals in a graveyard," he said. "The Bone Creature can come through. *Will* come through."

Sulawan's eye widened. "This gateway's about to close, and I ain't going to lose an arm to it," he told Finn, patience near breaking point. "So give me Gantrua right now or all these beautiful friendships you've made in our world are gone for good."

Finn pushed through the conflicting thoughts and demands in his head, the impending collapse of the gateway. He knew what he had to do.

"The Bone Creature is about to break through here. I have to stop it," said Finn, readying to run.

Realizing the gateway was about to close, the Legends retreated, Sulawan growling. "We will find you again, and next time we won't be so polite about taking Gantrua."

The portal slapped shut as violently as it had opened, replaced by only a drifting wisp of sparkling dust.

The loudest sound in Finn's world seemed to be of birds caught in the sap, fighting to free themselves. He wanted to help every last one of them, but there was no time for that now.

He had a town full of people to save first.

When the people who built Smoofyland first arrived in Slotterton, they had no idea what kind of place they'd chosen for it.

It was, its owners thought, a quiet little village with nothing amiss other than, perhaps, the enormous number of tremendously nervous people who happened to live in it.

It wasn't that they could really tell what those nerves were caused by. The townspeople were a friendly bunch. Really friendly. Maybe a bit too friendly. But, thought the owners, maybe that's to the advantage of a theme park based on a popular TV unicorn.

The owners of Smoofyland were unaware of several rather important facts about Slotterton.

Fact no. 1: If they'd checked the sign on the way into it they'd have seen that someone had changed the original name of Slaughtertown to Slotterton using some white paint and letters stolen from a nearby house.

Fact no. 2: Hundreds of years ago, the patch of land on which they planned to put Smoofyland had been a burial site. A very *well-used* burial site.

Fact no. 3: Slotterton had the worst fast-food joint in the entire country, largely as a result of its owner using turnips instead of potatoes for his fries. This had nothing to do with dangerous Legends, but was something the Smoofyland planners really wished they had known *before* they bought an order of them.

All these bits of information would almost certainly have helped to inform the decision whether to build Smoofyland at Slotterton. The team would have had a meeting at Smoofyland HQ to weigh the pros and cons.

"On the one hand," they would have said, "it is a lovely big piece of land, with great roads in and out, space for a Smoofy Hotel, and a corner where we could put the sparkliest roller coaster ever built."

"On the other hand," someone else might have added, "the gates of hell might reopen one day right inside Smoofy's Happy House of Rainbows."

They'd have thought about this for a while, until someone inevitably asked, "Do these fries taste like turnip to you?"

Fries were not on Finn's mind right now. Something else, far nastier, faced him as he double-checked the map.

Then looked up at where the graveyard was supposed to be. Double-checked the map again.

Triple-checked it.

This was Site Two. No doubt about it. The map was clear. This was where the experiments had been planned, were being carried out right now, if the sap on the trees was anything to go by.

But where is the graveyard?

Only then did Finn realize the map was out of date. The graveyard wasn't there anymore. Something else had been built on top of it.

Which is why he now stood, a great sigh welling in the back of his throat, beneath a huge sparkly arch, with a giant unicorn at either end and lettering so richly, ridiculously purple they must have used every drop of available purple on the planet to make it.

It read:

Welcome to Smoofyland.

DO NOT PUBLISH

Report by Tiger-One-Twelve

Word came through to me that our agent had found Emmie and Estravon quickly, parked up on the road out of Slotterton, the car pointing toward Darkmouth.

She heard an argument in the car. Two arguments, to be precise.

One was between Elektra and Tiberius in the back seat. They were shouting over who had been the quietest in the silence competition they'd been asked to take part in for the duration of their journey. Each was claiming victory in the loudest possible terms.

Our agent wasn't concerned by this; instead she tuned in to the argument between the driver and his front-seat passenger.

"I know it's wrong," Estravon was saying. "You don't have to tell me what's wrong. I could write the book on what's wrong. I have seen every type of wrong there is!"

"Then do something," Emmie replied. "Change it."

"How?" Estravon asked. "What power do I have?"

"I can help you."

"Oh, that will end well," Estravon said. "That always ends so wonderfully for all concerned."

Our agent is unsure of what exactly was said next, as Elektra and Tiberius began to shout particularly viciously about who was the quietest of all.

"I left Finn behind," was the next thing our agent heard Emmie say. "But I won't abandon him completely."

"You don't know what he's capable of," said Estravon.

"Yes, I do," replied Emmie. "And so do you. More than most. And you also know what Lucien is capable of. You can help me show everyone the truth."

"Show who?" Estravon asked, exasperated.

"We're all on our own."

Finally, our agent tapped on the driver-side glass.

Apparently Estravon was quite surprised as he lowered the window.

"Anne," said Emmie immediately.

"Actually, my friends call me Wolf-Three-Five," our agent replied. "But, do you know what? Anne will do just fine."

Elektra and Tiberius had both fallen dead silent in the back seat.

"Right," said Anne. "Now it's time to talk."

Smoofyland was closed for the day, the place empty now but for seagulls pecking through discarded food wrappers, and a rogue apprentice Legend Hunter searching for assistants opening gateways to a hellish world.

Finn had made his way in through the entrance, whose attendants had left their posts now that there were no more tourists expected. From a souvenir stall left unstaffed for the night, he grabbed a small Smoofy Snaps camera that would take pictures of the experiments, though it would also add glittery frames to them. From there, he moved past the Smoofy Superstore, various burger joints and slushy stalls, to a ridge overlooking the entire park.

It gave him a view of Smoofyland, its rides of various heights and sizes and speeds, each a sparklier color than the next. The park culminated—at the farthest point—in a shining purple roller coaster. It was, the guide map confirmed, the sparkliest ever built.

Pickles the Porcupine
TUNNEL OF TICKLES
FONDANT FALLS

SPRINKLE STORIES
BABYCAKES
Smoofy Sub

Finn didn't doubt it. Right now, in the low warmth of the setting sun, its glitter was mesmerizing enough to almost distract him from his mission. He was sorry his mam wasn't here with him now. She'd love this—if you ignored the whole on-the-run-from-the-authorities part of things.

Finn saw something move in the park. Someone. Far off among the rides was a gray suit, a flash of gold. Hard to make out.

He was sure it was the assistants. That briefly seen gold had the hue of a gateway. They had started—he knew that for sure now. But he hoped that he wasn't too late to stop them from bringing the Bone Creature into the world.

A single path looped the full way around the theme park's higher ground, from which smaller paths branched off to the various sections and rides. He kept on this higher path, keeping as far back from its edge as possible while still being able to look for anything down below. He couldn't be sure who was there. Running in while screaming something about a killer Legend could get him desiccated all too quickly.

He caught another glimpse of someone down there among the rides. Another spark of light, as if someone was striking a flint. It lit up two assistants trying to open a gateway. Here. In a theme park. In the last minutes of daylight.

Finn could only assume that his actions—the Skin-Walker, the chase, his own gateways—had forced them to carry out their reckless tests ahead of schedule.

He moved quickly, quietly, to a part of the path overlooking them, and saw them almost immediately, at a patch of narrow ground between rides, specifically the Upside-Down Umbrella Spintacular and the Magic Flying Manatees. Finn recognized Scarlett and Greyson right away, the scientists he'd seen working in the ruined cliffs of Darkmouth. She was crouched at a large case, whose contents were blocked from Finn's view. He was making notes, scribbling away while occasionally chewing his pen.

"Again, at twenty-two centiliters," said Greyson, looking at his notebook.

Finn hid behind a trash can shaped like Smoofy's sidekick, Prickles the Porcupine, checking first to see if they were alone. For all he knew, a trigger-happy assistant or two might be lurking among the stalls, observing and guarding the scientists.

Scarlett turned from the canister with a small lump of yellowish rock in her hand. Finn knew it was a crystal, or their clumsy attempt at re-creating one. Impure, dirty, it had none of the beauty of the crystals he had seen, held, and used. Theirs had been concocted in a lab, while the

Coronium he had seen and used grew naturally in the fissures between worlds.

The crystals in his Gatemaker were precision tools, opening swift, small gateways.

The bad imitations the assistants were using were crude approximations, polluting the very fabric between the two worlds as they tried to tear holes in it.

Finn took a picture, scanned again for any sign of watching guards.

Through Prickles the Porcupine's open mouth, overflowing with the day's discarded burger wrappers and soda cans, Finn watched as Scarlett held the crystal in a gloved hand, the thickness of the material making it difficult for her to press it against the air and hook it there.

Finn took a picture.

Scarlett got a spark.

The crystal stayed in the air, its tip lost in the space between worlds. Scarlett and Greyson both stood back, their expressions telling Finn this was something they hadn't quite experienced before.

While they were staring at the crystal, Finn moved down a side path to get a bit closer, to get a better look. He didn't know what might happen, but needed to be prepared. He stopped to hide at a vending machine filled with stuffed toys, its grabber poised as it waited for someone to put money in the slot.

Another spark in the air. The crystal was trying to catch fire, to work up the energy to split the world, to open a way to the Infested Side.

"Come on," said Scarlett.

"You can do it," said Greyson.

It sparked again. Fizzled. Died.

Scarlett and Greyson sagged, disappointed.

Finn sighed with relief.

The crystal popped, flamed.

A gateway opened.

It was small, unstable, but very real.

Scarlett and Greyson gasped with wonder and delight, and actually high-fived each other, Scarlett's thick glove soft against Greyson's hand.

Leaning forward to see what might come out, Finn knocked against the vending machine with his shoulder. It burst into life, its claw moving while speakers blasted out a chunk of the *Smoofy* theme song.

"*Who's got hovering hooves and a healing horn?*

"*Smoofy! That's who.*

"*Whose pal is a porcupine with tickly thorns?*

"Smoofy! *That's who.*"

Scarlett looked up instantly. She edged forward, away from the gateway, to see what might have caused the noise. Finn ducked down, heart hammering, his back to the machine, making himself as small as possible and hoping she'd just go away. If she found him now, he'd have to run. He'd done enough of that for one day. For one lifetime.

"What is it?" Greyson asked her.

"I don't know," said Scarlett. "You sure there was no one around?"

The gateway closed, its light going out instantly, not even a smudge left to drift across the park.

"Look at this," Greyson called to his colleague.

Scarlett stopped searching for the source of the commotion, returned to see what Greyson had called her for. Finn heard her go, peeked around the machine to see what was happening. The scientists were kneeling, examining something on the ground. Dust. Prints.

Something had come through, sneaked in while they were distracted by the song.

"Uh-oh," said Greyson. "Did a Legend just come in here?"

Yes, Finn screamed silently.

"Should we look for it?" Scarlett wondered.

"What if it's dangerous?" asked Greyson.

Finn had to restrain himself from getting involved. *Look at the drag marks between the paw prints. It's only small and slow. It's probably nothing more than a Basilisk. It'll be very close.*

"There," exclaimed Greyson, pointing at the gap between the ground and the Magic Flying Manatees.

A Basilisk stared back with the full force of its not very powerful paralyzing glare.

Finn checked around, this time looking not just for assistants, but for bones too. He was relieved that nothing appeared to have jumped out of the ground. No bones. No rising skeletons.

Quietly, he snapped with his camera. *All useful evidence of this crazy and dangerous experiment.*

"Why's it looking at us funny?" asked Greyson.

"Does it bite?" asked Scarlett. "We should alert Lucien."

"They'll already know. The gateway will have set off their alarms," said Greyson. "But we should trap it ourselves if possible."

"Trap it?" said Scarlett. "With what?"

"This," said Greyson, picking up an orange traffic cone from nearby. He shuffled gingerly toward the Legend, cone in his outstretched hand.

The Basilisk stared at him, the lone feather on its skull shaking with fury. Or fear.

Greyson dropped the cone over it. Scarlett picked up a couple of rocks and plonked them on the square rim of the cone for extra weight. The scientists then stood back to assess their handiwork, relieved that the Legend didn't seem to be making an effort to escape. Or attack. Or do anything other than, presumably, stare at the dark inside of a plastic cone.

"Well, that was fun," said Greyson.

"We'll be famous Legend Hunters yet," said Scarlett.

"Those Legends aren't so tough after all," concluded Greyson, grinning.

Finn wasn't watching them, though. Nor was he watching the orange cone to see if the Basilisk might slip free. Instead, he had noticed something else. Something he wasn't sure had been there a few seconds ago.

On the slope between the path and the rides was an imposing, rectangular flower bed, spelling out the letters of SMOOFYLAND in roses. A white, pocked object was sticking up among the stems.

It flopped down, leaning against some bright-pink flowers.

A thighbone, it looked like.

Scarlett and Greyson high-fived each other again at the adventure they were having, utterly oblivious to the fact they'd just invited the Bone Creature into the world.

The bone lay there among the flowers. A sliver of skeleton resting in the fading light of the day, as if it was just getting some air.

The scientists whooped.

Maybe this is as far as the Bone Creature will get, thought Finn. Maybe it was busy ripping apart the Infested Side while Finn held the only way of stopping it. The Legends hadn't tracked him down and grabbed it from him yet, so their fears about losing the signal must have been realized.

He peered at the flower bed more carefully. Was that another bone beneath the blooms?

Scarlett and Greyson were oblivious to this occurrence and were too busy watching a shuffling traffic cone, inside of which was an increasingly panicked Basilisk.

"Needs another cone," said Scarlett.

Greyson reached for one, added it on top of the first, but it only sat at an awkward angle while the pile moved more slowly now.

"The others better be here soon to capture this thing properly," said Scarlett, looking around for any arriving colleagues.

While they were distracted, Finn tucked the desiccated Gantrua under his arm and crept farther along this higher path, tracking bones where they had pushed up through the grass of the slope. At each small flower bed, the bones grew more numerous.

And where the Smoofyland arrangement was in full bloom, Finn saw his first skull, upside down at the S, displaying the hole where a spine had once been. The spine itself was wrapped around the Y. Like all the other bones so far, they were unmoving.

This must be it, thought Finn. *Bones, but no Bone Creature. A close call.*

He looked back to where Scarlett and Greyson stood,

saw them assessing the state of the walking traffic cones. They fished out another homemade crystal.

Finn stood up from his position, in plain view, ready to warn them not to do it.

It was too late.

The crystal sparked; a gateway opened. Small but fizzing.

Scarlett and Greyson looked at each other to see who was going to lift the Basilisk and chuck it back in. Scarlett sighed and, using her gloved hand to cover the bottom of the traffic cone, lifted the whole thing—Basilisk rattling away inside—and flung it in through the gateway. The portal closed almost immediately after that, leaving behind the grinning scientists.

Content with their day's work, Greyson actually smacked his hands together for a job well done.

Finn could see the true results, though. He saw that the bones were being called into action. Across the SMOOFYLAND flower bed they slid, shook, one hovering in the air. A couple of bones joined together. Found more.

Bones were rising through the earth everywhere Finn looked. Moving. Meeting.

Across the park, beyond a small purple pond, a lone park cleaner stopped, bemused at the sight of what might have been a bone, but *surely* couldn't be. He swept it up into a tray. The bone hopped out again. He swept it in again. The bone jumped out again.

A foot joined it. The cleaner dropped his brush and ran away babbling.

Finn had no time now. He could see the formation of the Bone Creature happening before his eyes. It was slow, a little shaky, almost like a newborn calf finding its feet, but Finn had seen this before. He knew what would happen once the creature was released into the world. He'd seen its colossal size and power. He needed to get to it, to thrust the charm into it before it had time to do any damage.

"For someone with the ability to move between worlds," said Lucien's voice behind him, "you proved remarkably easy to track down."

Finn turned to see Lucien at the front of a small souvenir shop, his head framed by a rainbow. Lucien was accompanied by several other assistants, once again pointing Desiccators. Why weren't they shooting? Finn realized it was because he was holding Gantrua. They still wanted him, and he and Gantrua would be mashed up together if Finn was desiccated now.

"Something terrible is about to happen, Lucien," Finn said. "You have to let me stop it."

“We have to stop *you*,” replied Lucien, “before you do any more damage.”

Finn looked at what he held. “Listen to me,” he said. “Look at the bones over there, all over this place. They’re moving. They’re going to become a Legend that you will *not* be able to stop.”

Lucien looked in the direction of the roller coaster, the carpet of bones surely obvious to him now. He squinted, perhaps unsure what he was looking at.

“And now that you’ve released it, it will keep coming back,” said Finn. “It’ll destroy as much of this world as it can, for as long as it is free.”

“That sounds like a threat.”

“It’s not a threat,” said Finn, frustrated. “It’s a warning. I can stop it. There’s a charm that Gantrua was wearing. See it? It’s the only way to stop the Bone Creature.”

“More threats.”

“I understand that you don’t trust me,” Finn said. “No matter what I do, you’ll find a reason to destroy me. When that thing comes through, though, you’re going to need me to deal with it. And I’ll still do that, despite everything. Because I know what the right thing to do is. I’ve *always* done the right thing, even if it hasn’t always looked like it. So, here's my promise. Once I stop the thing from coming through into this world, you can do what you want with me."

"Why don't we just do it now?" asked Lucien.

"Because you would have done it already, if you really wanted to," Finn said. He held up Gantrua, gripped tight with both hands. "I think you wonder if maybe I'm telling the truth, if the charm in here really is the answer to whatever is coming through, and you don't want to risk shooting me in case it is."

Lucien rubbed his head. Adjusted his glasses at his ears, considered this proposition. "You're right," he admitted.

From behind Finn, Greyson's hands reached in and grabbed Gantrua from him, tossing it high for Lucien to catch.

While Finn was distracted, Scarlett grabbed the camera from him and threw that to Lucien too.

Lucien held Gantrua tight, crushed the camera under his foot, looked around at those holding Desiccators.

"Fire," he ordered.

"Lucien!" a voice interrupted. A girl's voice. "Lucien! Over here."

Lucien raised a hand to halt the Desiccation just as the weapons were wheezing into life, and sought out the source of the voice.

"Lucien!" shouted a boy.

Elektra and Tiberius were sprinting through the park, past the Smoofycopters, around the Prickles the Porcupine Tunnel of Tickles.

"Lucien!" they shouted, because they were the kind of kids who called their father by his name instead of "Dad" just out of badness. "Look!"

They ran.

Straight for the huge purple sparkly roller coaster.

Finn considered running while Lucien was distracted, but he wouldn't get far. He calculated the likelihood of his getting the Gatemaker out of his jacket in time to press it against the air, open a portal, and escape before someone desiccated him. He didn't like his chances of doing that either.

Looking like his last remaining hairs might pop out from his tensing scalp, Lucien shouted down at his children. "Elektra. Tiberius. What are you doing here?"

"Having fun," shouted Elektra, belting past the Smoofy Swings.

"Why aren't Estravon and Emmie with you?" Lucien asked.

"Lucien," said Finn, "it's not too late. Please. Give me Gantrua and I can stop the Bone Creature."

"Get out of here now," said Lucien to his children. "It's dangerous."

Elektra stopped, looked at the ground, kicked at something. "This place is all bony," she said.

"The floor is moving," squealed Tiberius.

"Excellent!" squealed Elektra. "Look, a fun house!" she announced, spying Smoofy's Happy House of Rainbows.

Stepping on bones as they went, Lucien's kids dashed straight for the fun house squatting in the center of the park, a two-story purple rectangle with swirling rainbow murals outside.

"Tiberius, Elektra," Lucien called after them, but they

didn't hear, or just ignored him. Where they had stood, bones were shifting, massing.

"Something terrible is coming through," Finn told Lucien urgently. "We have no time. Give me Gantrua. You've got to understand: he's the only thing that can stop it."

Lucien did not betray any particular panic. If anything, he now appeared interested, thoughtful, as if eager to see what might happen next. Finn suddenly understood the full extent of Lucien's ambitions, of his madness.

"You *wanted* this to happen," Finn said, wonder in his voice. "You've been opening gateways because you wanted a *war*. It doesn't matter who gets hurt."

Lucien walked to him, slowly, and spoke darkly into Finn's ear. "We were born to fight Legends, not sit behind desks. We were meant to live in a world of chaos, not order. War, not peace. We should have had all these things. We *will* have them. Why should *you* have all the fun?"

Around Elektra and Tiberius the bones began to lift, to coalesce.

"You have no idea what you've unleashed," Finn said.

Lucien finally saw it. A twitch of a bone. The creep of a few more.

On the ground, hip bones joined with leg bones. Legs joined with shoulders. Spines ran into feet.

"Well, that is . . . ," Lucien started to say, but did not complete the thought, simply craning for a better look, as if not yet believing it. Or not yet *wanting* to believe it.

He seemed trapped between his need to save his children and his dangerous desire to see the chaos he had so yearned for burst into the world.

The bones began to flow, to lift faster into the air. That made Lucien's mind up.

"Tiberius, Elektra, get over here," he shouted. "*Now!*"

It was too late. Around them, bones took shape, quickly assembling until a loose and enormous skeletal figure, the height of a house, towered over everyone.

Elektra and Tiberius screamed, and Finn couldn't tell if it was with delight or fear.

The Bone Creature's face was a mass of hips and shoulder blades. Its teeth were a line of ribs. It opened its mouth and let out a spray of dirt and the flecks of ancient cloth long since buried with the owners of those bones. This must have been its attempt at a roar. Yet no noise came. No air either, only the smell of soil and severed roots.

And in the moments as it loomed over them, stretched to its full height, the late sun flashing through its rib cage, all that could be heard were clods of dirt splatting on the ground, the breeze whistling through bones.

The Gashadokuro, the Bone Creature, had risen.

The assistants stood frozen, as if waiting to see what might happen next. Or for someone to tell them what they should do.

A pigeon landed on the Bone Creature's shoulder, pecked a couple of times, flew away again.

Lucien spoke beneath his breath. "Oh my . . ."

With a force that sent a tremor through the whole park, the Bone Creature smashed down on the flower bed, punching the MOOF out of SMOOFYLAND.

Then it lifted its other makeshift fist and swung it at the humans.

As if jolted from a daydream, Lucien and the assistants jumped away, scattered immediately, ducking from the splinters of bone raining down on them.

Finn dodged between the creature's legs as an assistant fired his Desiccator, and the blue fiery blob hit the Gashadokuro at its right elbow—but where it sucked a

section of bone down into an ivory ball, the bones simply rearranged themselves around the damage, reassembling even as the other arm swung down, clobbering the souvenir shop behind them, sweeping through its facade like it was no more than a line of dominoes. The crash of brick, canvas, and toys pushed dust into the air all around, smacking Finn with a shock wave, knocking him sideways.

Coughing, he got up and ran from the scene toward the clearer air and open space of the theme park, ducked down low behind a stall, and watched.

The Bone Creature marched through the cloud of dust, one foot pushing against the slope of rubble where the gift shop had been only moments before. It had eyeholes, or at least roughly shaped gaps in its semblance of a skull where eyes might have sat. But there were no eyes. Yet it appeared to examine the scene, searching for victims.

All was still, except for the tumble of pulverized brick and the twinkling song of an electronic toy trapped within.

And the assistants were nowhere to be seen. Lucien too. All buried, Finn assumed.

The dust was thick in the air. Finn suppressed a cough, clasped his hands across his mouth and nose to stop himself from breathing in.

Then the Bone Creature heard something, off to Finn's

left, and moved through the newly created gloom toward it, its torso and head above the rubble cloud.

Finn heard the noise too. It was Elektra and Tiberius.

She was screaming at some sort of excitement in the fun house, pressing buttons that lit up disco lights inside.

Tiberius was shouting with gusto, "Best theme park ever!"

Finn was closer to them than he was to wherever Lucien lay beneath that rubble. He could try and dig his way through to get the charm, but if he did that it would be too late to run and help the kids. There was no time to think about it. Finn didn't even realize his legs were moving until he felt himself running.

He sprinted for Elektra and Tiberius, straight into the path of the Bone Creature.

Finn scrambled up the ladder of a slide that went straight through the window of the fun house, depositing him into a ball pit in which Tiberius and Elektra were already half buried.

The Bone Creature pushed its claws through the top window, just over their heads, missing Finn's nose by a fraction of an inch. Elektra and Tiberius, finally realizing the danger, screamed. As the vast monstrous hand withdrew, it scraped against the window frame, snagging a couple of fingers and simply detaching them, so they fell apart into the bones they had been made from.

Elektra and Tiberius swam through multicolored plastic balls and scattered, ancient bones.

Finn grabbed something that looked like a thighbone. "Come on!"

He ran down another slide. They followed, clattering into each other on the mat at the end.

The Bone Creature reached into the fun house again. Finn hit it with the thighbone, only succeeding in sending a jarring shudder back up through his own arm. For all that it was concocted of whatever bones made its way to it, the creature was tough enough that a whack made no impact. Instead, the bone wriggled in Finn's hand, as if it had a mind of its own.

There was no way out of the back of the fun house—they needed to go through the front. He pushed the two kids forward, across a spinning floor, until they literally fell, half dizzy, out of the exit door and onto the grass. The thighbone began to burn his palm as it struggled in his grasp, until Finn let go and it shimmied to be reabsorbed into the foot of the Bone Creature, which was still rummaging for them inside the fun house.

Multicolored balls flew from the structure. A giant unicorn head fell from its roof, impaling the ground beside Finn.

"I don't like this anymore," said Elektra.

"Is this a ride?" Tiberius asked.

The Bone Creature became wedged in the fun house and as it tried to free itself, Finn sought some kind of shelter. There was only one thing that offered any sort of solid cover. A large tubular building at the very bottom of something very tall, very long. And very sparkly.

"The roller coaster!" Tiberius shouted with glee.

They ran for it, the small ones fueled either by excitement or fear or both. Behind them the Bone Creature shook itself free of the fun house, mirrors slicing the ground beneath it, debris showering all around.

"We're in trouble," said Finn, as if this wasn't already obvious.

They reached the snaking fence at the roller coaster's entrance, meant to corral customers in line when the theme park was open. There were three layers of fencing, and Finn had to vault them while Elektra and Tiberius ducked in between.

The Bone Creature threw a hand, a volley of bones smashing around them, spraying shards. One sliced off Elektra's left pigtail. She screamed. Another narrowly avoided taking Finn's left ear off.

He kept going, jumping the last rail. It brought them to a gate into the start of the roller coaster, next to a measuring chart telling tourists exactly what height people needed to be to go on the ride. Tiberius ran straight past it, clearly too small, but Finn didn't think it was the time to enforce the rules.

"It's here!" cried Elektra, looking over her shoulder.

The creature was striding toward them, a chunk of pink-plastered wall skewered on half its head. Elektra screamed again, and kept screaming. Worse, she stopped at the entrance to the roller coaster so she could scream some more. Just before the Bone Creature scrubbed her from the earth, Finn grabbed her and hauled her into the small building.

The Bone Creature's foot hit the ground where they had stood, splintering bones spraying toward them.

"Woo-hoo!" cried Tiberius, and Finn wondered if he shouldn't just throw the boy back out there.

No. That was not what a Legend Hunter did.

They were inside a worryingly open building—a tunnel really, through which the roller-coaster track ran. The light was dim, and there were more railings for the lines, each leading to a numbered square on which visitors would stand before getting into their car. Parked up for the night was the roller coaster itself, a purple affair, each car bright with sparkles, its seats empty, its harnesses raised.

The Bone Creature punched the outside of the building. The rafters trembled, loose plaster dropping from it. In the booth, something sparked, a fuse blowing perhaps.

Finn realized the thing could see somehow. Maybe the

microscopic organisms that controlled it acted as one giant eye. It bent down for a better view, and pushed a hand in again.

"Hide in the car," Finn told them.

Elektra dived in. Tiberius jumped in beside her.

"Heads down," Finn advised, sliding into the row behind.

The Bone Creature smashed against the side of the building again, shaking more plaster from the ceiling, triggering a flurry of light and carnival music.

The children screamed.

"Quiet," begged Finn of Elektra and Tiberius. "That thing will exhaust itself eventually, so until then we just need to stay in here and let whatever is happening outside happen."

The giant crept along, over a skylight, an eerie softness in its skeletal step.

Finn hoped it really would exhaust itself. He wasn't so sure, though.

"I think it's going away," Elektra said and sat up.

Finn also sat up, just so he could tell her to get back down again.

Wondering what was happening, Tiberius sat up too.

Thunk. The Bone Creature hit the building.

Something frazzled in the booth.

The restraints dropped down in the car, securing the three of them to their seats.

"No," said Finn, trying to force the bar back up. It wouldn't move, locked in by a safety mechanism that had clearly been designed without the slightest consideration for people needing to escape a rampaging monster skeleton.

The roller coaster shunted.

"No," repeated Finn, still trying to pull free.

"Yes," said Tiberius.

"I'm going to be sick," said Elektra.

Alerted, the Bone Creature reappeared at the exit of the building, stooping to try again to scoop out the human contents of the tunnel. Its head appeared just as the roller coaster jumped forward, kept moving, and then shot forward like it had been fired out of a cannon.

The ride—on the sparkliest roller coaster ever built—had begun.

49

Finn and the children ducked as the car smashed through a rib cage, slowed a little as it climbed up the rails. The Bone Creature came back at them, swinging wildly as the car plunged downward at terrifying speed. Finn gripped the rail. Elektra kept shouting she was going to be sick. Tiberius had his hands up like he was on a vacation somewhere other than hell.

In ordinary circumstances, Finn might have joined him—he might even have admitted that the sparkliest roller coaster ever built was also about the most fun. But this was not fun. They were not in control. And the Bone Creature was preparing to smash down on the rails ahead of them.

The car broke through, however, taking a few fingers with it, and steadily, slowly climbed the peak that Finn only now realized was a shocking height. But it was high enough to be well above the reach of the Bone Creature. For a few awful seconds the car crawled at the crest of the climb, the roller coaster's highest peak. A bird flapped by, and Finn wished he could fly away too.

Down on the ground, he saw Lucien scramble free from the smashed-up souvenir shop, lit absurdly by still-twinkling lights.

"Elektra!" he called up. "Tiberius!"

Tiberius waved at his dad.

The Bone Creature seemed conflicted about which of them to go for first. Then the roller coaster dropped, leaving Finn's stomach behind as it plummeted at horrendous speed.

A flash went off. An automatic photo of their great adventure. If Finn were to ever see it, he would see the twisted, gravity-deformed laugh of a six-year-old boy so small for the ride he was in danger of falling out. He would have seen the crying terror of the boy's eight-year-old sister, who had never asked to be on this thing in the first place.

And he would have seen himself, frozen with his arms over his head as the car smashed through the Bone Creature's hip, splintering it so that it hovered momentarily as if trying to find a way to hop. It couldn't, and instead crashed down to the ground.

Its toppling was temporary. As the roller coaster shot

Smoofy Hug!
say "Smoofeee!"

along the track, the Bone Creature quickly regathered itself, stood again.

They zipped through a strobing tunnel, then stopped. Suddenly. Completely. Maybe a hundred feet in the air. Silence again, and darkness. The Bone Creature was looking around as it rose, unable to locate them.

Sparkling purple glitter sprayed from either side of the car.

The towering giant of death saw them again. There was no way out. Even if they could get out of the restraints, the only escape was jumping off the roller coaster to the ground far below.

The roller-coaster car blinked its lights.

The Bone Creature lifted its arm to grab them, blocking out the world around.

Then, shockingly suddenly, the rail dropped away steeply beneath them. The car plunged downward, nearly vertical, away from the crushing reach of the Legend.

Tiberius and Elektra screamed, of course. They screamed so loudly Finn could hear nothing but that and the whoosh of the world as they fell.

He gripped tight as the monster moved away from them above, and the ground rushed up to meet them below.

Krunk.

The ride was over. The car cruised steadily toward the point at which they'd gotten on. The fall had been its final thrill, a last moment of joyful terror for the patrons to experience. It was meant to scare the life out of them. It had worked.

They were back in the tunnel. The lights dropped. The ride sighed its last. The restraints lifted. And everything went dark.

They heard the crunching steps of the Bone Creature outside, getting quieter, as it left them behind to seek out a new victim.

Finn looked around the dark tunnel.

And realized something.

"It's the lights," he said to the kids in the seats in front of him.

They were too busy sweating and babbling and whooping and crying to listen.

Finn kept talking anyway. "It can't see in darkness, so the lights are what attract it most of all. The fires on the Infested Side. The sparkle and strobes here. They lure it." He began to lift himself out of the roller-coaster car. He had an idea.

“Where are you going?” Elektra asked, wiping her nose with the back of her hand.

“To do something really stupid,” he said, stepping onto the platform.

50

The Bone Creature was not diminishing. It was not collapsing. It was not retreating into the earth from where it had come.

If anything, it seemed to be growing stronger, more solid. Every splinter that fell from it, every bone that was jarred loose, found its way back, fixed itself to whatever point was needed. It was a structure held together by millions of unseen organisms, but together they created something singular. Something almost indestructible.

It had its pick of the theme park. The Ferris wheel at its farthest edge was a ring of light against the darkening sky. Swing chairs bobbed in the breeze, their chains clanking, light running up and down the central stem. And in there, though the Bone Creature couldn't see him, was Lucien, creeping through the dark, trying not to make any noise.

He was clinging to the ball that was Gantrua, knowing

now it was a charm that would protect him, but with no idea how, or what he should do if the Bone Creature approached.

And for the first time, Lucien had the look of a man who wanted all this to go away. The right lens of his glasses had a crack running down the middle. Dust covered his head. Because he'd been standing beside something glittery at the time the Bone Creature struck, his hair kept glinting under the artificial lights.

But the Bone Creature didn't seem to have noticed him as he made his way toward the exit, creeping along under the cover of the settling dark.

The Legend sent a shudder through the ground with each step, its rattling bones loud and terrifying. Lucien half tripped on a curb and when he righted himself, flustered and hurried, he found that the Bone Creature was practically down at his level. Its attention was on some small toy scuttling along the ground, an escapee from the souvenir shop. It was a brightly lit duck, with rotating feet on its side pushing it along.

Lucien did not dare breathe.

The Bone Creature picked up the toy between what might be considered its fingers, held it to its face, and, deciding it was of no interest, dropped it again. The duck landed on Lucien's head, bouncing off and causing him to shriek. Just a little, but enough.

The Bone Creature liked lights, but it couldn't ignore noise either.

Lucien fell backward, dropping Gantrua, who rolled away from him.

"I've changed my mind," he was saying as he tried to crawl away. "I don't want to fight now."

The Legend loomed down at him, jaws wide.

Lucien covered his head. "Noooo—"

Behind the Legend, a streak lit the air, burst into phosphorous light, drifting across the sky.

"Hey, over here, you big . . . big . . . made-of-bones thing," Finn shouted, throwing aside the now-empty flare gun. He rested a foot on the desiccated Gantrua.

The Bone Creature turned and saw him.

But it was not what Finn was doing that earned its attention.

It was what he was wearing.

Finn was wrapped in strands of decorative lights—twinkling, flashing purple, red, and white crisscrossing his torso. He had a sparkly, flashing belt of them around his waist. Another was slung around his chest like a cowboy's bandolier. On his head he'd strapped a Smoofy the

Unicorn souvenir horn, lit bright white by the LED bulbs inside. On top of that were glowing ears. On his back, a porcupine bag with light-up quills. In one hand he held a long paddle from the boating lake, luminous like a giant orange glow stick.

There was nobody in Smoofyland, possibly on the whole planet, more lit up right now than Finn. At least it covered up the raging redness of his embarrassed cheeks.

"Come on," he continued to shout, and flung the paddle at the Bone Creature.

It bounced off the Bone Creature's leg harmlessly, but the idea wasn't to hurt it. It was to encourage the creature to come at him.

"Do me a favor, Lucien," Finn shouted, picking up Gantrua while keeping an eye on the approaching giant. "Never tell anyone about my unicorn headband."

He lifted Gantrua up, kept his nerve as the giant skeleton reached for him, and then launched himself into the heart of the Bone Creature.

The Bone Creature had no actual heart, though.

No blood pumping through veins. No organs jostling for space below the rib cage.

There was only the space between the lines of bones, the tiny gaps where one misshapen or broken piece met another and another, until they formed some crude part of the puzzle.

No, the only heart in here belonged to Finn. And it was beating hard enough to echo around the interior of the vast monster. He heard the blood rush through his ears, could feel the veins bumpy on his skin. Sweat greased his palms, and he had to hold on tightly to Gantrua as he jumped, clutching him close to his chest like a football.

He ran-climbed up the creature's leg, then skipped in under the grasping hand of the skeleton, through a gap between its makeshift hip and jagged ribs, lighting up its interior with a garish and bizarre twinkling display.

Finn looked for a foothold, grabbed a row of connected, layered spines that made up the creature's backbone as he pushed his foot against a row of wide bones brought together to form some sort of pelvis.

For a moment, the chamber of ribs was lit up, and he thought he saw the tiny creatures that had brought life to this giant, writhing in their millions, an ever-shifting, swirling mass of organisms coating the entire structure.

It—*they*—responded to him. Pulling away from the bones of the rib cage, the writhing, pulsing microbes moved toward Finn as he climbed higher, aiming for the point where the head met the body. That was where Sulawan had said the charm had to go, right? He just hoped he didn't have to reanimate Gantrua first. There was no time for that.

As Finn hauled himself up, the Legend jolted, twisted, shards of torn bone spraying across the space.

He pulled the lights from his shoulders, threw the headgear off, let them drop, quickly left behind by the Bone Creature as it flailed across the ground, carrying Finn inside it, crashing through a fence below, hooking onto a bumper car and dragging it along.

The creature's hands reached in through the ribs, scattered bones latching to the arms, to the fingers, lengthening them. One hand ripped at the ribs; the other thrust in toward Finn.

Finn stretched up, straining. As he did so, doubt flooded in.

What would happen if he failed?

How long after he died would *his* bones become part of this creature?

No matter now—the fleshless claws were almost on him.

One last effort.

One last try.

The desiccated ball of Gantrua, containing the charm, touched the neck.

A million creatures screamed.

The Bone Creature imploded in a hail of ivory blades.

52

As the Bone Creature fell, the park lit up.

It outshone the Ferris wheel, the sparkliest roller coaster, the dancing fountains. A shock wave of light thrust outward in a perfect circle, sweeping across Smoofy-land, carrying no dirt, pushing no air, leaving no damage.

The light dissipated, dropped, and the theme park's radiance seemed almost dark by comparison.

Except for the shower of bones raining down on the ground where a Bone Creature had stood only a moment before.

It was gone.

From the far end of the park, Emmie, standing beneath the entrance archway, watched the Legend's sudden, total collapse. She scanned for Finn, but couldn't see him.

Not on the ground where the Legend had last stood.

Not anywhere nearby.

It was as if he was gone, had disappeared along with the creature he'd destroyed.

When Finn had touched the charm against the nape of the Bone Creature, things had gone weird.

Weird*er*, anyway.

As Sulawan had told him it would, the charm activated once he touched it against the place where the creature's neck met its head. Sulawan *hadn't* told him he'd hear the torment of the organisms holding it up, though, or that there would be the brief but skin-crawling sound of them being sent back to whatever half death they'd come from.

Finn knew there and then he wasn't going to get out of this in one piece. Not a normal-size piece anyway. After all, the whole structure of bones was beginning to fall apart in a hail of daggers, and he was inside it.

He was strangely accepting of this.

Maybe it was living so long with the prophecy that had prepared him for the moment when he would reach a point of no return, where he would sacrifice himself to save others, when he would die a death *greater than any other.* That's what it promised.

Maybe it was the fact that he had exploded before.

Maybe it was that he knew his luck had to run out one day. Or that he had run away from his hometown and had to reach the end of the line sooner or later.

Maybe he was just distracted by being inside a giant creature formed from the bones of the long dead.

Whatever it was, he was more ready for the end than he thought he would be.

He had accepted his fate, found a strange calm in the moment of the implosion.

This was the end.

He was wrong.

A solid, fleshy, somewhat green hand grabbed him, hauled him backward through a gateway and into the Infested Side.

54

Following the usual—and now incredibly familiar—scrambling of his entire being, Finn found himself in the arms of a very annoyed-looking Sulawan.

"Do you know how long it took us to find you this time, kid?" Sulawan said, his one eye filling Finn's field of vision. "Your signal has faded so much that little old Beag had a very hard time doing whatever it is he does with that weird looking-through-the-worlds trick."

Beag was crouching behind one of Sulawan's mighty calves, sheepish, any excitement drained from his wide eyes.

Finn smiled at him. Sulawan seemed only then to realize he was cradling Finn like a baby, and quickly put him down on the ashes of the Infested Side.

Finn was still holding Gantrua, so tightly a couple of his fingernails were bruising.

"I can't begin to tell you how glad I am to see you two,"

said Finn, taking a deep breath to fight the familiar but lessened nausea.

They were standing in a particularly gloomy spot, on the side of a hill—which Finn supposed explained how they'd been able to grab him from so high up in his world—the gray ground and sky colored as if by one bleak palette. The gateway had closed. Finn hadn't even noticed it, so wrapped up had he been in Sulawan's huge arms.

"I stopped the Bone Creature," he announced.

"You did?" asked Sulawan, intrigued.

Beag peeked out from behind his leg.

"I think so anyway," said Finn. "That's what I was doing when you grabbed me."

He noticed for the first time that Sulawan had a Gatemaker in his left hand.

"Great, you have crystals," said Finn. "You can get me home again. Maybe drop me off somewhere far away from here, so I can figure out what to do next."

He felt a bit giddy. From the battle inside the Bone Creature perhaps. Or his escape. Or just tiredness. And hunger. He suddenly realized how hungry he was. "There was a burger stand a bit that way—that would be a good stop."

Finn noticed that Sulawan's right hand was holding something else.

"Is that a knife?" Finn asked.

Sulawan didn't need to nod in reply. A mild grunt worked fine.

Finn's giddiness began to dissipate a little.

"Are we in danger?" Finn asked, looking around.

Sulawan shook his head, bent over Finn with that eye boring into the top of his head.

"You did well getting rid of the Gashadokuro. That's impressive for a thin strip of flesh like yourself."

"Thanks," said Finn.

"In fact, it's saved me a job that I wasn't looking forward to," said Sulawan. He spat the rock from his mouth, and it ricocheted off the hard ground like a bullet.

Beag flinched.

"But, and here's where I have to be straight with you, kid," continued Sulawan, "I have another job to do too. So listen up, because here's what's going to happen now."

It should have been a triumphant moment for Finn; instead it felt increasingly threatening.

"Where are Cornelius and Hiss?" he asked.

"What's going to happen," said Sulawan, "is that you're going to give me Gantrua and then I'll use this Gatemaker to send you back home and we'll say nothing more about it."

"Why do you need Gantrua now? The Bone Creature is

gone. You don't need the charm. You don't need this guy at all." Finn held up the desiccated Gantrua. "Why would you even want him?"

Sulawan glared at Finn, his single eye so close that Finn could see the little red capillaries in it, like tributaries spread across a white landscape. "I could say it's for honor and glory and as a victory for our kind in the eternal battle against the ruinous humans, and so on, et cetera," he said. "But the truth is more simple. Beag?"

"Gantrua paid us more to release him than the others paid us to just grab him and stop the Gashadokuro," said Beag, almost apologetic.

"There you have it," said Sulawan, matter-of-fact. "We're mercenaries and we work for whoever needs us. Cornelius and Hiss paid us to help them. But Gantrua had *already* paid us to help him in case he didn't make it back. So, everyone wins. Well, *we* win. Now, hand him over."

"That wouldn't be right," said Finn.

"Listen, kid, you've done a good job getting rid of the Gashadokuro," said Sulawan. "You've saved us. Maybe that's your prophecy fulfilled—didn't that occur to you?"

It made some sense to Finn. He hoped it was true and he could finally be rid of that prophecy.

"So maybe you can go on and live whatever life you

have left, safe in the knowledge that you saved a couple of worlds," said Sulawan. "That's not something to sniff at."

Sulawan wiped his nose with the back of his hand. "Look, kid, it's nothing personal, you understand. Not against you. Not against old Doggy Snake Bottom. Not against those unfortunate souls who think you're important. No. I'm just a mercenary. It's just a job. If you, or they, or anybody, could pay me more, then I'd do whatever you wanted. But you haven't, so that's the way all this works. But me and Beag only get paid if you hand Gantrua to me, and I get to finish my job. If you don't . . ."

He held his Gatemaker up with one hand and the knife with the other. "Well, I'm your only way out of here," said Sulawan. "It's up to you which one you choose."

Sulawan raised his hands in a "What are you going to do?" gesture, looked around as if to emphasize that it was just the three of them here, although Beag was still keeping as out of sight behind his leg as possible. It was as if he was ashamed.

Finn knew instantly he had no option left. But he still had so many questions. One in particular. "What are you going to do with Gantrua if I give him to you?"

"Stick around and we'll show you," growled Sulawan.

Finn's options were limited to the choice of handing the

Gantrua ball over, or having it torn from his hand. And maybe having his hand torn from his arm while he was at it. He remembered, though, that it was only the desiccated *remains* of Gantrua. There was no Reanimation fluid to go with it. Besides, a long time ago, he had seen a serpent reanimated here, and it hadn't worked nearly as smoothly as it did back home, but had left a horrible, mutated mess.

All this convinced Finn to do the thing least likely to result in losing a limb. Reluctantly, he handed over Gantrua.

Sulawan greeted this with a measure of respect. "Good decision, kid," he said, examining the ball. "So, that's what happens when you shrink one of ours."

"Maybe you'll get to find out in person someday," said Finn, surprised—and a little perturbed—by his own boldness.

Smiling a little, Sulawan put the knife away in his belt. Pulling a fresh rock from a pocket, he examined the ends of it and, settling on the one he wanted in his mouth, gripped it between his teeth.

The one-eyed Fomorian held Gantrua in his left hand while he ran the Gatemaker through the fingers of his right.

"Beag," he said, and the Sprite emerged around a leg

twice as wide as his armspan.

For the first time, Finn realized Beag had something with him. It was a wide shell, rounded and closed, a spine sticking out of either end.

He placed it down on the stubbly ground, prized it open carefully. There was a smooth muddy-green substance inside.

"Gantrua has a Troll who does the science-y stuff for him," said Sulawan, crouching and placing the desiccated Gantrua into the substance. "Mixing dust. Tickling the air. All that stuff. He brought your half-dead human into this world."

"Mr. Glad?" asked Finn.

"Is that what you called him? Well, Gantrua had him working on something before he left. This"—he rolled the desiccated Fomorian in the mouth of the shell, coating it in the sticky stuff—"goo."

Once the ball was fully covered, Sulawan stood and rubbed his hands on his leg to clean them. "Anyway, the Troll warned me not to lick my fingers or my head could end up the size of a mountain." He leaned in. "I said, 'Would anyone notice?'"

He placed the ball on the ground. It hopped, like a

jumping bean. It rolled. Shook. Shuddered.

"We should probably stand back," said Beag, scampering away.

Gantrua unfolded.

He grew, widened, stretched in stages. Legs into hips into chest, out of which unfurled arms and, finally, like a flower reaching into the daylight, his head and face.

All was not right.

It was Gantrua, but pieced back together like broken pottery. He was disfigured, a tooth pushed through his cheek, his hands more like claws, the muscles in his chest a patchwork of lumps and thick sinew bulging against the leather, and metal plates that looked boiled, half melted.

There was the sound of the shell crushed beneath his feet.

Finn's jaw had dropped so wide it began to ache.

"This is bad," said Sulawan, taking Finn by the shoulders, his grip making Finn feel like he was being squeezed like a tube of toothpaste.

"I meant it when I said it's nothing personal on you, kid," said Sulawan. "I meant it when I said you could go back. You're a brave human. And not a bad one. You've just stopped something big and ugly and very dangerous, and you almost died doing it. You've saved us all. Maybe you're done now. Maybe you've fulfilled the whole prophecy deal. So, here's my advice: quit while you're ahead."

Gantrua was opening his eyes. One was half in its socket, like it had been pushed back in place hurriedly.

"In a moment Gantrua is going to be conscious again, and not very happy," said Sulawan as he held a Gatemaker up in the air. "You don't want to be here for that."

With a spark and the now-familiar screech of the benighted scaldgrub within, a gateway ruptured the air.

"One last thing," said Sulawan. "Now that he's back, it's going to get messy here. Make sure your side stops opening gateways or it will get very messy for your world too. And make sure you don't come back here. You won't always have someone to save you at the last moment. Understand?"

Finn nodded.

"Good," said Sulawan.

Gantrua let out a roar of awakening that rumbled through the ground, kicked up a wave of dust.

Sulawan shoved Finn through the gateway home.

Finn was back in Smoofyland.

He used his last dregs of energy to drag himself into a seated position, back pressed against a sparkly purple umbrella lined with prancing unicorns.

All these times he had switched between worlds, found himself dragged between different realities, but he would never, ever get used to it.

In contrast with the sight of Gantrua in the blasted landscape of the Infested Side, peace had settled on Smoofyland after the fight with the Bone Creature. The calm felt so total it was almost perfect. A carpet of bones littered the ground, but there was no noise, no movement.

Finn didn't envy the park's maintenance crew. All those bones to pick up. They'd be finding them for weeks. Kids would be picking them out of their burgers, seeing them bob up out of the boating lake or sticking out of the shelves of Smoofy's Sparklemarket.

Sitting there in the cool of the early night, Finn felt he could almost trick himself into believing he was just relaxing here after a busy day at the theme park. He felt like getting an ice cream—until he moved a little and he realized that, no, he actually felt so tired and sore that he might just stay in this spot for the rest of his life. Maybe after that he'd get an ice cream.

There was a noise nearby. Footsteps. He groaned, wondering who this was coming to bother him. *What* this was. An assistant? A rogue Legend?

"Not now," he begged. "Please just give me a break."

"Finn . . ."

He looked around quickly, ignoring the pain and exhaustion shooting through his shoulders. He laughed a little.

"Emmie."

She stood at the corner, beside a vending machine full of candy. He still felt really hungry.

"You should have seen it," he said to her, trying to push himself back up to his feet. "You'd have loved it. *Loved* it."

He moaned as he stood, like he sometimes heard his dad do in that exaggerated way dads did when they had to pick something off the ground.

"Bones. Legends. Things breaking. Me needing rescuing."

He smiled at this, was slightly disconcerted that she didn't smile back. "Although Gantrua is back. Over there." He pointed at thin air.

"Finn, I'm so glad you're safe, but you'd better come with me now," Emmie said, serious.

Stooping, he tried to read her emotions. "I thought you didn't want to be near me after everything. You said you didn't trust me."

"I just had to be sure, that's all."

"And are you sure yet?" he asked, and shuffled a little toward her.

Emmie took one step back.

"No," he said. "You're not."

"You've done things you shouldn't have, made some crazy decisions," she said. "It was very difficult. I needed to figure it out myself."

"I did make some crazy decisions all right," he acknowledged. "But they were for the right reasons. I hope you know that."

"I've figured a lot of stuff out," she said. "Come on."

She moved to the corner, with Finn following gingerly.

Remembering something, he stopped walking.

"You know they call you Red Warrior?" he said, smiling.

"Who?" she asked without breaking stride, walking

through the surreal, blinking lights of the half-standing amusement park.

"The Legends," said Finn, following her again. "They worship you—some of them anyway—but they . . ." He started to laugh, and it hurt his ribs. He couldn't stop, though. "They argue about whether you're smelly or not."

She looked insulted and confused in equal measure.

"Don't worry, I told them you're not," he said. "At least, I think I did. It's just that we left a lot of stuff behind when we last went to the Infested Side, and they think those objects are important. Schoolbooks and things like that. It's kind of crazy." He winced.

"I know," she said. "Some of it anyway. Things have been showing up all around the world. Those things we left behind. I've been told all about it, but right now we need to go. Come with me and I'll explain everything."

"I don't blame you for getting away from me," Finn said, shuffling after her. "I really don't."

Emmie dropped her head. "It was important," she said, then looked him in the eye. "It was never about leaving you. It was about saving Darkmouth. You. All of us."

"Well, it's all gone for me now," said Finn. "I have little hope left. Darkmouth is yours if you want it."

"Finn—" Emmie started, but before she could finish

that thought they were interrupted.

"You," said Lucien, standing among scattered teddy bears and squashed plastic unicorns.

His last strands of hair were sticking up, his head was scraped, his glasses cracked. He looked caught between anger and shock.

Elektra and Tiberius stood, one under each of his arms.

She was subdued, with one surviving pigtail, and looked like she wanted to go home.

He was giddy and looked like he didn't.

From behind them, other assistants, covered in concrete dust and dirt, were slowly making their way toward them. Axel was among them. The scientists Scarlett and Greyson too. They looked shell-shocked, unsure, as if lost and needing orders and certainty.

Finn sighed. "Here we go."

"They could have died," Lucien snarled. "Your big bony friend could have killed them. Could have killed all of us."

Finn's exhaustion dragged so hard on him that he should have had no energy to stand up to Lucien. But he managed it anyway.

"You messed with the gateways," he told him. "In Darkmouth. Here. Maybe in Blighted Villages all around the world, for all we know. *You* brought the Bone Creature in here. *You* did this, not me."

Lucien looked around at the assistants. It was clear they just wanted orders, someone to tell them what to do. Lucien lifted his chin. He was going to be the one to do it.

"Interesting theory," said Lucien.

"I have the proof," said Finn. The camera was crushed, but he remembered he had the computer tucked away safely up a chimney in an abandoned Slotterton building.

"You mean this?" said Lucien, pointing at an assistant holding the bag Finn had thought was tucked away safely up a chimney.

Finn felt the hope drain away again.

"I have another theory," said Lucien, "which is that while we did scientific experiments with the crystals to make sure we knew how they worked, and to be sure they wouldn't open any gateways again, you were off working with the Legends on how to bring that giant into our world and kill us all."

"Do you really believe that?" Finn asked softly, peering at the rubble in the hope of finding something to eat. He was so hungry.

Lucien appeared troubled, looked at his children, then

back again to the bruised and beaten assistants behind him, their suit pants ragged, ties askew, shirts blood-specked. He lifted his chin. "What I believe is that there are two theories. One blames me. One blames you."

Smiling, Finn lifted a small purple bag from the ground. A package of chocolate Smoofy Snacks.

"Oh, finally," he said, relieved.

As he lifted it, all the candy fell out of the burst bottom of the bag. He groaned.

"And for all you've said about me, you have no proof," concluded Lucien. "This is finally the end for you. The last paragraph in your entry in *The Most Great Lives of the Legend Hunters*. The last line before the black page is lowered over your place among the traitors."

Finn slumped again, slid down the wall, exhausted.

"I don't know," said Emmie. "I mean, what if there was something else? A few more words for the writer of *The Most Great Lives* to hear before it goes to print? Something really juicy?"

From the speakers along the park came a scratchy sound, the squeak of them being turned on, and a voice.

"Is this thing on?" asked Estravon over the loudspeaker, triggering a painful whistle of feedback broadcast to the entire park.

"What's going on?" Lucien asked.

"Just wait," said Emmie, as much to Finn as to Lucien and everyone watching. "This is really, really good."

"Okay," said Estravon's echoing voice. "Let's press Play."

A sound carried over the whole of Smoofyland, so loud it was like a tear in the cosmos.

But it was not a tear in the cosmos.

It was the noise of a zipper. A humble, ordinary zipper, amplified to almost deafening levels.

"That's the bag being opened," Emmie explained to them.

"What bag?" asked Finn.

"Wait," she said, smiling.

A thud.

"The apple dropped on the table," Emmie said.

Lucien tried to give the impression that this was all some kind of charade he must endure before getting on with the pressing business of wrecking Finn's life for good. But as he tried to smooth his hair, his palms were clearly sweating.

"Is anything going to happen?" Lucien asked. "Or are

we just going to stand here waiting for the noise to drive us all crazy?"

"Just wait," said Emmie.

"*The crystals are not working,*" a recorded voice said, loud enough to scatter birds from a nearby fake plastic tree.

The final word echoed across the theme park. The voice was Axel's. Everyone listening turned to him where he stood, jacket torn in two, among the throng. He rubbed and dropped his head.

"*We've made so many of these using the dust from that Darkmouth cave, but we haven't opened any proper gateways yet,*" his voice continued.

Lucien's eyes had widened, but he attempted, still, to maintain an outward calm that Emmie and Finn could see was false.

"*Why isn't it working?*" asked another voice.

This one really grabbed Lucien's attention: it was his own.

"*We don't know. We've tried everything. Every combination of sherbet. We've tried different flavors. Different colors. We've used jam, marmalade, peanut butter. You name it. We've done everything we can, but all it's doing is opening gateways for maybe a second or two. Small ones at that.*

"*It has to work, Axel,*" Lucien said. "*I'm not sitting behind a desk all my life. And I doubt you want to go back to your exciting role in the Office of Snacks."*

"Turn it off now," Lucien said to Emmie.

"No way. This is my favorite part," Emmie said. Finn saw she was smiling now.

"*We've used this dust on seven continents, every Blighted Village we can, trying to open gateways,*" Lucien's voice said. "*If it is going to work anywhere, it should be here, in this claustrophobic, scared little town.*"

"*Lucien, should we be doing this? It could be dangerous. Is it right to continue experimenting with the fabric between the worlds?*" asked Axel. "*What if it causes something terrible to go wrong? Something terrible to come through?*"

"Oh, hold on," said Emmie, her words tinged with an edge of drama. "I meant this *next* part is the best part."

"*Rip open the entire sky if we have to,*" Lucien was saying. "*Let in every Legend that wants a bite of this place. Just open those gateways.*"

"*What if someone gets hurt?*" Axel's voice asked.

"*It's a war. People get hurt. We are meant to be warriors. Bring me a war!*"

"Yep," said Emmie, hardly able to hold back her satisfaction. "*That's* my favorite part."

"It's a trick," said Lucien, as the voices were once again

replaced by the roar of background noise. "It can't be real." But there was a crack in his demeanor. Those behind him began to shuffle, to move away. Lucien looked shocked—he had the face of someone who had been caught and had nowhere left to run.

In the recording, there was the sound of a door opening.

"*My jacket!*" said Emmie's voice.

"That's really weird," she said to Finn. "Is that what I really sound like?"

"*I left it behind, sorry.*"

"You will never become a Legend Hunter now," Lucien told her, restrained fury twitching in his cheeks.

"*This is going to work out really well for you,*" Lucien's recorded voice said.

The recording stopped, replaced only by the empty hiss of the speakers.

"Should I turn it off now?" Estravon's voice suddenly asked over the PA system, giving everyone a bit of a jump. "Oh, I can't hear you where I am. I'll turn it off. I'm turning it off now . . ."

With a squelch, the loudspeaker turned off.

"Arrest that child," Lucien ordered his assistants. "Both of them."

The loudspeaker came back on.

"By the way, Lucien," said Estravon's voice, "what you're doing with the experiments outside Darkmouth is against the rules. All the rules. But I guess you know that already."

The speaker cut out again.

"I said: arrest those traitors," Lucien demanded again.

His assistants didn't move. The reality of his actions was being exposed, and theirs with it.

"Under sanction 126 of the rules on treason, I order you to . . ."

Lucien didn't finish the order. It was pointless.

The assistants were backing away from him.

Realizing they wouldn't do it themselves, Lucien stepped away from Elektra and Tiberius, grabbed a Desiccator from an assistant, and lifted it toward Finn and Emmie, switching between the two.

The assistants gasped, stepped back farther.

Finn flinched a little too, but Emmie remained calm under the threat.

"I am doing this for our future," said Lucien, cracking. "I didn't mean to get my children mixed up in this, no matter how much they might test my patience. I just want them, *us*, to be able to fulfill our destiny as Legend Hunters. All of us. Elektra and Tiberius. Me."

He hadn't dropped the Desiccator.

Neither Finn nor Emmie said anything.

"I can't just let you take that away from me. I can still get hold of that recording and destroy it. And then what? No one will believe either of you after all you've done, all your escapes to the Infested Side. You can shout and shout and shout, but no one is going to listen to *you*."

Emmie stepped forward.

"You're right that no one would listen to us," she told Lucien. "But they might listen to *her*."

Emmie pointed.

On the hill near the entrance of Smoofyland was a figure.

It was clearly a woman, silhouetted against the flashing neon lights of the archway. She had something in her hand. In each hand, in fact. In her left was what looked like a small notepad. In her right was a pen. She jotted something down.

"Her name," explained Emmie, joy lifting her voice, "is Tiger-One-Twelve. She is the woman from *The Most Great Lives of the Legend Hunters*. She is the one sent to investigate what's going on and to write the entry everyone has been waiting for. She is the one who can tell the truth. She has investigated everything. And she has just listened to everything."

All eyes were on Tiger-One-Twelve now.

"I wouldn't go after her, either," Emmie warned Lucien. "She didn't come alone."

Beside her, another person appeared, strolling forward in full armor. Strong, resolute, and—even from this distance—obviously very, very angry.

"Dad," said Finn, relief bursting through his chest.

Lucien finally lowered his Desiccator.

It was a standoff.

On one side, the assistants were still ranged in various degrees of exhaustion and confusion.

Finn and Emmie stood opposite them. Finn felt a lightness creep across his shoulders, the crush being lifted away.

On the far slope, Tiger-One-Twelve and Hugo waited.

Lucien stood apart from all of them. They could almost see his mind cranking around like the Smoofyland Ferris wheel. He was doing calculations. Trying to work out his next move. He pushed the cracked glasses up his nose, smoothed down his hair, started to speak, changed his mind. Then he turned to give orders to his assistants.

Before he even spoke they began to leave, filing away rapidly, minds made up. They had decided they were better off out of this.

To Finn, it looked like when you lift a rock and the

insects suddenly exposed beneath it run for cover.

Lucien stuck the tip of his tongue between his teeth, clenched and unclenched his fingers, tried not to let himself look defeated. Failed utterly.

He finally opened his mouth to speak, but was interrupted by shouting children.

Elektra and Tiberius had started sword-fighting with discarded bones.

"Ouch!" the boy screamed, and wailed about how she'd hit him too hard. He picked up a skull and flung it at his sister, then ran, with Elektra belting after him, away toward the exit of Smoofyland.

With one last deep exhalation, the visible deflation of a defeated man, Lucien turned to follow them.

"Lucien," Finn called after him. "Don't go back to Liechtenstein without leaving us the keys to my house."

Finn sat again. Half fell to the ground, really. The tiredness just wouldn't let go of him.

He didn't care that he was surrounded by the remains of so many ancient skeletons, in a half-destroyed theme park. It didn't even bother him that when he sat, it set off a singing sparkly purple Smoofy belt he'd forgotten to take off.

"*Who's the sparkly unicorn with magic in his mane?*

"*Smoofy! That's who . . .*"

Emmie laughed as she dropped down to join him.

"So," he said, shaking his head, "basically everyone was double-crossing everyone else. Everyone was keeping secrets from everyone else. No one was who they said they were, or doing what they said they were doing. Except for me. And no one believes me anyway."

Emmie sat beside him. "I believe you," she said.

Finn was trying to remember when he had last eaten

something, and was sorry he hadn't taken a bite of a candy apple he spotted down the back of the roller-coaster seat. His stomach felt like it might implode with hunger.

"Tell me the truth, Emmie. Did you always believe in me, or did you doubt me like everyone else?"

"I didn't doubt you like they did, Finn. No way."

"But you did doubt me. Even just a bit."

She looked at the ground. "A bit, yeah. But things kept happening. And I knew you couldn't be a traitor . . . but then *more* stuff would happen. You'd disappear over to the Infested Side. Or you'd steal a Legend and release it on a train."

"*That* was an accident," said Finn.

"And you kept running, and that made you look really guilty," said Emmie.

"I couldn't exactly walk back in there with my hands up, could I?" Finn said, and then thought about that. "Even though, you know, I did actually walk in with my hands up in the end. But that was different."

"I had to make a decision about whether to keep running or whether to find some other way," said Emmie. "So I gave myself up because I thought it would gain Lucien's trust and help me find out what was really going on."

Finn thought about that, but other priorities kept poking at his brain.

"You don't have any snacks, do you?" he asked her.

Footsteps approached, and they looked up to see Hugo arriving with Tiger-One-Twelve.

Finn raised a hand, telling his dad not to speak. "I know, I know," he said. "You had a plan all along."

Hugo put a hand on his shoulder. Finn winced at the grip, landing as it did on top of the bruises left behind by Sulawan's fingers.

"Your mother is going to be very unhappy you got to Smoofyland before her," Hugo said.

"I have to admit, the roller coaster's pretty good," Finn said.

"You owe her one very long vacation here," his dad said, looking around. "Whenever they rebuild the place."

He held a hand out for Finn to take and hoisted him back to his feet. Dusted his shoulders off. Shook his head, yet looked proud all the same. It was as if Hugo was trying to decide if he should scold Finn or lift him up in triumph.

"Finn, this woman here is Tiger-One-Twelve. We have known each other a long time. And we now owe her a big debt."

Tiger-One-Twelve shook Finn's hand.

"I come from a Legend Hunter family too," she said. "I met your dad when I was younger and in training, but our Blighted Village went quiet long ago. I never became a Legend Hunter. Instead, I ended up working for the publishers of *The Most Great Lives*."

"This is the person writing your entry in the book," said Hugo.

"Well, I lead a team of us looking after your entry," she said bashfully.

"What's the story with your name?" asked Finn.

"It's coded. Just as names always are for those writing up *The Most Great Lives*, to keep us anonymous. I guess I'm not so anonymous now, though," she said, smiling. "But your father knew me back when I had a real name."

"And she was part of my plan, Finn," said Hugo. "Because I *did* have one all along. I wasn't planning on spending my life giving pedicures to cockatoos. I took that job at Woofy Wash so I could stay under the radar, and I just quit it, by the way. Although maybe I shouldn't have thrown that snake at Mr. Green as I did it. Being there meant I could steal the supplies, sure—and I hear that saved you on that train—but it was also about looking like I was doing nothing. I couldn't leave Darkmouth or we would lose everything. So I asked for help."

Finn was relieved. He'd wanted to feel that his father had a real plan. But he was also feeling a bit guilty for not believing him fully.

"Your father contacted me when he heard I was going to be writing the entry about you," said Tiger-One-Twelve. "An entry that, I'll be honest, was going to be a pretty dark chapter in our history. I wasn't sure I could help Hugo. It really did look like you could be up to some bad things, Finn. And this whole escapade would have made that look even worse if it wasn't for what I found along the way."

She fished something from a pocket, handed it to him.

"A Darkmouth Pet Shop pen?" he said.

"That and other things were found very, very far from here," said Tiger-One-Twelve. "Where they shouldn't be. And where certain things shouldn't be happening. Old Blighted Villages, some of them untroubled for decades, but where I now know Lucien had ordered assistants to try and open gateways to the Infested Side."

"So they didn't just try their experiments here and in Darkmouth," said Emmie.

"Far from it," confirmed Tiger-One-Twelve. "Lucien had all this dust from the cave in Darkmouth. All these pieces of crystal crushed into powder. And he wanted to find a way to make it work wherever he thought it was most likely."

"Like old Blighted Villages," deduced Finn.

"Gateways used to open in places like here in Slotterton, so they were the natural locations to experiment in."

Finn became aware of a couple of other people out there among the bones scattered across the ground. He couldn't make them out, as they were in a dark spot between Smoofyland's gaudy lights.

"So Lucien sent undercover teams out to dormant Blighted Villages all over the world," Tiger-One-Twelve continued. "Anywhere they could find. Old villages swallowed by cities. Deep jungle. Deserts. Wherever."

"It finally worked," said Finn. "Here, before the Bone Creature came through. They figured out how to open a gateway."

"Which is why it was so important that you stopped them before it was too late," said Tiger-One-Twelve. "Before this, they only managed sparks, scratches, tiny tears. But the skin between worlds can only take so much damage."

Hugo spoke. "Each time they try, even when it doesn't work, it weakens the wall between the worlds, thins it. That's what allowed the Bone Creature to come through, and . . . well, it could have led to even worse things. Still might, if we don't make sure they stop."

"Dad," said Finn, waving a hand at the destruction all around. "What do you mean by 'even worse things'?"

"If you weaken any wall too much," said Hugo, "it will eventually collapse."

"Which would mean . . . ?" asked Emmie.

"Bad things," said Hugo. "Very bad things."

They each let that sink in.

"I still couldn't figure out why the bones were appearing aboveground," said Tiger-One-Twelve. "Not until it happened here too. Not until Emmie told us you had seen that Bone Creature on the Infested Side, Finn, and I knew it must be happening here too. What I still don't fully understand is why these bags, pieces of armor, and other things of yours are showing up all over the world."

"I think I know the answer to that," said Finn. He looked at Emmie. "There are Legends in the Infested Side, ones I met, who kind of, like"—he felt embarrassed saying the word—"worship us, I suppose. Worship Emmie and me."

Hugo raised an eyebrow.

"I know it sounds stupid, Dad," said Finn, "but that's what they told me. I left a few things behind when I exploded on our last visit there. They said they were relics."

"Like the way religions have relics of saints," said Hugo, amused at this idea of his son being such an icon.

"I suppose," said Finn. "I know it sounds weird, but they buried them in the ground as gifts to the Bone Creature. Offerings. All over the Infested Side. They thought the relics might stop it."

A couple of people Finn could not identify were still out there among the bones, scanning the ground for something. Hugo and Tiger-One-Twelve seemed unconcerned.

"They've buried things like this pen all over the Infested Side," Finn went on. "When the Bone Creature was pushing through from there—"

"It was pushing the relics through with it," concluded Tiger-One-Twelve. She pointed at the two people among the bones. "That's what those two are looking for out there."

She gave them a wave, and the pair came closer, lit by the glare of a low unicorn-shaped lamp.

Finn recognized both people immediately. One was the man from the Bubble Blast Car Wash, who Finn had said a passing hello to back in Darkmouth. The other was someone they'd spent more time with.

"Anne," said Finn, seeing it was the woman who had given them a ride from the train station to Slotterton.

"She calls herself Wolf-Three-Five," said Emmie. "Which I think is cool. Anyway, it turns out it was no coincidence that she was near the train station when she picked us up. She'd been following us all along."

"We'd heard about you breaking out of Darkmouth," explained Anne, walking over.

The man from the Bubble Blast Car Wash, meanwhile, carried on searching through the bones.

"I was sent to keep an eye on you, and almost lost track of you to be honest," Anne continued. "I didn't expect for us to run into each other like that."

"Your recklessness caught her by surprise," said Hugo, matter-of-fact.

"I wanted to tell you, and I called Tiger-One-Twelve to see what I should do next," said Anne, "but you were gone by the time I hung up."

"As a team, we're pretty comprehensive when writing *The Most Great Lives*," said Tiger-One-Twelve. "But while we started by looking at you, it became more and more obvious we needed to keep an eye on Lucien. It became clear that your father was right to worry that Darkmouth was being taken away from your family through a conspiracy."

Hugo saw a look flit across Finn's face. "And that you were right too," Hugo said, to please him.

"What will happen with Lucien now?" asked Emmie. "They'll lock him up for sure, won't they?"

"I doubt it," said Tiger-One-Twelve, and Emmie's shoulders slumped. "Without a Council of Twelve to do it, he'll go back to Liechtenstein and argue his case with the other assistants. The problem is that there were a few of them who went along with his plan, and they won't want it all revealed through *The Most Great Lives*. And the problem for us is that we rely on whoever's in charge of the Legend Hunters for cooperation in the first place. I fear that when all this settles down and someone takes control again, the *Most Great Lives* publishers will come to some kind of agreement that will involve putting this part of the story at the back of a very high shelf to let it gather dust."

"It's not fair," said Finn.

"It's not," said Hugo, "but it might be better than the alternative, which was to put us in a jar at the back of a shelf. This way, at least, they all go to Liechtenstein and we get Darkmouth back. That's what matters."

"That's not all that matters," said Finn, weary but firm.

He looked at Tiger-One-Twelve. There was something he needed to ask. "Tell me, do you all trust me yet?"

Tiger-One-Twelve did not immediately respond, but looked around her, and to Hugo. Then returned to Finn.

Before she could speak, there was a shout from where the Bubble Blast Car Wash man was inspecting the bones.

"I found something!"

They stepped over bones and glitter, walked around debris and souvenirs.

The Bubble Blast Car Wash man was standing in a circle of grass, from the center of which rose a large plastic statue of Smoofy. Crouching down, he wiped dirt from a solid rectangular object half pulled from the earth.

Tiger-One-Twelve and Hugo reached them first, and stopped as Anne held a light up to the object.

"Oh no," said Tiger-One-Twelve, hardly loud enough to be heard.

"Wait there, Finn," Hugo said, putting a hand out to stop him just as he reached them. He then stood in front of him, blocking his view.

But Finn could see Emmie, and he saw that whatever was there caused her to clasp a hand over her mouth.

"What is it?" Finn asked, increasingly concerned and irritated that he was being blocked from seeing it.

"Maybe it's a hoax of some sort," said Anne.

"Maybe. It surely can't be real," said Bubble Blast man.

"Yes, it can," said Tiger-One-Twelve.

Finn tried to maneuver around his father to see it, but was blocked. "Why won't you let me see it?" he asked, worried.

"So far, we've been finding objects Finn left behind when he traveled to the past," continued Tiger-One-Twelve, crouching down to the object, whose cracked edge Finn could just make out.

It was stone, covered in a black sheen that reflected the colors of the Smoofyland lights.

"But the crystals in the Darkmouth cave didn't *just* open gateways to the past," said Hugo. "They took my father, Niall, to the future too. We don't know how far, but we know he went there."

"So you're saying . . . ," began Emmie, glancing from the object to Finn.

"That it's possible an object from Darkmouth could someday *in the future* travel to the Infested Side and become a relic," said Tiger-One-Twelve.

"And then be brought back to the present," said Hugo, sounding disturbed.

Frustrated, Finn tried to pull his father aside, without

any luck. "I need to see it," he insisted.

Hugo turned, put his hands on Finn's shoulders, squeezed. "It could be nothing," he said. "You need to understand that before you see this."

He stood aside.

The others parted too, letting Finn see the object.

They watched him approach it, each of them solemn. It felt strange, like he was at a funeral.

Then he understood why.

The object was a slab of stone, cracked at the top. But as he crouched and pushed aside the last flakes of dirt, the words chiseled into it were clear.

Meanwhile

Many thousands of miles away, the breeze was blowing from the wrong direction.

It flowed through the desert, pushing a tiny line of sand ahead of it, forcing it across the lip of a dune, down the slope toward the abandoned village, across the flat earth, and past the hut in which the old man Warmaksan the Unflinching waited. Dutiful. Patient. A little bored, if he was to be honest with himself. Which he wasn't, because that might let in the threat of craziness. This was not a place he wanted to go crazy. There was enough crazy here without him adding to it.

He noticed that breeze, though. Noticed how it tickled at his toes, how the sand settled in small piles against the legs of his chair. Most of all, he noticed it was coming from the wrong place.

Before, the breeze had always come from the west, running up against the back wall of the hut in which he sat. This one blew in from the east.

Warmaksan the Unflinching considered this, reached for the length of steel and blades that constituted his closest weapon, then withdrew a little before deciding, once and for all, to grasp it tight. Because he'd noticed something else in the breeze. Something far more ominous. Something he had not experienced since he was a child, that the desert had not tasted for decades.

Rain.

It was light, a spray carried into the hut by that breeze. He walked toward the door, slowly. The glare of the day outside had been dimmed; the temperature had dipped.

As he reached the doorway, he was startled by the slither of a lizard darting under his feet in search of shelter.

Warmaksan stepped outside and almost stood on another lizard. Then a third. The ground was writhing with them, pouring from the sand, scattering across the surface, all heading in one direction. Away. Out of the village.

He watched them go, tails flicking, each a rapid blur of panic, then turned again in the direction from which they were coming. Beyond was another building, a small outhouse long ago abandoned to anything but desert and emptiness. Behind it was a light, a smudge behind the building, a shimmering edge leaking from either side.

Weapon high, Warmaksan walked toward it. Slow, steady

steps. Reluctant but dutiful. Rain ran down his nose, tickled the edges of his mouth.

He rounded the back of the building, and saw the gateway.

It was about as wide as he could stretch his hands out. Thin, it was still enough for him to peek through. Against the blue of his sky it was a streak of ominous, sparkling gold.

There was a crack in the world.

And it was widening.

The house smelled of other people. Their clothes. Their food. Their mess.

Finn's bedroom smelled of Tiberius and Elektra in particular. It was a dump, torn apart by the unconstrained behavior of the two children who had lived there for a while.

He picked a broken sword off the floor. Discarded books. Something that looked like a mummified Basilisk. He could hardly see the carpet for the stuff thrown around and used the broken sword to poke through the piles a little, knowing he'd have to tidy it up sooner or later. He just hoped that smell—*their* smell—would go quickly.

Knock knock.

His mam stood at his bedroom door.

"You think that's bad? I found about half a ton of sherbet clogging the drains," said Clara. "The assistants were up to all sorts of things while we were gone."

Hugo stood behind Clara, rubbing his chin with his knuckles—always a sure sign he was not relaxed—while holding something in his palm. "This is a six-hundred-and-fifty-year-old Minotaur claw that's been in this family for generations, and I just found it being used as a toilet-paper holder."

Finn managed to navigate a way through the mess to open a window and let fresh air sweep in. It felt good as it cooled his face.

Emmie came into the room. "You should tidy this mess up," she said mischievously. "It looks like a Hydra ran loose in here."

"Hey, don't think all that Red Warrior stuff means you can go telling me what to do." Finn smiled. "I've seen your bedroom, and it's messier than a Hogboon's nostril hair."

"Did you talk to your dad?" Clara asked Emmie. "He'll be furious that he missed everything that's happened. Everything *you* did."

"Yeah, he's finishing up in Liechtenstein and getting back here as soon as he can," said Emmie. "He says there's turmoil over there at headquarters while they figure out who's in charge."

"There are a lot of messes to clean up," said Hugo, still rubbing at his chin. "Lots of things to worry about."

They all looked at Finn.

"Hey, I'm not dead yet. I'm not going to be dead. So all of you stop looking at me like that."

"There is *some* good news for you," Clara said, breaking the gloomy atmosphere by handing Finn a letter.

Finn opened it, saw the Smoofyland logo at the top of the sheet of paper.

"Oh, you've got to be kidding me. Mam, we can't go there on vacation, please . . ."

"Just read it," she said.

> *You are firmly instructed that you, and at least five successive generations of your family, are hereby banned from ever attending Smoofyland . . .*

Finn laughed. "Excellent."

"It's not fair," said Emmie. "I never got to go on anything. That roller coaster looked brilliant. You know it's the sparkliest–"

Finn's sharp glare stopped her. She grinned.

"Anyway," Emmie said, "I'm staying with you now until Dad comes back, and whatever happens here always tops any theme park."

Peeling some candy wrappers off his wall, Finn thought

about everything that had happened, and the one thing *yet* to happen, but which now sat like a weight on their lives.

Finn the Defiant. RIP.

He felt their stares on the back of his neck.

There was no choice. He had to head toward whatever future was written. It would meet him here or elsewhere, but it *would* meet him.

And right now, he had to take on one great task, though at least he knew he wouldn't be alone.

"Right," he said, picking up a Desiccator wrapped in tinsel. "You can all help me tidy my bedroom."